The
Plague

The Plague

KEVIN CHONG

ARSENAL
PULP PRESS | VANCOUVER

THE PLAGUE
Copyright © 2018 by Kevin Chong

ARSENAL PULP PRESS
Suite 202 – 211 East Georgia St.
Vancouver, BC V6A 1Z6
Canada
arsenalpulp.com

The publisher gratefully acknowledges the support of the Canada Council for the Arts and the British Columbia Arts Council for its publishing program, and the Government of Canada, and the Government of British Columbia (through the Book Publishing Tax Credit Program), for its publishing activities.

Cover Photo by Scott Webb
Cover and text design by Oliver McPartlin
Edited by Susan Safyan

Printed and bound in Canada

Library and Archives Canada Cataloguing in Publication:
Chong, Kevin, author
     The plague / Kevin Chong.
Issued in print and electronic formats.
ISBN 978-1-55152-718-5 (softcover).—ISBN 978-1-55152-719-2
(HTML)
     1. Camus, Albert, 1913-1960. Peste. I. Title.
PS8555.H648P53 2018   C813'.6   C2017-907214-5
                                              C2017-907215-3

This book is dedicated to the kids: Joe and Franny

"Abstractions are fascinating: they can cast light on the past, but not on the present. They can also kill."

—Kamel Daoud

Part One

Setting:
Vancouver, Canada,
in the near future.

1.

The remarkable events described in this narrative took place in Vancouver (traditional territories of the Musqueam, Squamish, and Tsleil-Waututh First Nations) in 201_ and into the following year. For many readers, this will be a tale told once too many times.

The collected literature that treats this historic calamity ranges from medical case study to onstage monologue. It has been offered in film documentary and comic book forms, relayed by storytellers and monologists, authored by those living outside the city, and pieced together from eyewitness accounts. They all attempt a futile struggle: to not forget what happened. Regardless of such efforts, we find that speaking of these events is often considered impolite, so it is mentioned without being named. For all of us, the process of un-remembering is steadfast and systematic.

How is this version of events different from the rest? It certainly offers no new information about the origins of the outbreak. However, the recollections from its primary witness, Dr Bernard Rieux, allow one of the first glimpses of the infection. Woven into this tale is material from Megan Tso, a writer previously known for her work on funerary rites and historical attitudes toward mortality, who was originally visiting this coastal Canadian city for only five days. Another contributor is Raymond Siddhu, a longtime city-hall and health reporter for a Vancouver daily newspaper. Through these three witnesses, we get a glimpse of this city and its people in a light that it was never under and has yet to be seen again. (Although these figures create a polyphonic work, do not consider them a true representation of the city. They represent only the limited social reach of this account's authors, whose identities will be revealed later. They represent a distinct band of the population—they are well-educated and middle-class. Don't misinterpret them as archetypes. In fact, they are well-heeled parasites subsisting on the anxieties of a more unreflective larger population.)

Before and after this period, Vancouver was an outpost coastal city in Canada. It was erected at the bottleneck of the province's lumber and fishing industries, the shiny ring that sealed the exit. Its now-renowned amenities were originally afterthoughts. A large city park was envisioned in a former logging camp and gravesite. An ethnic ghetto for redundant railway workers became a grimy tourist stop. Its public market had been a docking point for houseboats and shacks; before that, it was a fishing spot for the First Nations people (who are notably unrepresented in this tale). In its second century, the city went from resource to resort town. By happenstance, Vancouver's utility had become its ornament. The coastal mountains were no longer impediments but pretty to look at, and the waterways previously used by pulp mills and canneries were valued as ocean views for luxury homes and playgrounds for paddleboarders. Wealthy migrants were willing to overlook the damp cold of the city's winter months for its mild summer temperatures, the unceasing greyness and palette of bathwater hues for its clean air.

The people of Vancouver were, as you should expect, difficult to encapsulate. The easy generalization, at the time of the outbreak, was to posit that the city had become the backdrop for the dramas of ultra-wealthy layabouts and the casualties of the recently concluded opioid crisis. Either they emerged from jewel-box McLarens and Teslas like Mandarin-speaking insects between butterfly wings, or they decomposed, forgotten and overlooked in the alleyways. In fact, the city was made up, as it had always been, of people who worked too much for too little.

These people had forsaken living in smoggy metropolises where they could have made real money. They sought what they described as "balance"—in truth, just an abundance of pleasure. But still they felt harried. They worked two jobs or worked long nights at one job so they could spend their days in their studios. They had children with learning disabilities. They were alone but attended a church group. They were the oldest, by a good decade, at the board-game nights hosted at the community centres. They made sure to wish their exes happy birthday by text message. They visited their parents on weekends. They overate on Saturdays and hiked on Sundays. They lived here because they were from here (although no one believed anyone was originally from here). They ended up in Vancouver because no one else was like them where they grew up. They never knew their parents. They never knew their home towns.

This bustle precluded self-examination. Yes, there were activists in the city, but those people seemed unhappy and disagreeable. Others felt trapped in their lives, but didn't understand their confinement. They thought themselves free—as long as they remained within their own highly rated neighbourhoods and didn't reach out to where they'd been forbidden. Those without jobs, too rich or too old for employment, filled their days with fitness regimens and classes. They made their own bodies their worksites.

This was a city that had never seen a war. It had never been overrun, sacked, or bombed. An earthquake loomed in the distant future. The citizens rioted at sporting events and outside concerts. They came together for summer fireworks that celebrated ... fireworks. As a result, it was an anatomized city, a place in which joys and fears were contained within the spheres of self and family. Among the city's Indigenous peoples, its immigrant groups, its sex workers and LGBTQ population, collective traumas were experienced but barely heard by the rest of the city—including the figures in this narrative.

The epidemic described in this narrative, which lasted four months and took over fourteen hundred lives, was like an infant's first nightmare. It was formless and oppressive, stunning in its novelty, and never-ending until you woke from it, patting yourself to see if you remained intact.

2.

The first figure we will meet is Dr Bernard Rieux. His catalytic place in this story and his subsequent role grants him primacy. His status as a male physician also serves to foreground him as a protagonist. But his manner would not otherwise suggest that he fits the role. When it is first necessary to speak of him, it occurs shortly before the key incidents that took place in late October.

It was Halloween. To be more precise, it was a weekday that fell between the weekend when adults celebrated in their costumes and the holiday's actual date when they dutifully trudged the streets alongside their children. As someone who had no children (and found dressing in costumes distasteful), Dr Rieux was largely oblivious to the trappings of this festivity. He had, however, been awakened at five in the morning by a loud bang. It was a local tradition that fireworks and firecrackers were set off in the days around Halloween. The tradition had taken place for at least a few decades and was routinely decried by concerned citizens calling for a ban. The previous year, fireworks had caused a dog to be spooked and then killed by a SkyTrain car and fireworks were also held responsible when a house burned down another year. According to one blog Dr Rieux read, the peculiar fireworks tradition originated in Guy Fawkes' Night and could be traced to the city's British origins. For people who lived in Vancouver, this was how Halloween was experienced. If they relocated to other cities, ex-Vancouverites would wait in vain for the explosions expected at this time of year. Their chests clenched in the evenings whenever they saw a cluster of teenaged boys—knowing that there were people who didn't habitually flinch in this way.

Rieux was unable to get back to sleep after being woken. His day at the clinic would start in just another hour. He sat up in bed and noticed that his wife was no longer beside him. The sheets on her side were cold. He found her at the kitchen counter with a mug of tea still steaming onto her perfectly round eyeglasses. Her suitcase was already set by the door.

Elyse Rieux was a thin, precise woman whose severity had once been offset by a plump face and the expressiveness of her gesticulations. Since she had been diagnosed with breast cancer, the flesh on her cheeks had been overtaken by bone and shadow. Her teeth and jaw had grown in prominence. Her eyes, once pools of light behind those circular eyeglasses, now seemed permanently parched. As always, she kept her hair in a tomboyish bob—it was thick enough to withstand radiation. But where it once had accentuated her long neck, it now highlighted the deep recesses between her neck and collarbones. Her collection of scarves had grown expansive.

"I've already changed the sheets in the spare room for your mother," she announced. "Is that why you're up so early? Or did you miss me?"

"A firecracker woke me up," he said. Rieux took a seat across from her and squeezed her hand.

"Teenagers," she muttered. "They only get up early in order to wake everyone else up." She let out a dry laugh. Her humour had grown caustic in the past year. At least it hadn't been turned on him today, Rieux thought.

Soon Elyse would leave on her own; she was taking a cab to the airport. Her suggestion that Rieux work today had curdled into a command. Her friend Nicole, who was in remission and six months away from being declared cancer-free, would travel to the airport with her. This friend swore that the clinic in Reynosa, a Mexican border town, had turned back death with its herbal remedies and oxygenation treatments. Rieux no longer objected to her "scheme," as he called it, but she remained wary of his skepticism, a feature as elemental to him as his dark hair and his tendency to mutter in the shower. She worried that his presence would wither away her optimism before she even stepped aboard the plane.

Four hours after she departed, Rieux's mother would arrive from Hong Kong. That they would miss each other by a day went unacknowledged and, for the most part, both the women in Rieux's life refrained from speaking critically about the other.

He changed into his cycling gear for his work commute. Afterward, they spoke about the day that stretched out ahead of each of them. He would need to get through paperwork before seeing walk-in patients for the rest of the morning. That afternoon, he would leave his bike at work and board the SkyTrain to meet his mother at the airport; they would take a cab home. Rieux and Elyse usually spent their mornings this way, up earlier than necessary, too anxious to sleep well, exchanging information. And yet it had been different since Elyse fell ill, Rieux thought. It was the difference between going to church and feeling one's heart churn in the refrain of a hymn.

Her phone on the counter began to buzz. "Nicole is downstairs," she said.

Elyse braced herself against the counter to climb off the stool. Fixing her eyes on the granite countertop, she pushed herself off with an economy of strain that seemed like ballet to him. He grabbed his own bag so he could leave at the same time and then wheeled her deceptively light luggage to the elevator downstairs.

At the end of the hall, they saw their building superintendent, Mr Santos. He was in his fifties, a man with caramel-coloured skin, greying, bristly hair, a thin black moustache on his long upper lip, and a tattoo of an anchor on his forearm.

"Good morning, Doctor and Mrs Rieux." There was a tentativeness in his voice, which normally seemed ready to break into song in mid-sentence.

"Is something wrong, Mr Santos?" Elyse asked. Everyone else in the building called him by the name embroidered into his shirt, Miguel. But the Rieuxs thought it polite to return the formality.

"No, ma'am," he said. "I'm just worried about the way kids are raised today. We weren't brought up the same way. They eat too much sugar."

"We were just saying," Rieux said, thinking about the firecracker that woke him up earlier. But Mr Santos had another reason to be upset. That morning, he told them, he'd found a dead rat in the underground garage. There had been a garbage strike that ran from the middle of August through the first half of an unseasonably warm fall. Until only a few weeks earlier, even the most genteel parts of the city had a ripe smell that reminded Rieux of his childhood visits with his mother to Vancouver's Chinatown, where they would cut through alleyways full of open dumpsters and butchers seated on upturned buckets smoking Marlboros in blood-stained white smocks. The rats and raccoons that were occasionally glimpsed in the city had become more visible, wobbling from overflowing garbage and compost containers. People spoke of these pests as though they were obnoxious neighbours.

Every few days, Mr Santos explained, he might see rodents running from under a car, where they huddled for warmth. But this morning, a rat had been left in front of the garage-floor elevator. "Now imagine being a lady, taking your baby out, and seeing that?" He shook his head, whistled, and then disappeared into a supply closet.

They took the elevator to the front hall. Rieux had hoped to say something to his wife, something that might clear the fine mist of uneasiness that had come between the two of them; it was an obnoxious perfume that obscured a more offensive smell. But at the sight of Nicole waving from the idling taxi, Elyse moved briskly outside.

Rieux followed behind. He placed the suitcase—was there anything in it but toiletries and a scarf?—in the trunk of the taxi. Once he closed the trunk, he turned and collided into his wife, who had approached him to say goodbye. He had to catch her to keep her from falling.

"We can't even get this right," Elyse said.

"I'm sorry."

There was a kiss and a hug that could have been a handshake or a fraught wave goodbye. Elyse said she would call when she landed at the airport, but that the clinic had limited phone service and no internet. He watched the taxi circle the driveway and turn onto the road.

As the car grew smaller in his view, he felt a tension loosen from his shoulders with the absence of his wife. He took his commuter bicycle from the storage locker and rode out through the garage entrance. Normally he would take the Seawall to the clinic on Powell Street, but he wanted to buy a Vietnamese sandwich in Chinatown. There was a fire truck attending to a car crash at the intersection of Main Street and Second Avenue. He wove through the cars stuck in traffic, catching glimpses of the impatient commuters.

Near the intersection, before he could veer off on the crosswalk, he recognized Elyse's blue-and-white taxi. He saw his wife's head from behind. Nicole was on her phone. Rieux stopped between the cars in the left-turn lane and those inching forward and took a look at Elyse's face. There were tears on her cheeks, but she wasn't sobbing or looking especially grief-stricken. She wasn't crying because of him. She felt the same way he did—relieved, he thought. Likely hopeful, too.

Traffic lurched ahead, and he returned to the world. Before the taxi scooted into the intersection, he'd eased behind a Tesla in the left-turn lane. Rieux cycled past the man he saw most days. He carried a cardboard sign that read, "Everything Helps."

3.

At the risk of disrupting this narrative once more, it should be mentioned again that the authors of this piece will be revealed near the end of the story. There was some discussion about the best way to relate the testimony of each of these witnesses, and ultimately, a more distant, objective voice was deemed optimal.

Our next witness, Raymond Siddhu, offers insight into the city's power structures and communities. As a reporter, he also had a pretext to interview and collect impressions from an assortment of people. For the sake of simplicity, we begin Siddhu's story the same day as Rieux's. That day commenced with his commute.

Siddhu preferred to take public transportation into the city, departing before rush hour began. In such fashion, he could leave the car for his wife, Uma, who had another two months of maternity leave, and be out of the house before his twin boys, Ranjeet and Ravinder, woke each other up. This morning, Uma was still sleeping; she'd stayed up late, sewing together Halloween outfits for their ten-month-old babies. In Siddhu's mind, they already attracted too much attention, but his opinion, he was beginning to discover, counted for nothing. The boys would go trick-or-treating as salt-and-pepper shakers.

In the winter, taking the bus entailed stepping outside when the sky was still cobalt blue. The bus—and later, the SkyTrain—meant fifty-five minutes of enforced inactivity. Reading or checking email on his phone while in a moving vehicle turned his stomach. Eating or drinking was prohibited. Occasionally he would listen to streaming music or a podcast, but finding new music and podcasts was a part-time job in itself. The calm of the bus ride allowed him to rest before he launched into a work day that often left him both exhausted and buzzing. His job had always involved deadlines and compromises, but the latest round of buyouts and cuts at the newspaper induced stress hives. He'd already covered the health and city hall beats; the September workforce reduction brought op-eds into his portfolio. At least he now had a window-facing cubicle. And at the morning story meeting, he could find blueberry muffins. A perk, right? The fruit-stained fingertips of a laid-off staffer flashed before his eyes.

The newsroom meeting was brisk and uneventful as the editor-in-chief's rundown of top stories went unquestioned. Siddhu was asked to discuss his story about a clinic on the edge of an area contentiously known as the Gastown Annex; the doctors there had put a priority on treating patients who'd been displaced by the development. Siddhu got the sense that he was going on too long. Everyone seemed impatient for the day to proceed. Among a boardroom full of people who prided themselves in declaring every bit of news a poor copy of something that happened ten years earlier, there was an anxious energy surrounding an afternoon visit by Romeo Parsons.

The newly elected mayor had the heady glamour of a movie star, despite his near-sightedness and fluency in rezoning policy. The staff at Siddhu's workplace prized neutrality, but the swooning could not be concealed when his name was uttered in passing. Newspaper sales, stagnant though they were, rose to 2007 levels whenever his face appeared on its front page. Siddhu did not trust Parsons but would never have voiced his skepticism. It would have been a singular shame in the office to have admitted voting for the incumbent. Luckily, he lived outside city limits.

At his new desk, he reviewed a press release from the clinic, which had introduced an outreach worker to find patients pushed out by the Annex. The phone started to ring. He initially ignored it, thinking the call was for the desk's previous occupant, who was currently in a guest house in Mexico on an indefinite vacation. He checked the caller ID and recognized the name: Elliot Horne-Bough, the young owner of a popular news website, GSSP. The site had repurposed a few of his buzziest stories, leaving out his byline, to whip up their own internet traffic.

Horne-Bough told Siddhu that he wanted to meet with him, which Siddhu interpreted as a peace offering. He declined.

"How about instead of an apology, I hire you?" Horne-Bough said. "Sorries are for suckers."

"I already have a job. And I need to go."

"Okay, but I am persistent. I don't want you to work for me. I want you as a partner. Remember that: I am *persistent*." Siddhu hung up.

As the afternoon approached, LED camera lights were installed in the front foyer for photos with the new mayor. Women came back from lunch wearing more makeup, and men who lived in wrinkly button-downs had covered them with blazers. Siddhu kept a bottle of mouthwash in his drawer and wondered whether he should pass it around before he took the elevator downstairs.

Outside it was spitting rain. A handful of blocks separated his office in the city's financial centre from the Annex. He sidestepped the tourist shops in Gastown selling replica totem poles and Canadian flags and barrelled along the Annex's cobblestoned pedestrian thoroughfare. Siddhu's last meal out with Uma had been in the summer at one of the new sidewalk cafés. Coloured lights had been strung between the four-storey buildings over the thoroughfare, and he felt like he was in Europe. Now he missed the balmy weather if not the solicitous gastropub owners and sushi slingers hoping to entice him onto their patios.

The clinic sat at the end of the development, around suspiciously charred buildings that were now weeks away from demolition. He stepped foot inside the waiting area to sounds of coughing and told the receptionist about his appointment. "Our new counsellor called in sick—at the last minute," she told him, too harried to be apologetic. "Dr Rieux has offered to speak to you."

Siddhu agreed, knowing it was his best chance to avoid Romeo Parsons, and was sent back to the waiting area. None of the magazines on the table had been published within the past three years. Most of the waiting patients wore headphones and sat slumped on their chairs. One woman held a child on her knee. She was trying to comfort the boy who was no older than six years old, and held his own elbows as though he ached everywhere else. The mother seemed to think the child needed to be cajoled out of his pain, her admonishments delivered in singsong syllables. The boy grimaced but held back his tears.

Since Siddhu had become a father, he'd lost the ability to throttle his emotions. Once he could clench his mouth into a mask of calm; now the feelings bubbled onto his face. Siddhu knew that when his eyes began to water, soon he would be bawling. Just a month earlier, both of his babies had gone into anaphylactic shock after they'd first tried eggs. He remembered the step-by-step hurry of bundling the boys and latching them into their car seats, and his wife snarling at him because a strap was twisted. He remembered driving to the hospital in pyjamas, the headwind of paperwork at admissions, and then the wait.

Siddhu felt the yo-yo in his pocket. When the boy's glance landed in his direction, he flashed the silver Ricochet in his closed palm and slung it out. Then he stood up, threw the yo-yo behind him, and brought it up so it looked like he was walking a dog. He'd been given a yo-yo as a child but had only renewed his fascination in the last six months. The yo-yo he owned was an indulgence and aspirational purchase; it was made for professionals and produced a pleasant ratcheting sound as it unwound. He brought the toy up to his chest, flung it down, and separated his hands to recreate the trick he'd seen online. The boy's expression settled, and his mother quit chirping and smoothed the hair on the back of his head.

Dr Rieux appeared. He was a short man who wore his hair in a bouquet of wiry brown curls. He had a Mediterranean complexion but his eyes seemed to have some East Asian provenance. When he saw Siddhu's tears, he instinctively shrank back. Siddhu snapped the yo-yo back into his hand.

"I'm about to take a coffee break," the doctor told him. "Do you want to come with me?"

Everyone in the crowded waiting room watched him bounce out. The doctor was indifferent to their looks of impatience and disappointment. Rieux was arrogant—like many doctors Siddhu had met. "It's been crazy all week. There's a flu in the neighbourhood," the doctor told him. At the corner coffee shop—a place Siddhu would later describe as a "Scandinavian coffee laboratory"—Rieux told him to order a twelve-ounce latte. Siddhu followed his command, even though he usually took his coffee black, then Rieux led them to a set of stools by the window.

"Do you want to start your tape recorder?" Rieux asked.

The coffee had an unctuous flavour. Siddhu placed his iPhone on the counter to record the conversation. Rieux had begun talking before he could take out his notebook and had already veered off-topic to Siddhu's recently published retrospective on the first anniversary of the Annex. "The headline described the development as 'inevitable,' like the area was being remade in the image of the rest of the city," said the doctor.

"I was there. I spoke to activists and the big shots when the discussions and protests were underway," Siddhu said. "I don't know about 'inevitable,' but the article was written from today's perspective." He wanted to say that, in retrospect, the outcome seemed "predictable."

"People don't want to talk about it," Rieux said. "Nowadays they can drive through without locking their doors. But there's a reason why the previous mayor lost the election. What was here before—the people, the problems—may have been swallowed up, but they haven't gone away."

"I won an award for my Annex coverage," Siddhu said. He instantly regretted sounding so defensive. "And the editor wrote the headline."

"It's a matter of language. Inevitability suggests futility. *Why try if we're going to lose?*"

This was a person who argued to pass the time, Siddhu noted. "My story concerns the new outreach counsellor," he finally said.

Rieux's knowledge of policies toward displaced patients was general. "We want everyone to receive care," he insisted. "A patient is a patient." Siddhu would still need to interview the actual counsellor. The doctor had apparently agreed to talk with him only to set him straight on the headline's word choice. *Jesus.* And yet he didn't have the airs of a crank or know-it-all. He was too aloof. Rieux's emotional reserve was borne of his role as a doctor. Siddhu could never work in medicine; as a metro-beat reporter, earlier in his career, he'd covered fires and car accidents, beelining to be the first to interview firefighters and police officers, bracing himself before he approached the families who'd lost homes or loved ones. Now, he buckled at the sight of a child in pain.

It was clearing outside when they parted. Siddhu was preoccupied by a blade of light against a skyscraper in the distance when he felt something at his feet. He'd kicked a dead rat. Blood was coming out of its eyes.

He kept his gaze trained on the sidewalk until he was back in the newspaper building. Before he stepped into his office, he washed his hands in the washrooms by the elevator. A tall, broad-shouldered man, the kind of man who wore glasses to mute his dazzling handsomeness, stepped out of a stall.

Previously famous as a real-estate marketer and a social entrepreneur, Romeo Parsons possessed a baseline demeanour of ironic detachment

from the niceties of social life. Whenever he glad-handed in front of reporters, he made sure to signal that he was playing a role. To offset that
cynical aftertaste, he staged moments of unguarded pleasure. Last week,
he broke off from his daily 5K to join a group of teenagers playing basketball. A video of him making a jump shot was widely shared and re-posted.
As a result of his public gestures, people felt pre-acquainted with him.

"We've met, right?" Parsons asked as he took the sink next to Siddhu.

"I've been part of your press scrums," Siddhu told him.

"Of course," he said. He jogged his finger toward him. "Hey, did you
write the piece about the anniversary of the Annex"—a vein on his neck
bulged when he used that word—"last week? I made my staff read the entire story. I'm reminded of something Joseph Stalin said, something about
how one death is a tragedy —"

"A million is a statistic."

Parsons beamed. "*You get it*. People act as though the epidemic vanished, but it's the advocates like you who make us see the consequences of
inaction. We need more stories like yours."

The new mayor slapped him across his shoulder before he left Siddhu
alone at the hot-air dryer. Siddhu returned to the newsroom where everyone had repositioned themselves at their work terminals, back to their
unionized jobs with purpose. They stared at their screens with curtailed
grins and scrabbled away at their keyboards. It was as if Parsons was Santa
Claus and could see them being nice.

Siddhu had always considered inspirational books written by motiva-
tional speakers and pored over by his two success-driven brothers—each

of whom had an extra column line in their investment accounts—to be the
energy drinks of professional life. To feel inspired, as he did now, left him
twitchy, jumpy. He was perched for the sugar crash. It was inevitable.

4.

We now introduce our final witness, Megan Tso, on her flight from Hong Kong to Vancouver. She was pleased to be placed next to an empty seat. Since she'd been travelling so much, a thirteen-hour stretch without brushing elbows with a co-passenger, a place to put her laptop and e-reader, and a spare tray where she could leave her hot towel and glass of ice water—all of this gave her enough space to appreciate humanity.

She updated the talk she'd just given in Guangzhou. While there, she spoke about death as the impetus for ritual and then of its place in many civilizations, with references to social media. She took a selfie at her family's ancestral home, which received her eight-hundredth "like" before the plane ascended. Her social media popularity was a dubious achievement, and at least five of those likes were from dummy accounts created by Markus.

Then she took a two-hour train back to Hong Kong, gave the same talk based on her book, *The Meaning of Death*, and had dinner with aunts and uncles and cousins, relatives on her mother's side, eager to see her, and oversolicitous. Now she was on this flight for her final two engagements in Vancouver, which were spaced nearly a week apart.

Once she got home to Los Angeles from Canada, she would have been away for a month: L.A.-Chicago-Madrid-Seoul-Guangzhou-Hong Kong-Vancouver. She'd cycled through her outfits five times and had spent nearly a four-figure sum—an entire speaking fee—on hotel laundry and dry cleaning. She'd run out of toothpaste and lost her favourite notebook. Now she thought of getting home as the next stage in a triathlon—a chance to exhaust yet another set of muscles.

Before leaving, she'd quit her job of six years as an editor at an academic press. Tso had loved her job and hated freelancing and was barely afloat despite her book's unexpected success, but she'd needed to quit. She needed the bandwidth.

After she returned to Los Angeles, she planned to move her belongings out of the storage locker. Her first temporary address, a dog-sitting stint, was in peril because the rescued greyhound's owner, a documentary filmmaker, was no longer certain that funding was secure for his three-month stint in Appalachia.

Don't think about stuff.

To soothe herself, in her head she tallied the air miles she'd accumulated and imagined them like stars in the sky. She fell asleep tracing them behind her eyelids. Airplane sleep was a fraction as restful as it was in one's own bed, but when practiced well, it was a form of teleportation. One could nod off when the plane was lit like a cave, then wake with all the lights on and the flight attendants scurrying to their seats for touchdown. This time, Tso roused herself awake after forty-five minutes and watched parts of three movies. Her suitcase was the first of many black cloth bags to emerge on the conveyor belt; she grabbed it and dashed to the taxi stand. If traffic wasn't terrible, if check-in didn't take too long, she'd have enough time to take a shower and lie on a bed for another forty-five minutes before she was picked up and taken to the lecture venue.

She had been to Vancouver once before, a decade earlier, on a summer road trip with college friends. Tso remembered beautiful days and cool nights and seeing so many other Asians that she felt both comforted and swarmed. (She hadn't been to Asia yet.) This time, she felt like she was seeing the city indoors under fluorescent office lights. The patches of lawn that she glimpsed driving across town even resembled grey carpeting. The hotel overlooked the beach and backed onto a park, but sat on the edge between quaint and grubby.

Her plan to rest was thwarted on multiple fronts. When she got to her hotel room, she knew something was wrong as soon as she lifted her suitcase onto the luggage stand. She unzipped it and found a package of Chinese sausage inside, not the silk pyjamas that she remembered placing at the top layer of her packing. While she looked for an ID tag, the phone in her room rang. Her event's organizer started to apologize for arriving early. "I can wait in the lobby until you're ready," the woman said with the voice of someone preemptively disappointed. Tso told her that she would go downstairs immediately. She would have to deal with her luggage later.

Her guide—also the organizer of the event—was a woman named Janice Grossman. There was a look that people who organized death-related events cultivated. It wasn't so plainly "alt" as a high-school goth aesthetic, though black was often a default clothing choice. White people liked to dye their hair black. (Tso had purple highlights.) Grossman's frizzy hair was tinted grey, but she otherwise followed that look. She looked to be in her mid-forties, a decade older than Tso, and wore chunky brass rings that seemed to be refashioned from antique door hinges and brown leather boots. In place of a sign with Tso's name, she clutched a copy of *The Meaning of Death* to her chest.

"Sorry again for being early—the traffic was better than I expected,"

Grossman said, and Tso was reminded that "sorry" was a form of punctuation in Canada. Her talk was going to be at a converted adult cinema, followed by a reception at Grossman's house that Tso had already been dreading. "Normally, the other promoter would introduce you," she said. "But he's come down with the flu. There's something going around. He has a condo in the Annex—and that place is haunted. I'll host, but I don't enjoy the limelight."

There was no problem with traffic, and they had a parcel of time to kill that iPhone games and pocket novels had been designed for—a time best spent alone. Instead, Grossman suggested sushi. "Most of the sushi places here are run by Chinese, but this is Japanese," Grossman told her. "*Not that that matters*," she added quickly. "I live two blocks from here. My father and I come here all the time."

"Do you two live together?" Tso asked, as she signalled the waitress for more tea.

"Yes and no." Her father owned a large house that had been divided into apartments decades earlier. Since he was over eighty years old, she had taken on property management on top of her work as a guide on a city bus tour and volunteer for the arts community. "Downstairs in the house is a commercial space that used to be a corner grocery store. Across the hall, there's my dad, and I share the upstairs suites with a tenant. I have the biggest place—until recently, I was living with my spouse."

She let that last statement sit as she dipped her sashimi. People always wanted to confide in Tso, who considered a response. She decided to check the time on her phone. Finally, when that piece of sashimi was completely tanned in soy, she nodded and said, "My fiancé and I split up early in the year."

Grossman's face took on an energy that wasn't there before. "It's the worst, isn't it?"

This woman probably meant something else by worst, Tso thought. It hadn't been that bad, especially on the road. She could block Markus's e-mails and he hadn't yet learned her new cellphone number. He hated air travel, so the distance had made her feel safe. "I'm still processing it," she said.

"It is a process." She repeated, "*Pro*-cess," Canadian-style. "Janet moved out six months ago." *Hi, we're Janet and Janice*, Tso thought to herself. "I called her so much in the first month that she changed all her information. Eventually, she wrote me a letter. And then two more letters. I haven't opened them. Since she wanted more space, I figure I needed more time." Grossman asked for the bill. "We should go. I'll tell you more about it at the party."

The converted porn theatre was entirely respectable, even with the vintage nudes in the bathroom and the old marquee above the bar. This would be the "fun" event, the one that brought her to the city early; another, more mysterious obligation paid much more and justified her extended trip. Tonight's event was conducted like a lecture series with talks to be given by an embalmer and a spiritualist, as well as two others besides Tso. Grossman was, as promised, a jittery host, whose remarks tended to crumple in mid-sentence. Tso was saved for last. She felt like a jukebox, able to recite her speech, even the ad-libbed moments, as though it were etched into her throat.

As she gave her remarks, pausing for chuckles, a parallel talk took shape in her mind. *This was the book I wrote after I volunteered for six months, writing down life stories at a hospice*, she thought, *but I got a nice book advance— one I had to burn through to pay for the lawyers to throw a legal firewall between me and Markus—and the marketing manager told me to tell funny stories about the mummies of the Atacama Desert to make you feel comfortable about turning cemeteries into picnic spaces and taxidermying your pets. This is one of the reasons Markus used to say I was crazy.*

She got through the talk and signed forty-six copies of her book. This was pleasant. People spoke to her as though they'd read her book; they edged toward her like they were at a high-school dance. Their opening remarks felt rehearsed in their heads but not in their mouths. They posed for photos with her.

Tso watched Grossman strike down the stage and move folding chairs into the back room by herself. She meant to help, but one of the readers had bought her a glass of wine. The group of attendees, a dozen of them, had already been invited to Grossman's reception, and they all piled into cabs. Tso was pulled along. They arrived at a big house with an abandoned grocery store on the main floor and a side door with three separate mailboxes next to it, each one a different shape and colour. Grossman hadn't come back with them, but they pressed her buzzer. When there was no response on the intercom, another person in the group knocked on the door. An older man answered promptly. He had the same frizzy hair as Grossman, but he was bald on top and the hair cascaded from the sides of his head. This—and the buttoned-up pyjamas he wore—gave him the appearance of a mad inventor.

Someone that Tso recognized from the event emerged from a door upstairs. "Come on up!" she told them. Tso watched the group dash up past Mr Grossman until she was the only one left. The door was still open to his ground-floor suite.

"Where's Janice?" he asked, tightening the collar of his bathrobe. His blue eyes were small, hooded, downturned.

"She's on her way, Mr Grossman." She held out her hand. "I'm Megan."

His nostrils flared as he looked at her hand. He bunched his collar more tightly. "Janice told me about her party," he said. "Tell her she needs to check on Far-head. He's still behind on rent and November is coming around. I never wanted to rent to him. And you know what? That doesn't make me racist. I'm a good judge of character." Without another word, he turned back into his suite.

The lecture was unexpectedly pleasant, but she'd reached her half-life of fun. The party upstairs wouldn't have exceeded the delight she'd have unpacking her tightly crammed suitcase and slipping on her pyjamas. *If only I didn't have the wrong bag.* Back in the hotel, she wouldn't even be able to run her toothbrush across her teeth.

Grossman appeared at the entrance carrying a bag of ice under each arm. "Oh good, I was worried you'd left," she said to Tso. "I've set everything up."

"Do you always show up late to your own parties?" Tso asked. She followed her up the creaky steps.

"Who else is going to get ice?" she replied.

"I met your dad," Tso said as they reached the landing. The door had been locked, and Grossman rapped on it and waited patiently to be let back into her own apartment. "He mentioned someone named Far-head?"

"Farhad's our tenant," she said, looking across the landing to another door. "Dad doesn't like him, mainly because he's Persian. Plus he's rude and is always late with rent, so Dad didn't totally miss the mark. He didn't even have references when he applied. I guess I shouldn't have taken him on."

Tso looked at Farhad's door. On it a piece of loose-leaf paper was stapled that read: *Let this be over by nine*. It was already nine-thirty.

"Why did you rent to him in the first place?"

"No one else would," she said. It sounded like she'd heard this question before.

A party guest let them into Grossman's apartment, which was lit entirely by what seemed to be an assortment of scented candles. Tso offered her shoes to the pile that grew by the door. Grossman threw her jacket on an air mattress in her bedroom. The apartment was ample but half-empty. Tso saw a home full of missing objects: a space where an armchair might have been placed, a vacancy on the kitchen counter from a displaced coffee maker. The heavy and severe curtains belonged to a night person.

At the kitchen table, Tso loaded her plate from a mezze platter and filled her plastic glass from a box of red wine. *The Best of Leonard Cohen* was playing on iPod speakers. In the living room, the dozen or so death enthusiasts sat in a circle on the floor, their eyes closed.

Tso thought they were conducting a séance, but it was a game of Werewolf that had just started. She'd played this game before; it was called

Mafia when she participated, but it was essentially the same. The game's narrator asked the two werewolves to open their eyes. Next they pointed to the villager they wanted to "kill." Then the village doctor opened her eyes and tried to guess the next victim and save them. She failed. When this was done, all the participants were asked to open their eyes. "Dawn has broken," the narrator said. "And there has been another casualty in the village." Everyone else had to guess who the werewolves were.

Accusations, misdirection, and disavowals ensued. *People have fled their homelands to escape such conditions*, Tso thought. *Anything can be passed off as fun and every nightmare must be play-acted afterward.* Tso only editorialized when she was in a bad mood.

"I would have sat out this game even if they'd asked me to play. There's too much tension." Tso hadn't noticed Grossman standing next to her. She held a glass of punch that was filled to the top with the ice that she had brought to her own party. The way she held the glass, at chest level, seemed to suggest she was holding it for someone.

"Is it hard to get a cab from here?" Tso asked. "I'm feeling the jetlag."

Grossman said she would call one for her. "But first I need to tell you the rest of my story."

She grabbed Tso's upper arm and led her to an alcove with a computer. It was a quieter place to relate her woes, as "Suzanne" wafted in the background.

Tso was not particularly forthright about her own feelings. Friends described her default expression as haughty and disdainful, and yet people always confided in her. First, she asked questions (in order to avoid talking about herself). And she never passed judgement; to offer approval or criticism felt like overreach. For those who had guilty consciences, like a group of grave robbers she'd once interviewed in Arizona, she granted absolution. Their unhappiness was externalized into a paper ball, and she was the waste basket.

This was Grossman's story: She had met Janet for the first time twenty-five years ago, when Janet was still in middle-school. "I was her camp counsellor," she said. "I made sure she went to bed on time and was wearing enough sunscreen." Grossman had recently come out and wore T-shirts that celebrated her newly acknowledged sexuality: one had a rainbow flag on it, another featured an illustration of Gertrude Stein. The morning after Parents Welcome Day, she was called in by the camp administrator, who suggested she make wiser sartorial choices. In a fury, Grossman quit.

When she met Janet in a bar nearly a decade later, she neither recognized nor remembered her—that came later. What drew Grossman to Janet was her strong nose, dark unruly eyebrows, and a resting down-turned mouth—features that would age well. "She looked like the younger version of a portrait that might hang in a haunted house," she said. "She seemed mature beyond her age, but she was being herself." They had, Grossman admitted, a blisteringly sexual relationship in their first couple of months. "It was hot," she said. "We were two people used to getting sex twice in one week and then living off the crumbs of those memories for another eight months until our next opportunity." They bounced between hostels and beachside campsites in Mexico for two months. Then Janet fell ill with Lyme disease, and they grew closer during her recovery. Grossman loved caring for her. She even considered training as a nurse, but she didn't want to go back to school.

Janet, however, still wanted to learn. She was a painter, and Grossman supported her through her MFA. She deferred her own creative dreams for her wage-work in tourism. Grossman's father needed to be cared for, so they arranged to live with him. This saved them enough money that Janet no longer had to toil as a teaching assistant. By watching YouTube videos, Grossman learned how to fix leaky faucets and replace toilet bowl stoppers. After the corner store downstairs was closed, Janet used it briefly as a studio space, but the light was poor, and it was like trying to see to the bottom of a bowl of chicken broth.

At the beginning of the year, Janet's career had broken through to find an audience. After nearly two decades of painting, she won a major award, was profiled in an influential glossy magazine, and found a New York dealer. It all came at once. "In some ways, she no longer needed me to care for her. If we were eating out, I didn't have to pick up the tab," Grossman told Tso. "But then there would be a deadline for a big show, and the dealer was a shark who would drop her if she flopped. Her anxiety levels peaked. So she needed me more. However, now she resented it. One time, the day before one of her openings, we had a big fight because I wanted to wear the same suit I'd worn for her last show. When the exhibition turned out be a hit, she apologized. She moved out a few days later."

Unlike most of her contemporaries who explored mixed media and abstraction, Janet was a figurative painter. Her watercolours were inspired by both comic books and Mexican folk art, and her subjects were entirely young women—friends and family members in outdoor landscapes inspired by trips along the province's north coast. Grossman appeared in a number of Janet's paintings, but only as a stylized version of herself. She was painted in the Gertrude Stein T-shirt, but not in the way she looked when she was a camp counsellor. "My hair is asymmetrical in those portraits, but I didn't have that hairdo until years later," Grossman said. "Plus, I'm the only one who is fully clothed. Everyone else is topless or pant-less. It's like she doesn't want to imagine me naked. Either that, or she doesn't want to show the world the woman who she saw naked."

Tso shook her head. "I don't think that's what she meant," she told Grossman. *It's exactly what she means.* She realized again she was in a terrible mood.

Now that Janet was gone, Grossman said that she volunteered for many community arts events. "I'm taking a comedy course, too," she said. "I've always wanted to try stand-up."

Tso noted silently that Grossman had not attempted a single joke that night while introducing any of the presenters and that she seemed almost divorced from any sense of humour. Months later—when she had a standing order at a restaurant in Vancouver, when the city had been quarantined and she had seen people seriously ill—Tso remembered the restlessness of her first night with yearning. (She yearned for her agency.) By that time, she considered Grossman hilarious and endearingly damaged.

Someone at the party found Grossman and asked her to change the music to something more upbeat. Tso chose this moment to leave the party without a farewell. She crept to the front hall where she attempted to find her shoes from the bottom of the large pile. She took a picture of the shoes and would post it when she got home. She thought of a pithy caption: "This party is ghost-busted." Once she was outside on the landing, she glanced across to the door of Grossman's neighbour, Farhad Khan. The door was slightly ajar and the note had been changed.

I have killed myself, it read. *Call the police. You do not need to see this.*

The floorboards creaked as Tso inched toward the door. She could hear someone groaning. That meant he—Farhad—was alive. She heard a crash, the sound of feet, a body, and then the smack of a head hitting the floor. She jumped back. She would return to Grossman's apartment and make her go in and see what had happened. Her heart outraced the lazy beat of the eighties party music that had followed Leonard Cohen. Tso spotted Grossman at the far end of the living room, her glass full of ice.

Tso needed to get to her, but the people in the room—and the jovial, tipsy mood within it—made that distance feel impassable. She edged around the wall toward Grossman as the game of Werewolf finally concluded. The remaining participants opened their eyes. The final innocent villager had been killed, and one party-goer, the remaining werewolf, still looked circumspect. "I warned everyone," one of previously eliminated players complained. "But now we're all dead."

5.

Rieux and his mother had returned to his condo when he saw his first victim of the disease.

At the airport, Rieux's mother waited for him at the arrivals area, her Burberry jacket, handed down from her daughter, folded over her arm. He apologized for being late, but she had just come through the exit after waiting for a half hour for her bag to arrive on the conveyor belt. She only had her carry-on. "I got dizzy looking for it," she said. "Please, Son, will you help me speak to the airline?"

The man behind the desk at the counter said that all the luggage had been unloaded and claimed. "It's possible that the bag has been stolen," he told them. "It happens rarely. Do you have insurance?"

Mrs Rieux looked at her son in dismay and tugged the sleeve of his fleece jacket. It saddened him that his mother, once a woman who instilled fear among landlords, bureaucrats, and plumbers—as fearless as she was obsequious to her employers and the relatives who gave her money for her children's school expenses and tuition—now seemed so small and looked to him to make things better. Dr Rieux puffed out his chest and told him that airport security needed improvement. He gave the man his address and contact information should the luggage turn up.

"You've aged," she told him when they were in the cab. "That's good. Your patients will take you more seriously. That's not a bad thing. You look more like your father every day."

Rieux's father was only a half decade older than he was now—thirty-six—when he had been killed in a car crash. Rieux was five when his father died, old enough to have memories of him, though few remained—the sense of his father's moustache across his cheek was one of them. His father had been a doctor too, although Rieux had made no effort to emulate him. He'd passed on to his only son his hair, his slight stature, and according to Mrs Rieux, his taste for argument.

Mrs Rieux herself was a devout Catholic who believed in reincarnation. She saw joy in patterns and was the kind of person who, while eating a meal, was reminded of some place she'd visited as a child and would tell you all about it. She sometimes believed that the strangers she spoke to were dead relatives reborn. As she grew older, she became even more fanciful.

"Elyse sends her regards," Rieux offered.

"It makes me so sad for you two." She dabbed her eyes with a tissue. "When I look at her Facebook profile and see her most recent shots, it's like a light being dimmed."

"She's optimistic about this ... treatment," he said. "What's important is that she remains positive."

"Have you eaten?" she asked.

He'd conscientiously avoided dinner. Mrs Rieux would cook and clean while she was here. In Hong Kong, she was waited on by a Filipina helper hired by his older sister. When they arrived at his house, Mrs Rieux swept immediately into the kitchen before she even washed her face and wrapped an apron around her waist. Rieux set her jacket and handbag on the bed in the spare room where he would have taken her suitcase. It was the better room, with a mountain view, the one they had set aside for a nursery.

The phone rang. It was the seldom-used land line, a number called only by telemarketers and the woman who was now in the kitchen. "I am fine, Dr Rieux," a voice announced.

"Mr Santos?" Rieux asked.

"Do not worry about me," Mr Santos said. His breathing was heavy. "My wife worries too much."

"Are you not feeling well?"

The sound of coughing filled Rieux's ear. "Mrs Rieux looked very good today," Mr Santos said once he'd cleared his throat. "Is she going on a vacation?"

"She's in Mexico until the New Year."

"An extended holiday. How nice! It's too bad doctors have such busy schedules."

"Indeed."

"As you can tell, I'm feeling better as I speak. I won't take too much of your time. Enjoy your evening."

As Rieux puzzled over this phone call, Mrs Rieux prepared macaroni in broth with shredded ham and peas—a Chinese diner specialty. Her preference would have been to make a proper Cantonese meal, but first she would have to shop. She asked her son for bus directions to the nearest Chinese grocer. He worried that she'd have too much to carry and said they could go together.

She threw a hand against her forehead. "I forgot that I packed sausage in my luggage," she told him in Cantonese.

"We have that here," he answered in English. "You'll see when we get to the store. We can pick up some items—clothes, toiletries—tomorrow morning. It won't be long before your luggage is retrieved."

"You're already too busy. I'm here to help you."

"It's no trouble," he lied.

This was the extent of their conversation. As it had been in his youth, the meal was so devoid of chatter that every slurp and clink of spoons against bowls seemed to form its own language. At least in his youth his mother could ask him and his sister about schoolwork. This was the first time she'd seen him in a year and she would be here at least until January. Unless he insisted, she would not go sightseeing—she had lived here for twenty-five years, anyhow—or visit with her remaining friends. She would watch her Chinese TV shows through an elaborate black box whose installation Rieux had arranged last week. They would eat together, silently, and this would be the extent of their time together.

A firecracker went off nearby, causing Mrs Rieux to shudder. "Should we call the police?"

"It's Halloween," Rieux told her.

"Oh ... I'd forgotten about these North American customs," she said, recovering her composure.

Rieux had begun to explain the peculiarity of firecrackers at Halloween when the land line rang again. This time it was Mr Santos's wife. "I'm so sorry to bother you," she said. "My husband is unwell, but he refuses to visit the hospital."

It took Rieux a moment to understand what had happened: Mr and Mrs Santos had argued about calling Rieux, and Mr Santos had called him preemptively, thinking Rieux had already spoken to his wife. Mrs Santos described symptoms that resembled the flu. Dr Rieux said he would be down immediately. Normally he would have advised Mrs Santos to take her husband to the hospital, but he knew how stubborn the man could be.

"I have to speak to the superintendent," Rieux told his mother. While her back was turned, he retrieved the bicycle saddlebags where he kept some medical equipment.

The Santos's suite was similar to Rieux's, though their patio view offered more of the commuter traffic of Great Northern Way than the mountains. Mrs Santos led Rieux to the living room. Mr Santos was sitting on a worn brown leather couch, a wool blanket pulled up to his neck, his legs extended on a footrest. A water bottle sat on the armrest. The living room was dimly lit except for a floor lamp at the far end of the couch.

Mr Santos was visibly clammy. When he first saw Rieux, something like fear passed his face, which he covered over with a defiant, impatient look. The doctor realized that he'd always seen Mr Santos smiling, standing completely erect. The superintendent's features had never been more expressive, and he felt the superintendent's shame reflected back onto him.

"What did I already tell you, Dr Rieux?" he asked him.

"Mrs Santos asked me to take a look," Rieux told him. "I promise you, if this is not serious, we will leave you alone."

"There's swelling, Doctor," Mrs Santos said.

Mr Santos nodded and looked away as Rieux moved the floor lamp closer and retrieved a pair of latex gloves, a stethoscope, and a flashlight from his bag. Mr Santos flung his head back like a silent-film damsel-in-distress as Rieux pulled off the wool blanket.

Mr Santos was outfitted in a white undershirt and pyjama bottoms. The swelling on his lymph nodes startled Rieux. They looked like large blisters, each one the size of a robin's egg. Rieux could only recall seeing such swelling in photos.

"I'm sorry to tell you this," Rieux told the superintendent. "I can't say for sure what it is. But you need to go to the hospital."

Mrs Santos was already putting on her coat. Rieux helped them into their Toyota Camry in the garage. When he saw another dead rat, he again removed latex gloves from his bag, slipped them on, and placed the rodent into the trash can. He stood impatiently in the elevator on his way back to his apartment. After thoroughly washing his hands and throwing his clothes in the wash, he joined his mother in front of the television. Thankfully, no explanations were required by Mrs Rieux.

The doctor slept poorly that night. In the morning, he took the elevator downstairs and knocked on the Santos's door. He was about to return to the elevator when the door opened. Mrs Santos had gotten back from the hospital an hour ago. Mr Santos was still under observation and she would visit later this morning, she told him. Without explanation, Rieux asked for Mr Santos's keys. She pointed to a loop of keys by the door and handed them over. Rieux found his way to the supply closet where Mr Santos kept his cleaning equipment. Rieux took the broom and dustpan and went down to the garage where he was able to collect four dead rats.

There were also two dead squirrels and a dead raccoon—the urban wildlife Vancouverites were accustomed to seeing. He wrapped them up in two garbage bags, threw them in the trunk of his wife's Subaru Forester (they owned the car together but he did not generally like to drive), and delivered them to the incinerator in the suburbs.

The next morning, before work, he found six rats, including one lying belly up, feet pawing listlessly, that he killed; then twelve rats (and squirrels) the day after; and more in the days following that. News reports confirmed that Rieux's experience was shared in other parts of the city. Between the blasts and whistles of fireworks, Rieux could hear the moans of these pests as they died in the alleyway. And then, five or six days after Mr Santos discovered the first rat, after Rieux had filled three garbage bags with lifeless rodents, the doctor searched the garage for more corpses and didn't find a single one. The immediate relief he felt was quickly chased away by an uneasy feeling.

By the end of the next week, the city's hospitals saw about a hundred cases similar to Mr Santos's. For the first few days, the results were kept under cover to stave off hysteria as treatments were applied. The name of the disease had ugly historical connotations, and the antibiotics used to treat modern cases were highly effective. It was only after the first death that a press conference was called to announce the outbreak. Even then, the Minister of Health appeared to talk down the situation.

Mr Santos was not the first one to die; his death was part of a wave that occurred twenty-four hours after the first fatality. Because that initial death struck in one of the areas surrounding the Annex, many people ascribed the fatality to a resurgence in the drug problems that had previously afflicted the city. Roadblocks were set up within a two-block radius of the first casualty. Calls were made to protect taxpayers. Rieux learned of Mr Santos's death when a notice was posted in November by the strata management company. The company apologized for a delay in repairs and any decline in maintenance as a replacement was sought.

Part Two

6.

Now comes an intermediate period in our story, which covers the week when the quarantine was imposed. Each section of this narrative spans a different stage in the city, each signalling a refraction in the collective mood. As our story continues, the sections will extend to longer intervals when the days began to blur together. Our recollections are most imprecise in these later periods.

The first deaths set off, along with reports of the "inconclusive" nature of the illness, what could only be a rehearsal of panic. It was the reaction of people who had been drilled to deal with emergencies, who had watched them on their screens and been on airplanes with flight attendants wearing inflatable rings around their necks. Children were pulled from schools where they might become infected and taken instead to playgrounds and ice rinks. Some adults took a few days off from work, content to ride out the "flu." Very few of them left town. It was imperative for anxiety to be cloaked as an adventure. A local repertory cinema scheduled an impromptu selection of apocalyptic films, which ranged from Vincent Price's *Last Man on Earth* to Edgar Wright's *Shaun of the Dead*, from camp to comedy. The audience included Romeo Parsons, who made a point of looking confident and appearing in public every night that week. No one would characterize this period as "fun," but there was a heightened feeling in every Vancouverite's actions. A trip to the store to buy milk felt eventful. People said goodbye with tongue-in-cheek final gestures: "This may be the last time we see each other." And then they smooched like movie stars.

The Coastal Health Authority released information about hand-washing and warnings to stay away from rodents and urban wildlife, but only a few people knew of someone affected by the illness. The calamity became snagged in their consciousness as a catastrophe they were fortunate to avoid. The disease, with its absurd-sounding name, remained outside their spheres of concern. Until the quarantine, this threat only made people more outgoing. The shopping malls saw more business than usual. The bars were filled with people who spoke about how they wished they could still smoke inside. Singles eyed each other with deeper lust, knowing that yet another avenue existed for causing one another harm. On their profile photos they posted pictures of themselves wearing surgical masks. Others, hoping to look medieval, wore black cowls, but resembled nerdy sorcerers.

It's something that's happening downtown Vancouverites had said during a recent string of drug deaths that already felt like a bygone era. *They did it to themselves. Okay, they didn't start from the best places, but ...* Or when homicides reached new highs in the city, and people murdered each other in drive-by shootings at noodle houses, they said, *It's just gang members defending their turf. They're so professional that hardly anyone innocent ever gets killed. Don't deal drugs and you're safe.* And now, they ascribed blame to those who fell ill and drew walls around the casualties in order to protect their sense of safety.

During her first week in Vancouver, Megan Tso still considered herself a short-term visitor. Her second engagement, the mysterious but lucrative consulting contract mentioned in the first section of this chronicle, had been delayed. An intermediary for the wealthy man who'd engaged her services apologized for the need to reschedule. In addition to compensating her for her extra days, this executive assistant offered to upgrade her accommodations. With this offer, Tso moved into a room with a kitchenette.

Her extended stopover in Vancouver during a public health crisis was an opportunity for reflection. This break happened for a reason, she told herself. She would shake off her jet lag here. She would breathe clean air and enjoy the relatively underpopulated Canadian city.

In the week that ensued, she did the following: She returned the suitcase to a nice old woman; her son accepted the bag, a man with the face and stature of an Egyptian pharaoh who closed the door before she could offer the amusing explanation and apology that she'd planned in the taxi. (The airline delivered her luggage the same day.) She walked the entire length of the Seawall twice. More and more people were wearing face masks in public. She visited the library and read Thucydides's *The History of the Peloponnesian War* for hour-long stretches before returning it to its spot on the shelf. She couldn't help but notice how many people were coughing in the library, coughing into their hands and then typing their queries at the library internet terminals. Afterward, she went to the drug store and bought hand sanitizer. She checked in on Janice Grossman.

Grossman invited her over for a cup of tea. What Tso really wanted to know was the condition of Farhad Khan. Grossman had discovered him prone on the floor of his kitchenette next to an upturned chair. Tso had inched behind her into Khan's apartment, which smelled like sour laundry and empty liquor bottles. Khan lay slumped on the floor, cheek-and-jowl flush against the same checkerboard tiles she'd seen in Grossman's kitchen. Around Khan's neck was a tie knotted around a light fixture that had dislodged from the ceiling. Tso had called 9-1-1, anxious because she would have to pay roaming fees. Khan sat up. He looked to be in his mid-twenties, but seemed to have stepped out of a film noir. He had dark, slightly protuberant eyes, a stubbly muzzle, and wavy hair, slicked and shiny. There was a gash on his head from the fall, and he was mumbling to himself in Persian. Grossman crouched beside him, her concern alternating between her tenant and the hole in the ceiling that she had to fix. When Tso left, around the same time the police and ambulance arrived, Grossman's father stood outside his door, muttering under his breath. Occasionally, he shrugged his shoulders as though he were commiserating with himself.

"Farhad's in my spare room right now, napping," Grossman now told Tso. "He has no family, you see, and someone needed to be responsible for him. Otherwise he'd rot in the hospital. My father thinks I'm a sucker."

"I can see his point."

"I know how it seems—it's like Janet all over again. But it's easy to judge Farhad. We come from stable countries. He's from Iran, you might recall. Who knows how he's suffered?" Grossman admitted that she had not asked Khan about his background or suffering. In their period of temporary cohabitation, Khan had not volunteered much about his life except for an interest in dance remixes of Adele songs. In the two days that he had stayed with Grossman, he spent most of his waking hours on the phone. Earlier that morning, he'd left the building for the first time.

They were on their second pot of Lemon Zinger when Khan returned.
They could hear him singing, in Persian—syllables parked against a silent
drum machine beat—as he bounded up the stairs. Tso had only seen Khan
once, spread out on his kitchen floor, and didn't notice how tall he was.
Once he removed his jacket, Khan entered Grossman's kitchen. He presented his landlady with a bouquet of flowers purchased from a corner store.
Although he was still gaunt and pale, he was clean-shaven, and the circles
under his eyes had begun to fade. He introduced himself to Tso as though
they hadn't met.

Khan said that he'd spent the day visiting friends about a business opportunity. "It was good to go outside," he told them. "It wasn't too cold."

"You're not worried about getting sick?" Tso asked.

"Sister," he addressed her, as he looked in Grossman's refrigerator for
a bottle of beer, "I have been sick my whole life. Now I'm better. I've got
nothing to hide."

"You might be the happiest person in Vancouver," Grossman suggested.
She admired the flowers in their coloured cellophane.

Khan chuckled mirthlessly. He stood by the refrigerator wearing only
a white T-shirt and jeans. His arms were lean and wiry. His phone began to
buzz and he took the call in his own room.

Grossman invited Tso to ride on her city tour the next day. She initially
declined, preferring instead to read at the library, but when she discovered
Thucydides missing from his regular place, she changed her mind and headed toward the tour's starting point at Canada Place. Grossman pulled up,
driving a converted school bus and wearing a microphone around her neck.

There were about a dozen people waiting with Tso. A couple of men wore chambray shirts and khaki shorts and seemed obviously American. There were Chinese tourists and German visitors too. Grossman took their fares. Most of them spread out on the bus.

"Good afternoon, brave visitors to Vancouver," Grossman told the sparsely filled bus as it left the curb. Her elocution became brighter, gathering intensity mid-sentence, her words delivered as though she recited them from sheet music. "Thank you for making sure I still have gainful employment. It's been a little quiet the past week." She stopped at a light and peered back. "Was it because you couldn't get a refund? Or are any of you in town for the epidemic?"

There was an anxious pause. The European and Chinese tourists reacted with befuddlement. "We're here for an Alaska cruise," one of the ever-smiling silver-haired Americans said. She liked him better than the others. "We're more afraid of guns than the flu." Probably from California.

"Welcome to my hometown, the only city I've lived in, and I can tell you it's changed a lot. A mystique has developed around the city—one that might be visible to locals who like to think we live in the best or worst city in the world. Has anyone heard any of these myths?" She did not wait for a reply. "Let me dispel some of them. The first is that everyone here is rich. It's true that anyone who owns land here, for instance, is a millionaire on paper. And there are truly rich people, of course. But we also have millionaires who line up at the food bank. We have heiresses to million-dollar fortunes driving, for example, tour buses. The second myth is that Vancouverites are notoriously unfriendly. It's not true, but the city is clique-y. I think of it as a video game where you need to level up by acquir-ing high-user ratings. When it comes to social equity, inequality is high."

Her rambling digressions exhausted the tourists, whose attention returned to their copies of *Lonely Planet*. "Please note the stops on the itinerary. We will visit every one of those at the appointed times, but I may park a while at a couple of other personal favourites."

They stopped for thirty minutes at that shopping street, the Van-couver version of Rodeo Drive. New tourists boarded there, including a young woman who sat next to Tso at the front of the bus and wouldn't stop coughing into her phone, in which she was texting in Japanese. The bus started down another busy street toward the city's famous park.

Tso was looking out the window when the Japanese woman coughed again. As she rose Tso caught a glimpse of the bloody Kleenex she clutched in her hand. (If Tso's observation is correct, this would be one of the earliest indications that the infection had progressed to its pneumonic form. This would have preceded the first officially documented case by at least three days.) The woman walked to Grossman's seat while the bus was stopped at a red light. She whispered in Grossman's ear, but the driver's headset microphone broadcast the woman's brief statement: "I believe I have it." Grossman turned off the mike. The bus lurched into the intersection.

She switched on her mic. "Excuse me, ladies and gentlemen and those of you who are both and neither, we will not be going to Stanley Park, as I promised. Not yet. Instead we will be embarking on the off-the-menu part of our tour," she said. "Our first stop is the West End where you'll find many bike-rental shops, a fine pierogi place, and, oh look, the answer to your picture-framing needs. Famous residents include that dipsomaniac novelist Malcolm Lowry. Growing up on the east side, I thought everyone who led an interesting life in Vancouver—and there weren't many—inhabited these streets. I would take the bus down here as a teenager, look at comic books on Granville Street and wander these residential streets, hoping someone from one of the buildings would run out onto the street and kidnap me into their cosmopolitan life."

The Japanese woman was visibly sweating. She had taken a seat directly behind Grossman now. She shivered and repeated the same Japanese phrase in a baby voice. Tso tried to talk to her, but the woman waved her off. The bus turned down Nelson Street.

Grossman related the story of Errol Flynn's death as they entered the emergency department lot. She took a wide turn in the driveway and blocked an ambulance. The hospital, with its arched Edwardian windows and tin roof, seemed to contain the city's reserve of red brick. (It was one of only a few anomalous throwbacks in this city of steel and glass condo towers that were built to melt into one another.) "Well, I hope I haven't soured you on our fine healthcare system in the city and country. Here we are at St. Paul's Hospital where you'll be free to disembark and look around. The next tour bus will pick you up only six blocks from here. Please direct all comments and suggestions to our website or office number. Have a great day."

Grossman draped the Japanese tourist's arm over her shoulder and led her off the bus. People filed out after them. The Asians were spooked, the Europeans bemused. The Americans tried to give cash tips. Tso stood by the open bus door, watching as the Japanese passenger stopped and turned back.

"She wants her purse," Grossman told her.

Tso found the purse on her seat. As she stepped out, an ambulance driver told her to move her vehicle. Tso offered to check the woman in at reception so Grossman could re-park her bus. "You don't want to lose your job," Tso told her. "I'll handle it." Grossman's reaction—a slight recoiling—suggested that she didn't often get much assistance, and being offered help felt like a questioning of her competency.

In the waiting room, people took inventory of one another as they coughed and shivered in their chairs. Some were doubled over, others wore blankets. She found a seat for the woman and tried to check her in using the information in the passport that she'd retrieved from her purse.

"How are you related to this woman?" the nurse asked from behind a partitioned booth.

"I don't—I'm not. I met her on the tour bus. We're tourists."

"I see. And you were saying she was feeling uncomfortable?"

Tso hesitated. Should she mention she'd seen this woman coughing blood? What if she had just imagined it? She no longer trusted her memory. What she said would affect this woman's treatment. What if she withheld the detail—what would happen then? Finally, she told the nurse what she saw. The clatter of the nurse's data entry slowed.

"It was just what I thought I saw," Tso said.

"That's all you need to tell us. The doctors will check your observation."

Tso returned to the Japanese woman slumped in her seat. "Yuko?" she said, repeating the name on the passport. The woman looked up. Tso told her that she would be getting help. Did she understand? She nodded. How was she feeling? She nodded again. Did she need anything? She made a drinking gesture with her hand. Then she said, "Water."

At the vending machine she dug through her collection of Canadian coins. How lucky she was not to be sick in a foreign country. *Like Yuko.* People imagine the ideal death to be in your own bed. Tso thought that she'd be satisfied dying in a country in which she was a passport-holder.

She recalled that a doctor who'd treated an early SARS patient had travelled from Guangdong to Hong Kong to attend a wedding in 2003. He went through the security controls that kept Mainland Chinese from Hong Kong. The former British colony was under its own sequester. The first press report about SARS was a denial, but everyone knew better and began to stockpile vinegar, a traditional remedy for the disease. They cleaned their hands in vinegar, wiped bus seats with it. The doctor was aware that the case of flu he had seen was atypical. Over three hundred people had already become ill; five of them had died. But he had taken precautions and deemed himself safe to travel. He took a ninth-floor room in the Metropole Hotel in Kowloon. The next day, he felt too ill to attend the wedding but well enough to walk to a nearby hospital. When he was admitted, he told them to lock him up. No one at the Kwong Wah hospital knew what they were dealing with. A month later, the doctor died, and eighty-seven medical staff members and students had fallen ill. The disease spread from his hotel room to Hanoi, Singapore, Taipei, Toronto, and Vancouver. Only in Vancouver were necessary precautions taken—an infected fifty-five-year-old man was isolated—and an outbreak was prevented.

When Tso turned back, the Japanese woman was no longer in her seat. Only her purse remained; she had taken her phone. She was being wheeled down a hall by nurses in hazmat suits. The hall seemed to stretch further in Tso's head than in reality as she thought about Yuko's reaction to not having a purse. She had written something about how dying people reach for their wallets when they wake. We're trained to think of every process, even the biological ones, as a transaction. Tso grabbed the purse and called out to them. The doors closed.

7.

Raymond Siddhu needed the walk home from the bus stop to clear the exhaust fumes from his lungs. There was no sidewalk where they lived, so he would step into the outer lip of a grassy ditch whenever a car passed by. A neighbour once called the cops when he saw him on his evening stroll. Siddhu could not fault his neighbour; being a pedestrian qualified as a suspicious activity here. The physical aloofness of suburban life—different from the more social standoffishness seen within the city limits—would keep his family safe as long as they avoided the mall and cleaned their hands after paying at the drive-thru window.

When he came through the door, his boys tottered toward him, each holding out their arms like high-wire performers. They'd started walking only two weeks earlier, and he saw their steps grow more steady with each new day.

Perhaps, Siddhu considered, the image of their father grimacing at them would have no effect on their psyches. They would not remember the days when Daddy pried them off with a closed umbrella on the way to the sink to scrub his hands. He returned, eyes smiling, grabbing each of them under his arms and spinning around until they squealed and giggled.

"Put them down," Uma Siddhu said. She was wearing an apron and a high-school era sweatshirt. "Time to eat."

"You should have started without me."

"Don't tell me what to do."

"You know you get angry when you're hungry."

"And you know you get stupid when you open your mouth."

So far, there had been no reports of the disease outside the city's downtown core. Uma still suggested that he take a leave from work. "You're being an alarmist," he said accusingly as Uma placed their dinner on the messy table where their boys had already eaten.

"What are *you*, then?" she asked back.

"Being rational."

She scoffed at him. She was the even-tempered one in their marriage, the one who found compromise. He was the impulse shopper grabbing fistfuls of chocolate bars at the checkout counter. "There are no rationalists in these situations," she told him. "There are those who *let it happen to them* and the *alarmists*. Pick a side."

As they ate, they watched their boys in the living room ambling around, looking for something to topple. Before too long they would find each other. They would fight over a box. Tears would follow.

"This tastes good," he told her. He didn't even know what he was putting in his mouth. It was brown—it had been pressure-cooked—and served on rice. Her parents, who lived on the other side of the duplex, were in Asia, so he and Uma relished their ability to eat quick meals.

He didn't want to make her angry. He did not want to tell her that he'd spent the day at a hospital speaking to health officials, who claimed to be waiting for results, and doctors. Or that he'd been in a hospital with people who didn't cough into their elbows. Maybe Uma had a point about safety—he couldn't take chances, now that he was a father. That's why he'd sold his motorcycle and stopped playing rec hockey after he broke his ankle.

And he wanted to have sex with her that night, even if he needed to put the boys to sleep on his own (so she could relax) and take a shower. He listened to himself chew, to the clack of cutlery on plates.

"You know this is a great story," he said. "It'll be the only chance I get to write one."

He could hear one boy creak, a prelude to angry sobs of a wish unheeded. The other one was cackling wickedly. Siddhu was reminded of the fact that his own younger brothers hadn't called him since the summer.

"If you took on the metro beat, you could write about gang warfare. You could be first on the scene of every drive-by execution. If you pry enough, we might get threatening phone calls at night. You might even get killed, but you wouldn't bring disease into this house," she suggested. "Would that be exciting enough for you?"

"It's not about excitement," Siddhu told her. Correction: It was only partially about thrill. He was carrying out a promise he'd made to himself: The newspaper would die, but not because of his departure. He was a self-appointed officer aboard a sinking ship.

"Let that website cover the story," she told him. "They've beaten you so far."

It was true that GSSP had broken the news about the first fatalities. They had been the first to comment on the delays between setbacks in infection management and reports from the Health Authority. On one level, Siddhu had been glad that someone had reported the story. And yet he was stunned—up until then, GSSP's reporting had been inept, even with its click-generated wealth. Until recently, they had only one reporter, the website owner, Elliot Horne-Bough, whom everyone referred to as Hornblow. He dressed in skinny neckties and took photos using a Polaroid camera. *How could I be losing stories to him? And why does he want to hire me?* Meanwhile, Siddhu was interviewing city councillors about the restricted access to disease flashpoints. In these areas, signage had been erected advising only local traffic to enter. Other notices strongly advised wearing face masks.

Today, he'd attended a mid-afternoon special council meeting that ended in a fight when a councillor from Romeo Parsons' party attacked the mayor for his inability to immediately provide better temporary housing and showering stations in economically disadvantaged parts of the city. It represented Parsons' first broken promise in his initial month as mayor, the councillor told him. Siddhu watched Parsons' face as it tightened into something rigid and clenched before loosening back into appealing handsomeness.

The councillor, a twenty-nine-year-old advocate for sex workers, had been personally recruited by Parsons. When the mayor deflected her earnest pleas, she rose from her seat in the cherry-panelled council chambers. She was seated at the far end of the room from the mayor, and as she rushed toward him another female councillor, a Parsons loyalist from the same party, took her by the arm. The first councillor struck the other one with an open hand and left the council chambers.

Siddhu tried to change the discussion with Uma. He asked her about the boys' music class—they banged tambourines on play mats while the teacher sang nursery rhymes. The range of their conversations had narrowed to two sharp points since the boys were born.

She brought out her smartphone. He decided not to repeat his question.

Siddhu offered to give the boys a bath while his wife watched Netflix. He decided against washing their hair to avoid tears and let them play with a plastic tea set. After their bath, he dried and dressed them, then flashed his yo-yo as both boys pulled themselves up against the crib railing. He was working on a more intermediate-level trick: Split the Atom. It started out like a Brain Twister but involved another step. The boys lost interest as he worked on the pushing motion. He won them back with his old stand-bys until they had slumped back into their cribs. Then he waited at the door until they cried themselves to sleep.

In the weeks that ensued, he would summon each of these moments to savour like heirlooms from a lost world.

His wife waited for him under the covers, already naked. As he stripped down, she held up a corner of the duvet for him like an open car door and he felt the chill of the air on his chest. He rolled toward her in bed, and they reached for each other, pulling all the compulsory levers. There was no time to tease or upgrade from the basic package. They felt grateful for the certainty of their flesh. A cry from the other room would force them to freeze; a longer wail would shut things down. Hurry, hurry. Success, success.

Siddhu lay there afterward in the light from the hall. The bedroom took on a grainy quality, and he slept poorly. Uma and the boys were still asleep when he awoke and packed his lunch. When he got on the bus, he found a seat—normally, he had to stand. On the SkyTrain, he was one of only two people in his car. From the station, he stepped outside to see that the sun had broken. The office buildings glinted in the damp air with the sheen of plastic wrap.

It had taken a potential health crisis for the mood in the office to brighten. People moved quickly. No one here thought that their work would gain new subscriptions or earn them kudos, but it seemed like a rewarding diversion. Like Siddhu, they saw opportunities for noble career deaths.

At his mentor's retirement party, the paper's thirty-year veteran—the Chicago-born wife of a draft dodger—took him aside and asked him to start sending out his résumé. "I'm not worried about old goats like me," she told him. "And I don't know the newbies well enough to give a shit. But I'm worried about you. You've been here for all of the bad years and none of the good ones. The paper looks like it'll die by the end of the work week, but it's going to keep sputtering for a few more years. I'm worried that, by then, you'll be too long in the tooth to be employable. Even worse than that, I'm concerned that it'll make you a good family man, at the expense of your work. They say no one dies wishing they worked more. *Absolute bullshit.* Maybe if you're selling hot dogs. Not so much when your job is looking at the world." Siddhu remembered her talk verbatim. She had never said that much in their entire working relationship.

He took his place at her desk and started her old computer. In his inbox was a notice from the city's communications director about a press conference. It related to the fight in council. He caught the train to City Hall and arrived early, taking his place in the front row next to Horne-Bough.

"It's definitely about the fight," Horne-Bough said in a stage whisper. He held his Polaroid camera with both hands. "The mayor's ego has been clipped by the radical wing of his party. They're going to lift the restrictions on the area around the Annex. 'Freedom is given to everyone in this city, or no one.'"

"Maybe you should be holding the press conference," Siddhu said through glassy laughter. He had a feeling that the mayor would repeat those same sentiments, in those words. "Who's your source?"

"I'll tell you, if you answer my own question. Where does one get the best craft Kölsch in the downtown area?"

"Are you counting Strathcona?" Siddhu asked. He'd occasionally post about breweries for the paper's food and drink blog. Horne-Bough had been doing his research.

"Anywhere within a fifteen-minute cab ride."

Siddhu offered a detailed and comprehensive ranking of breweries that any reasonable person would describe as overkill.

"As you know, I've been trying to get you to our offices for two weeks," Horne-Bough said after Siddhu's disquisition. "Maybe you're afraid of me. I don't take it personally. A more informal venue might help. What if I were to invite you for one of those Kölschs tonight?"

Romeo Parsons bounded in front of the podium. Siddhu noticed that he had a habit of mouthing certain phrases, the money lines of his prepared

remarks, before he spoke. He wore a blue tie that matched the curtains behind him. Those curtains were a lighter tint of blue than the blue used by
the previous mayor. The colour change had been a recommendation from
a branding firm—at a cost of $12,000. "They really bring out his eyes,"
the reporter from a local radio station snickered. It was the first time that
Siddhu had heard an unkind remark uttered about the mayor.

Parsons began with an apology for the fight in City Hall. "These are
tense times. There's been unnecessary panic and finger-pointing," he said.
"We've seen nothing like this in our city since the Spanish Influenza at the
end of the First World War." Siddhu had heard that the city councillor
who'd attacked him had left the caucus. (Later that day, she announced she
was sitting as an independent.)

What made Parsons an electrifying speaker was a modest amount of
eloquence refracted through joyfulness. Even now he smiled, but it wasn't
a hayseed smile; Parsons was a Rhodes Scholar, and he sat on the board
of directors of the Art Institute of Chicago. The rest of his remarks fell
in line with Horne-Bough's prediction. Parsons added that he regretted
the advice he'd been given from the Coastal Health Authority about the
neighbourhood restrictions.

"What happened was that we needed to balance health safety with
our concerns about our city's most marginalized people. We failed in this
regard. We have heard stories about harassment from our most desperate
people. We have further demonized our most vulnerable people. Meanwhile, rates of infection haven't decreased. The roadblocks have caused
traffic congestion." New measures would be announced soon to take the

place of the old ones. "These new guidelines will be fairly applied to all. Until then, we all must proceed carefully. We don't know the true extent of this health situation."

The question period followed. Most queries were couched in praise for the mayor's demeanor. There was still an aura about him, and the press still wanted him to succeed. Their own work as political reporters had been lifted by Parsons' lofty profile. Voter turnout had risen by a quarter because of his presence. People talked about residential zoning and garbage collection with the same depth of feeling as they would about the all-time greatest hockey players. Relatives and friends of reporters inquired about their work with interest.

To his credit, only Horne-Bough asked a question that unnerved the mayor. "According to some accounts, twenty-nine people have died. When will we know this is a crisis?"

"I—I don't think it's, uh, twenty-nine," Parsons stammered. "That's not confirmed." The rest of the mayor's mumbled response could not be stitched into a coherent reply.

As the mayor finished the conference, he approached Horne-Bough and Siddhu, who had stood by the exit. "I hope you don't mind some tough questions," Horne-Bough said.

The mayor smirked. "I'm still standing."

"Care to be in a Polaroid with a colleague?" he asked. "It's for my private collection."

"Anything involving Ray-Ray here is okay," the Mayor insisted. He put one arm around Siddhu. The mayor smelled like he had been outside all day. It wasn't a bad odour. He gave off the smell of someone who'd spent the afternoon hiking through a rainforest path. Parsons held the same camera-ready smile even as Horne-Bough tried his shot from various angles, finally holding the Polaroid over his head.

Later, at a nearby gastropub, Horne-Bough confessed that he was trying to see how long the mayor could hold his expression; the Polaroid shots caught only the tops of their heads. Each of them had the brewery's tasting flights arranged in front of them on wooden trays. Horne-Bough seemed taken aback by the set-up—it looked like a science project. "I am more of a soju drinker," he confessed. "I don't even need fancy soju."

Horne-Bough looked to be in his mid-twenties. He came from a wealthy Toronto family and had arrived in Vancouver only two years earlier. Although he was privileged, he claimed that his money was largely his own. Four years earlier, he'd placed most of a small inheritance into the hands of some boarding-school friends who'd launched an app that was later sold for what was rumoured to be a nine-figure sum. He had little experience in news besides a CBC internship he'd completed after high school.

With the exception of that internship, Horne-Bough's work experience consisted of a string of odd, low-skill jobs: he played the "white guy" in a number of Korean TV shows after working on a documentary in Seoul. He cared for a falcon in Antwerp owned by an eccentric Belgian industrialist who dabbled in illegal arms dealing. He herded yaks in Tibet for two brothers married to the same woman—a local practice meant to keep land within a family. He so enjoyed recounting these workplace tales that Siddhu wondered whether that wasn't the point in acquiring them. After all, he didn't need the money. As he listed his jobs, he bounced between the mannerisms of a fey layabout and the more aggressive language of a bootstrapping start-up head.

"I don't do well if I don't have something to do," he said. "Or something in my hands."

"You should work with wood," Siddhu suggested.

Horne-Bough's eyes flashed then dimmed. "Except that I'm so absent-minded, I'd lose a finger."

"Better yet," Siddhu said, palming the yo-yo, "you should get one of these."

He let the yo-yo slide out between their two stools at the bar.

"I love how it whirs," Horne-Bough said, his eyes following the yo-yo. "That sound is wonderful."

Like the mayor, this spindly young entrepreneur was fascinating to Siddhu. Horne-Bough was not the stingy kind of rich person, nor was he oblivious to cash. He saw money not as lifeblood but as a social lubricant. "Contrary to what you newsmen think, I want to pay for content," Horne-Bough told him. "Maybe not a unionized shop, but wages and benefits and options." His model was not just click-driven, but also used a subscription/patronage model from individual subscribers and institutions. GSSP's initial staff included a couple of Siddhu's ex-colleagues, including a formerly fresh-faced investigative reporter who'd been laid off before he could qualify for a buyout. Another staffer was a journalism grad who used to work as the mayor's executive assistant and knew where he did his dry cleaning. "The city has grown enormously in the past decade in terms of wealth. There are people willing to pay top dollar for the best cars and food and sunglasses and ski chalets. There's no reason why they wouldn't want to pay more for the best news coverage. There are no better circumstances for this model to flourish."

GSSP saw itself not only as a reporting service but a private knowledge hub, a "data concierge" for the wealthy. Horne-Bough was certain people would pay a four-figure annual subscription for, among other things, a phone number that got them a cab five minutes earlier. "Everyone else will get the news for free, but there will be a time lag—sometimes a day, sometimes fifteen minutes," Horne-Bough suggested. "Others will still get news free before your paper can give it away. But those who have paid will have a piece of—you guessed it—gossip."

Between their two tasting flights, Horne-Bough checked text messages on a 2007-era vintage flip phone. He'd explained he liked older technology—not as a conversation piece but because it reduced the time he spent not focusing on his present surroundings, yet he checked it and set it aside several times throughout their conversation. This time, though, he gaped at the phone. After a prolonged silence, he signalled to the waiter for a bill.

"It contradicts our workplace culture to leave a drink for the office, but this one is big," he told Siddhu. "I need to write this story and get it out there. I won't even have time to use my electric typewriter."

"What is it?" Siddhu asked. He added, "I can keep a secret."

Horne-Bough hesitated. The World Health Organization, in dialogue with Vancouver Coastal Health, had recommended a city-wide quarantine. The announcement would come quickly and leave people with the least amount of time to flee. The city wanted to avoid the situation that had occurred in Surat, India in 1994, when the disease struck and three hundred thousand people evacuated the city in fear of being quarantined.

Flights coming into the city were being rerouted. Roadblocks would be erected on all highways and bridges to the metro area within an hour. "You live in the boonies, don't you? I figure you should get a head start," he said, reaching for a wallet that was stuffed with hundred-dollar bills. Horne-Bough, whose loft was only steps away in Railtown, preferred cash because he'd lost his wallet too many times to use plastic. He carried no ID for the same reason.

Siddhu began to run toward the nearest SkyTrain station. He was not physically fit, so he found himself staggering at the foot of Water Street. The city scene outside, give or take a few face masks, could have passed for any day in the past decade. The sun beat down benevolently, and the air was worth paying money to breathe. He swiped his Compass Card as he rushed through the SkyTrain gates, then ran down the steps to catch the incoming train. He was huffing and puffing when he took his seat.

The crowd on the half-full SkyTrain car was occupied by commuters who were bored, jovial, or solitary. There was a couple in their twenties making out, an extremely tall cyclist in spandex with his racing bike, one guy singing along to music with his eyes closed. He recognized a face or two: people he didn't know, but who, like him, rode this train until its terminal point in Surrey. They had fit themselves snugly into their compartments of private space, pressed against window seats, their brief-cases and purses on their laps.

He checked his phone for news coverage as the car slowed into Burrard Station. Nothing. He texted his wife to say that he was coming home. She texted back to ask him to buy string cheese. He checked his phone again. Nothing on his paper's app or website. It occurred to him that this had been a prank and he was rushing home based on misinformation. Siddhu told himself that this could not happen. At Stadium-Chinatown station, a two-sentence item appeared on Horne-Bough's website. When they stopped outside Science World, he received two calls from his paper's editor-in-chief. He left them unanswered and the voicemails unopened.

On social media, there were unofficial reports about the roadblocks and the airport closure. By the time they reached the Commercial-Broadway Station, the SkyTrain had started to fill. Siddhu gave up his seat to a pregnant woman. People pushed into the car, their faces red from running and squeezing. Heads remained bowed toward their devices, and thumbs tapped screens to refresh web browsers. People whispered to one another, looking out from the corners of their eyes.

At the Joyce-Collingwood Station, the last one before they crossed city limits, Siddhu had a sense of what it might be like to commute in Tokyo or Shanghai. Many passengers who stood could no longer hold onto a strap or rail or pole. They propped themselves against other commuters desperate to get home. They still held phones up to their faces, sometimes pressed to their cheeks. They tapped and tapped.

When the train left the station, the suburbanites in the car heaved

one collective sigh. When the automated voice, heralded by the ubiqui-
tous three-toned chime, announced the next stop to be Metrotown, Siddhu heard cheers. The city limits came within sight as their train began to
slow down. Siddhu waited for it to halt, but he still felt surprised. Groans
flushed out the sighs. The mood spoiled. Siddhu heard someone complain
that they had trouble breathing.

Five minutes passed. They began to move again. Those who were
standing wilted as the car inched in the opposite direction. Everyone
was quiet. They were going back into the city, back toward death. Siddhu expected an announcement over the PA system, but all he heard was
the chime followed by the pre-recorded voice announcing the next stop,
Joyce-Collingwood Station.

The train thinned out, more or less in the same order, with people returning to their offices and workplaces. Siddhu got off behind the man in
spandex rolling his bike. He wanted to completely reverse his course and
go back to his stool at the gastropub. He sent Uma a terse text message and
called his boss to say he was returning to the office. Night swallowed the
skyline, and the city became busier. All around were people who looked
like Siddhu: stunned, moving uneasily, moving because they would look
crazy if they just stood there.

8.

It is now difficult to recall our bafflement in those first forty-eight hours. Up came barbed wire fences and outposts manned by camouflaged men in body armour with assault rifles. Only essential products, groceries, and medical supplies were allowed in after being screened by security officers with dogs. Dystopias were evoked, liberally. Friends and family from "outside" shared our alarm, but we resolved our cognitive dissonance at every turn. We drove our children to school and scraped our plates into the compost (picked up by sanitation staff in hazmat suits). Our devotion to routine was how we sought comfort in the moments after the hot flare of annoyance tapered into disquiet—when we noticed, say, a co-worker absent from a meeting. Or when we saw entire aisles in markets picked clean.

Once the quarantine was imposed, Dr Bernard Rieux remained busy with walk-in traffic at his clinic. According to the diary he kept, a few patients presented the swelling and flu-like symptoms associated with the disease. He lanced their buboes and advised them to check into the hospital. They asked him how worried they should be. Rieux learned to parry back that worry didn't matter, treatment did. "Take your time getting there," he instructed. "How important is it to rush if you get hit by a car crossing the street?"

He told a handful of patients who had become infected to pack a good book. It was solid advice, innocuous enough, but the first time those words left his mouth he felt a twinge of disbelief. He didn't usually offer suggestions like that and was wary of any overreach in a doctor's authority. Why had he changed course? The disease had done this to him. He wanted to offer patients something, but he had no reassurances. His work frequently involved batting away unfounded fears, contextualizing symptoms, and limiting expectations. Patients often explained away danger, and he could frighten them into worry. But the surge of preparation that followed alarm would not do much to save his patients. He had nothing else to offer but to suggest they read while waiting.

To his relief, patients responded pleasantly to his advice; one asked for recommendations. Rieux named Leo Tolstoy, Chinua Achebe, and Virginia Woolf. "Stick to the books written by dead people," he added. Contemporary literature, to him, felt too much like posturing.

His favourite patient, Walter, came in regularly, as expected. Walter was difficult. Aside from an occasional cold and high blood pressure, he was healthy, but he visited the clinic at least twice a week. Rieux did his best to hasten their appointments, but he knew that Walter's interaction with him amounted to his only social outing of the day. His chart indicated that he was fifty-seven years of age, but he could have passed for any age between forty and sixty. His hands were rough from years as a dishwasher and a labourer in construction, but his face was remarkably soft (more remarkable because of the smoking). And he had the slight, hairless body of an active pre-teen.

Rieux looked at his file. "I understand you feel you were infected?" he asked.

"Of course I am," Walter said, speaking into the fluorescent lights above him as he lay on the table. "Why wouldn't I be targeted?"

Rieux inspected Walter thoroughly for signs of illness, knowing this might be the only time he was touched today. (Rieux's theory was that Walter had once been a sensualist, but had forsworn human contact.) Walter explained that this variant of the disease had been manufactured in a laboratory, refracting theories he'd dug up from library internet terminals. "Of course it was manufactured," Walter said. "Let's talk about how small-pox exists only in the world in two laboratories. One in the States, and one in Russia. It's a fact. Look it up. How easy would it be to manufacture the plague?" Disease had been exposed to the public as a form of population control. "Look at the deficits the government is running. Just think," he said, tapping his head. "How much money would we save if all the poor people died? This outbreak is finishing the work that was started by the Annex."

"I pay enough taxes as it is," Rieux joked.

"You fucking doctors," Walter said, sitting up. "You never get sick. You never know how it feels."

"How are your hemorrhoids?" Rieux asked him. "Did the cream I give you work? Did you try it? I know it's awkward to apply."

"That's where it begins." He buttoned up his shirt. *The thing with Walter was that he wanted to be sick*, Rieux wrote in one of his diary entries. *I'm not his healer but his witness.* By disposition, Walter did not use any drugs, he remained homebound, but he had not yet exhibited any urges to run into traffic.

"A lot of us are getting swept up in the concern over this epidemic,"

Rieux told him. "You don't have it. Who knows? Maybe you'll get it later."

Walter's mouth wobbled in withheld delight as he refocussed. "Dr Rieux, I come from a group—we've been beaten up by people who look like you. People who look like money. Do you know how many people I've seen die? Hundreds. *Literally*. Loved ones, friends, enemies. People who lived better lives than me. People who never did one thing wrong to anyone. This isn't 'survivor's guilt.' Everyone says that."

Walter left as soon as his exam was over—for once. His appointment came before Rieux's lunch break. That day, the second one of the quarantine, Rieux saw his friend and mentor, Dr Orla Castello. They had run into each other earlier in the fall at Whole Foods. In the produce aisle, they made a lunch date on their respective smartphones. She had only two white potatoes and half a pomegranate in her basket. Since that interaction, the date had been pushed back twice already. In Vancouver, the effort of staying in touch and the affections stirred by seeing an old friend's name appear on your screen before you messaged them to postpone felt more friendship-affirming than actual socializing. Seeing that old friend, once excuses could not be summoned, often underscored the growing chasm between two people.

As Chief Medical Health Officer at the Coastal Health Authority, Castello could credibly claim to be engrossed in her work. Rieux expected another postponement, if not an outright cancellation. Instead, she'd called to confirm their get-together. "I need a break," she told him. "And you owe me a distraction."

Long ago, Rieux had been Castello's student at medical school. As a teacher, Castello was a divisive figure. Rieux's peers felt she rambled too much, openly contradicting information on her own PowerPoint slides, and assigned grades by whim. Others, like Rieux, were charmed by her anecdotes and her tailored tweed suits. To them, her laughter seemed like champagne, acidic and sugary. They became part of her coterie. Rieux was her unsurpassable favourite. After Rieux had been evicted from his basement apartment, Castello and her then-husband, Victor, took him in for a month. Rieux stayed in the guest room. He tutored their sixteen-year-old son, Adam, for his essay on *Brave New World*. He walked their bull mastiff on rainy days. She would serve him tea and biscuits in the afternoon and they would talk about anything but medicine. Rieux would describe her as a polymath—she spoke five languages and was an accomplished violinist—if not for the implied strain of being good at many things. To be around her was to waft in the webs that connected science and culture.

Castello chided him for being too serious. She felt that he carried a weight that originated in his father's premature death and later, the sense of shame he experienced as his mother struggled to support two children. For years she had prodded him to find someone to love. Vivid descriptions of fascinating, lovely women accompanied by cell-phone snapshots would erupt from Castello every time they visited. Elyse, the daughter of a partner in Victor's law firm, had likely been mentioned more than once. Castello had decided that her protégé needed to marry. He'd turned down all the offers and refused the invitations to her garden parties where chance meetings with eligible women could be engineered.

Today, Castello picked a favourite downtown lunch spot, a place crammed with mismatched second-hand tables and chairs. This café, normally so busy at lunch hour, was nearly empty. The menu items were listed on gilt-framed chalkboards. As he expected, Castello was waiting for him, contained in a pool of light. She already had tea and a sandwich.

"I don't have much time so I ordered. Thank you for giving me an excuse to leave the office," she told him. "I've been living there."

"You seem upbeat," Rieux told her. "I expected you to look more like a mess."

In his mind, Rieux aligned the woman before him with the one he had once known. When she set her teacup on its saucer, her trembling made the china clatter. "How is it that you've stayed married for so long?" she teased him. "You must raise your compliment-giving game. I'll be your practice. The stakes are so low."

He ordered a coffee and panini at the counter and tried to catch a glimpse of her as she watched the scant foot traffic. She seemed grotesquely thin. She was still perfectly made up and wore tailored skirts. But when they'd first met, she had been fuller-bodied, more vigorous. She used to smooth out her fidgety energy with a Negroni; now she needed to bolster it with caffeine and sugar. She had not been the person he knew for many years; he still saw her losing parts of herself and exhibiting the fixations of a careless woman who'd once been curious and delighted with her discoveries.

"How bad is this outbreak?" Rieux asked, settling into the chair.

"*Everything is under control.*" She looked from side to side. Then she added, "We've never seen anything like it."

The infection rates were higher than any other cases of *Yersinia pestis* recorded in the past two decades. The incubation times were double the normal speed and typical treatments had failed. Hospital staff—a doctor and a nurse—had contracted the pneumonic form of the disease. Another several hundred beds had been dedicated to treatment in an auxiliary hospital in False Creek. The number of deaths, obfuscated in news coverage, had been severe. Still, the Health Authority hesitated to order the proper number of early-detection kits.

"No matter what we do, we're going to take some heat," Castello admitted. "Some of it will be deserved. So far, the disease hasn't spread to other cities, but no one will thank us for that. By the way, I'm so glad Elyse is out of town. Even if she is being swindled in Mexico."

Elyse Rieux knew nothing about what people were calling "the P-word," in varying degrees of delicacy, from her Mexican treatment centre. She had sent an e-mail to her husband the night before from an internet café in the town nearest the clinic. She wrote about her tan and the view from her room, and the patient kindness of the doctors and nurses. Rieux needed to write back. He would tell her about seeing Castello—or not. She'd always thought his friendship with her Aunt Orla was odd. His mentor and his wife had known each other since Elyse was in diapers. Elyse had once babysat Castello's son, Adam.

"She is doing well," Rieux said. "I would rather she do this than see her waste away."

Castello shook her head. "It would ruin your eyesight."

Adam Castello's funeral was the occasion of Rieux's first encounter with

Elyse. He had been shot in a house in the suburbs. There were circumstances around his death that Castello never talked about. Her son had had a drug problem and the wrong set of acquaintances. In a crowded church meeting room, Elyse introduced herself to Rieux. "Every time I see Aunt Orla, your name comes up," she said. All the speeches made in tribute to Adam and the sight of Castello being propped up by her husband had made Rieux eye the exit. After speaking to Elyse for five minutes, Rieux knew why Castello had wanted them to meet. They were both slight and fine-boned and liked outdoor activities. He was assertive by nature; she was deferential but knew where she would not budge. He felt at ease with her. She later told him that she'd first noticed his hands. He needed a ride home from the church, she was driving, and both lived on Commercial Drive. They bumped into each other the next day. They had acquaintances in common. It seemed unlikely that they hadn't seen each other before.

Castello left half of her sandwich untouched. She told Rieux to eat it. Rieux didn't want it, but wrapped it in a napkin to take home at her insistence. They stepped outside, and he followed her a block in the wrong direction. "Is that all you're wearing?" she asked him. He had left his jacket at work. She offered him her scarf. He declined.

Rieux should be the one caring for Castello, he thought. Victor had enclosed himself in work. They had long kept separate rooms because of his snoring, but he'd recently moved into a condo of his own. Through Elyse, Rieux knew that Castello had collected her dead son's clothes from the room he rented in a punk house on Heatley Street. She kept those unwashed clothes in a sealed bag and opened them periodically to recapture his scent.

"Let's make an appointment again for two weeks from now," he insisted. "My mother will cook dinner."

"That sounds delightful," Castello said, but something streaked through her eyes.

Only as he was turning to his bike, after he handed over the sandwich to a panhandler, did he understand. Castello viewed his mother as a rival. *That's it.* Once he had this insight, he feasted on a goulash of feelings. He remembered once being in Adam Castello's room, which had the ripe smell of a teenaged male. The boy disappeared for long bathroom breaks, and as Rieux waited he looked at his trophy case. "Pokemon Player of the Year." "The Boy Most Likely to Build the Perfect Sandwich." "In Recognition of Two Weeks Spent Without Electronics." These awards, commissioned by the mother of a mediocrity, were tucked behind a set of free weights. Rieux would have denied it, but it burned him inside not to have the chance to earn what this boy accepted so grudgingly.

And Rieux had gotten his wish. Castello had anointed him as her surrogate son even before the real one died.

When he got home, Rieux's mother was on her knees, back turned to him. "I sent your cleaning lady away," Mrs Rieux told him. She was scrubbing the bathroom tiles with Dettol. Elyse had declared their house chemical-free before her previous treatment, so the cleaning lady had been using vinegar. Dettol was the British antiseptic that his mother had used to clean when there was illness in the house; Rieux and his sister would be bathed in diluted Dettol. He thought the brand had been discontinued and wondered which Chinese grocer had stockpiled them. Dettol smelled the way he imagined a tree smelled to a robot.

Mrs Rieux took pleasure in asserting her presence in her son's life. She had chosen to respect the chasm between herself and her daughter-in-law and neither to bridge nor widen it. Filling in the space Elyse left behind, she returned the scents of Rieux's adolescence: the spice of sandalwood soap in the bathroom, bitter melon in the kitchen—and Dettol. Someone could make a fortune packaging olfactory memory, an album of odours.

They had established a pattern during her stay. She made dinner and asked him about his work. He gave her a point-form version of his day, as she seemed interested only in information that she could use to prove that he worked too hard. For the rest of the evening, as his mother knit, he would have been content to spread out on the couch, reading e-books in the public domain. (As someone whose views could be described as libertarian, Rieux was strictly against copyright, but nonetheless felt uneasy about online piracy.)

"Mom," he told her. "Let's go out tonight."

She looked to him, then turned back to his bathtub. "I made dinner."

"We can put it away for tomorrow," he said. "I have tickets for something." He'd purchased them on his iPhone on his way home. "It's a surprise."

"Okay, let me finish here," she said and continued scrubbing without turning her head.

He had noticed the advertisement for a Cantonese opera on a telephone pole between posters for improv comedy nights and now-cancelled concerts for touring bands. Mrs Rieux frowned when her son told her about the performance. The lines on her face deepened when she learned the price of the tickets.

On her iPad she'd been listening to Cantonese opera in her bedroom. Only a few years before, when she was still lacquering her hair in black dye, he remembered her describing the musical form as old-fashioned and boring. Rieux himself recalled his grandmother listening to cassette-tape recordings of operas. To his untrained ears, they sounded like cymbal clatter and alley-cat yowling.

His mother put on makeup and changed into the dry-cleaned slacks she had brought with her. The performance would take place at the Jewish Community Centre. They were outside the auditorium when he received his first text from Castello. She thanked him for lunch—he had paid—and confessed that she had been feeling lonely. In the volley of texts that followed, more messages than Rieux had received from her in a year, she mentioned her ongoing difficulties with Victor, the persistent grief over her son. He had no time to respond. Rieux held his phone in his hand as it continued to buzz. The veins in his neck bulged.

Outside the auditorium, a note added to the original poster indicated that the opera was being held over. The Guangzhou opera company had decided to occupy their protracted stay in Vancouver by working. But judging by the audience—only a dozen people in a theatre that seated a few hundred—their extended run exceeded public demand. The other members of the crowd were like the Rieuxs, women in their sixties accompanied by their adult children, the rest of them daughters.

They took their seats. Someone made up to look like a member of the

Ming Dynasty royal court came onstage and apologized that the Chinese and English subtitles were not working for this performance of *Fragrant Sacrifice*. Rieux's phone began to vibrate as a call came in. Castello, again. He thought about answering until the lights dimmed. He turned off the phone.

Two actors came onstage in heavy robes and headdresses, one playing a princess and the other a suitor who woos her with poetry. Their skin was powdered white, their eyes winged with red eyeshadow. The princess sang *a capella* before a recording began to lift her tune. Rieux did not understand a word. As the prince sang along, Rieux fell into a stupor—or what people might now describe as a dissociative state. His mother, however, was entranced. He watched her lips moving to the songs. He had never seen her transported. Even when she watched her TV shows, she broke off to chat with him, rewinding when necessary. Some essential tension was released from her face, and in its slackness, he saw a younger version of his mother unfastened.

Rieux caught sight of a moth. He'd been reading Virginia Woolf the previous week, and the gist of these lines rang in his mind: "It was as if someone had taken a tiny bead of pure life and decking it as lightly as possible with down and feathers, had set it dancing and zig-zagging to show us the true nature of life." For a moment, he inhabited Woolf's sentence. That moth was the most vital bead of life.

The first half of the opera ended. During the intermission, he listened to three separate voicemails from Castello. She was angry in her first message, weepy and apologetic in the second, and then demanded to meet him for a glass of wine in the final one. He realized then that he was normally prompt in replying. Had she demanded this promptness from him, or had he provided it in anticipation of her impatience? For some reason, Rieux felt that Castello knew he was out with his mother. She was laying claim on him.

"Are you needed?" Mrs Rieux asked. "Is it work?"

He shook his head. She seemed alarmed that they might have to leave and then relieved that they could stay.

"They're quite good," she said about the performers. "How did you know this was my favourite opera?"

"I just knew." He didn't.

They returned to their seats, and the lights dimmed once more. They'd never gone to live theatre when he was growing up. He occasionally saw a movie as part of a church group activity or on his or his sister's birthday. As he got older and took part in after-school band practices, he missed his mother who was always busy with her babysitting and cleaning jobs. He'd come home to find dinner in the oven for him and his sister, who helped pay down the mortgage by selling jeans during the school year and dream-home raffle tickets at the Pacific National Exhibition in the summer. He would often eat alone in front of the TV. His mother insisted that he study instead of work because one day, he'd provide for the family. And yet his sister still ended up the wealthy one with a two-thousand-square-foot flat in Hong Kong Island.

"It's almost over," his mother whispered to him. "This is the scene where the lovers kill themselves on their wedding night. Watch now. It is very sad." Rieux looked up from his lap. There was a squadron of performers onstage surrounding what seemed to be a wedding banquet table, then just the two lead performers. Rieux began to pay attention again, but then the moth returned. He'd forgotten to turn off his phone, and it started to vibrate once more. By the time he shut down the phone, the moth was gone. The lovers onstage drank from poisoned goblets after the last cymbal gong, then lowered themselves to the floor.

He turned to see his mother in tears as the lights dimmed and the audience began to clap. Then the stage lights came back on. The audience waited for the couple to rise. Some applauded impatiently as they adjusted the collars of their rain-resistant parkas. Rieux could see the male actor speak to his leading lady. Their makeup was so heavy, he could not tell at first that the actor was breaking character, nor could Rieux see the urgency underlying the woman's painted face.

The audience was too polite not to leave before the performers could be acknowledged. A stagehand was waved onto the set, at which point Rieux knew. He asked his mother to wait for him before he climbed onto the stage. He told the sick performer that he was a doctor and she nodded. Her chest felt warm when he loosened her gown to let her breathe. He asked the other performers to back off in English, and when they didn't he waved at them and told them to step away in his baby Cantonese. The audience figured it out before the cast did. He could see them moving from the stage, up the aisle, faces in their cotton masks. They fled—to exit but also to undo.

9.

For days after meeting her, Megan Tso was preoccupied by Yuko. She emptied the woman's bag to try to find contact information for her, since she'd taken her phone with her into the emergency room. Along with her passport, Tso found a guidebook, a wallet-sized photo of her boyfriend (or fiancé—Yuko had been wearing an engagement ring), a wallet, and a day planner. Most of her writing was in Japanese except for one entry later that week: there was a first name, a time, and a location.

When she returned to the hospital with the bag, she was told that Yuko had died. A woman behind the desk offered to take Yuko's bag, but suggested that it could be returned to her family sooner if Tso dropped it off herself at the Japanese Consulate.

It was only a fifteen-minute walk, so Tso agreed. Outside, she noticed more people walking. At first, she had concluded that Vancouverites were pressing on defiantly against the infection. When a half-empty city bus passed her by, she realized people didn't want to get close to each other in a confined space.

Tso made, then retracted, a number of generalizations about the disease-stricken city. Her first great love had been a communications postgrad who had once, with a dramatic flourish of his father's credit card, taken her to a conference in Dubai. In the cab ride from the airport, staring at a newly constructed office tower backlit in magenta, he sniffed and said, "This is a city in vertical decline." He needed to be coaxed out of their taxi. Although by now she knew better, she was still drawn to "pronouncers," even while she smirked at their over-simplifications and dismissals.

In Vancouver, there was no reason to hurry. Vancouverites sought survival—in body, in mind, and this forced them to slow down. They didn't want to die. They also sought purpose. Some stepped inside a church for the first time, even though their blood boiled as they were offered communion wafers by coughing priests. Others found themselves untangling themselves from long-held beliefs for the first time.

Tso kept notes. She took photos. This was the first extended holiday she had taken since she finished college. Even then she knew she had an internship lined up for September, followed by the rush of grad-school applications. This stay in Vancouver was indefinite.

That week, Tso quit social media because her electronic interactions with the outside world made her dizzy; it spun on a faster axis than the city did. A friend working at a publication that she once dreamed of writing for asked for an essay on life within a quarantine zone; the friend wrote back two hours later to say that the story idea now felt "dated." But there was interest elsewhere. Her niche expertise overlapped a cataclysmic event—and she was on the ground. "This will make your career for the next five years," she was told. "If you don't die."

She dropped Yuko's bag at the consulate and returned home to rest. To her surprise, her hotel had grown to full occupancy since the quarantine. The new residents did not look like tourists. Most of them were solitary men. They stepped out of the elevator with stale eyes, and pinched their noses through their face masks as if trying to avoid an offensive smell. Afterward, they shuffled in their sink-washed shirts to fill the restaurant bar, drinking down draught beers until there were only lips of foam at the bottom of their glasses. Tso sat alone at the bar, cradling a notebook and a Cape Cod. She knew she was a target for these men, but she didn't receive a single unwanted remark or proposal.

Most of the men only wanted to talk. They offered theories on the infection: A few suggested that the disease had been introduced by angry Communist Party officials in China in an attempt to temporarily depress the price of real-estate held by Chinese tax evaders. Given her heritage, she tried to work through her mixed feelings about being Westernized enough to be included in such dubious conversations.

One hotel resident, a criminal court judge named Jeffrey Oishi, told her that the disease had prompted his wife to kick him out of their home. "The missus prefers dying alone than waiting on me at my deathbed or being waited on by me," he said right after he introduced himself. "How could I question her resolve?" He drank apple juice through a straw, a habit that contributed to his aura of listlessness. He had taken time off from work to find a new home, but admitted that he hadn't looked around—a hotel room was better for him now in his uncertain state.

The camaraderie inspired by the hotel lounge allowed them to confess to one another their fear of dying alone. The judge had elderly parents in assisted living and younger siblings preoccupied with their own families. "I was raised to be the responsible, self-sufficient one," the judge told Tso. "If I die, I don't want it to interrupt anyone's life. Not even my daughter's." He was a compact man in his fifties with a round bald head. He had married later in life, and his daughter was still a child. His manner, lacking the usual membrane between thought and speech, made him seem youthful. His demeanour as a judge must have been the complete opposite, Tso surmised.

"Let's make a pact," Tso said. "If we don't see one another for twenty-four hours, we will call the front desk."

"Okay, but let's call the police in case there's a false alarm," the judge said as they shook hands. "I would rather piss off the 9-1-1 operator than the hotel staff."

———

Only two weeks earlier, Megan Tso had felt desperate not to be found. She had changed her numbers and blocked her ex from everything, fearing that he would chase her down. The day before she left Los Angeles, she found an unopened bottle of his antipsychotic meds—the ones she'd begged him to take—in a shopping bag hanging from the front door of the AirBnb cottage that she'd been renting under a friend's name. Now, to want to be traced created a cognitive whiplash.

As Megan crossed Denman Street on a pedestrian light, a car veered into the intersection and stopped just short of hitting her. The driver threw his hands up in the air as though she had gotten in the way. She spit on his car. He blasted the horn at her. His tires squealed onto Denman. She hurried back to the hotel. *I don't need a biblical disease to die, or a chemically unbalanced ex, just an idiot behind the wheel.*

It was in this hotel that Tso also became a friend of Raymond Siddhu.

They met in a way that is typical of Vancouver acquaintanceships. They saw each other and each felt a vague recognition. Siddhu's image and by-line filled the city newspaper, the one she used to track local reactions to a story being reported globally. In his columns, the new mayor's efforts to curtail a pandemic were being compared with his predecessor's handling of a garbage strike and the bulldozing over of an opioid-ravaged neighbour-hood. For his part, Siddhu recognized her from a photo and write-up that appeared in the free weekly before her event. They Googled biographical data on each other after they shared an elevator to their rooms on opposite ends of the fourth floor. But they refused to acknowledge one another for several days.

On the day Tso was to meet her mysterious consulting client, she found Siddhu in the restaurant for breakfast. The eating area had become fuller, homier, more like a rooming-house kitchen. The waitresses brought everyone their drink of choice without being asked. Judge Oishi was lingering at a table with the reporter. "Hey, everyone's here!" he declared. This time he drank milk through a straw. He told her to pull over a chair. Mint tea was brought to her.

She often saw Siddhu early in the day speed-shuffling from the far end of the fourth-floor hallway, slinging one arm into a tweed blazer as he panted toward the elevator. He reminded her of the scene in Disney's *Fantasia* when the hippos mince around in tutus. He appeared effeminate in his gestures and mortified at his bulk. He swirled the stir stick in his black coffee like the wing of a hummingbird, seeming to take pleasure in the motion. A gold wedding band stood out on his dark, hairy hand. Siddhu had the same frayed appearance as the other men in the hotel, the same melancholy, but he projected the purposeful desperation of a man worried about missing his last chance.

"You're up late," Siddhu said to Tso as she sipped her tea.

For any true Vancouverite, Tso learned later, proximity precluded introductions and served as the larval stage of acquaintanceship.

"I've been getting ready to meet a client," she told him. "Shouldn't you be at the newspaper?"

"I'm starting a new job today," he said, lips curling into a smile as she acknowledged him. "Their workplace culture involves oversleeping. I'm surprised you haven't gone for your run today. What kind of client does a woman who writes about death meet with?"

Now that's a big small-town introduction, Tso thought to herself. "It's a secret," she told him. "He's press shy."

"My daughter is visiting me tonight," the judge interjected. "If you two get in early enough, please join us for dinner."

Tso agreed. A black SUV picked her up outside the hotel, as had been confirmed. The driver, dark-haired, vaguely Slavic-looking, wouldn't respond to her questions. *This better be good.* They crossed a bridge to the other side of the city. The driver took an off-ramp that led them to a busy street, then turned onto a road that ran alongside the water. The houses facing the water were built on the cliff side below. She could only see hedges and gates. Then they reached the longest hedge of them all and then the biggest gate. The car approached a roundabout driveway that encircled a marble fountain. A man was waiting at the door.

He appeared to her to be around sixty, but trim and youthful. As she approached she noticed his blue eyes. He had a full head of greying hair, side-parted, that was a shade lighter than his goatee. He introduced himself as Graham. "First off, I must apologize for the timing of our meeting," he told her. "There are better cities to be trapped in. I mean, I would be happily trapped in Barcelona. This city—ugh. It's like Hong Kong run by the Swiss."

"No problem," she said blithely as she took in the gold-encrusted decor. *He's not putting me up in a nice-enough hotel.* "I mean, I was the one who initially delayed." He had wanted to meet a month earlier, but she'd needed to combine her two Vancouver events.

"I hope you're getting good material," he said, leading them into a kitchen that looked recently remodelled. Graham offered her a coffee as she looked out the floor-to-ceiling windows. Beyond the pool and tennis court, there was the ocean dotted with stranded oil tankers that were hemmed in by red-hulled Canadian Coast Guard boats. Past them were the mountains in the far distance, outside the quarantine zone. Despite this opulence, Tso felt as though only a fraction of this man's wealth was being flaunted. His leather shoes were expensive, likely Italian, but battered.

"Perhaps I can occupy you for part of this layover," he said. Graham stood alongside her and began by explaining that he was not religious. "I wish the idea of the afterlife felt credible. Not believing in hell led me to self-indulgence. World-class stupidity! But I am preoccupied with leaving a mark." He was divorced, childless—"There's a shitty nephew of mine who will be sorely disappointed when he gets nothing from me"—and he wanted to spend all of his fortune creating a legacy. "I didn't accomplish much to get so wealthy. Not blowing it was my achievement. My grandfather and father were rich, and I took over the business when my older brother developed a cocaine habit. I've done well simply by not screwing up."

Some of that accumulated wealth he'd spent altruistically. He had donated to a local hospital to erect a wing in memory of his parents. A greyhound rescue foundation received a large sum in the name of his favourite aunt. "I'm a pretty good guy, within reason. I want you to know that before you get your panties in a knot," he told her, eyes flaring with provocation. Tso ignored it. "Now I want to do something for myself." He led her to a glass-topped kitchen table, and handed her an iPad. First there were images of a snow-covered mountainside with a mirrored glass cube jutting from it. She saw images of a room with grey concrete walls and maple floors. The lighting and displays seemed to suggest a museum, but the images didn't look like simulations. She swiped until she found the image of a rectangular metal object which looked at first like a martini shaker, before she realized it was much larger.

"You look like someone who grew up fascinated by mummies," he began. His eyes traced her body from head to toe. Tso felt like he was running his finger over her for dust, like she was a window ledge, only to stop halfway with a fingertip blackened by soot.

"Well, I did, but I never grew out of it," she said.

He told her that he wanted to construct a monument in the Canadian

Arctic. It would be buried a thousand metres within a mountain on Elles-mere Island. "I could tell you what I've already spent on this, but you'd be furious, and I don't have time for class warfare." Within this structure would be a sarcophagus. "When I die, my executors will have instructions to announce to family and shareholders that I have been cremated. What will actually happen is that they'll transport my body to this location in my bespoke casket."

The mirrored cube entrance, inspired by the front door of the Sval-bard Global Seed Vault in Norway, would be covered up for a century with a façade made from natural materials that would disintegrate in that time. Graham envisioned the monument going undiscovered for at least that long. He wanted it to be found accidentally by people who would not recognize it. "My best-case scenario would be for aliens to happen upon it after our species has become extinct. Realistically, people will probably find it in fifty years when the Arctic Circle becomes habitable after more climate change."

"What do you need me for?" she asked. "You have this figured out."

His mouth puckered with displeasure. "I have put a lot of thought into this. You get a lot of input when something like this enters your head. You get a lot of static. You don't know my family's line of work, do you? We're in advertising. My work is about messaging. What I want to do is advertise to the future. But I realize I might need some outside input, you see? Come, since you want my song and dance, I need you to follow me. *Come.*"

She didn't so much as decide but feel compelled to follow him. He had the voice of a high-school principal. She was led down a corridor until they reached a mudroom—shoes, boots, scuba gear. He took her through an ordinary door to an unexpectedly grand room, about the size of a gymnasium. The concrete floor had been lowered. At the centre of the room was a glass cube.

"This is a replica of the structure on Ellesmere," Graham told her. "It's my playroom."

They walked down a ramp that took them to the floor and approached the cube. Two panels swept open like the doors of a spaceship. They stepped into a dark void.

A light came on slowly and she saw that the space was decked out like the drawing room of a tony country club, with wine-coloured leather chairs and leather-bound volumes in glass-fronted bookcases. In a cabinet were family photos and a set of war medals. What stood out in this tableau were two metal caskets that lay in the middle of the room like unpacked furniture.

"We had a number of concepts that emulated ancient Egyptian and Chinese cultures," he told her. "I couldn't wrap my head around them. They weren't *me*. But I want it to be *more*, you see."

"Ancient burial sites spoke of an afterlife; they served to bridge this world to the next," she explained. "That they were discovered was incidental."

"I know that—I've hired you to tell me something I don't know."

"Why are there two caskets?" she asked him.

"I don't plan to die anytime soon, even with this pandemic outside. I am going to take the long view. And, as such, there is a chance I could meet someone." He paused to suggest an unrelated thought. "You know, I was really taken by your author photo. Obviously, photos convey a subjective truth." When she didn't respond, he laughed it off. "It's a shame that I've gotten pickier in old age. I used to be one-size-fits-all, but now I'm looking for someone tailor-made for me, like a hand-stitched glove."

She shivered but allowed him to enumerate the qualities of an ideal tomb mate. This gave Tso the necessary time to perform a series of calculations. How much of her consulting fee would she have to eat if she left now? How long would she be able to stay at her hotel without his financial backing? What were her chances of being locked in his sarcophagus should she rudely dismiss his project? She looked toward the door.

"I probably should have demanded more information about this project," she told him. "I don't think I'm the right person for it."

His face flushed. "Wait a second—wait—I shall be the judge of that," he stammered.

"I'm going to return your fee. Most of it now, the rest when I get out of here."

"The money is nothing to me."

"I should go."

He pointed to one of the club chairs. "*Sit down.*"

"Your tone is scaring me."

"I'm sorry," he said. "But sit down."

She eased into the chair and was surprised by how comfortable it felt, like a broken-in pair of slippers. From one of the cabinets he brought out two glasses and a bottle. Graham held out one glass with two fingers' worth of scotch in front of her. "You don't need to accept this project," he said, settling down in the other club chair with his drink. "But you had a gut reaction to this place. It wasn't the one I wanted. And I want you to explain it to me. Just tell me why you hate it and you can keep the money I gave you."

She took the glass. The whisky tasted like the ocean, a shoeshine, and a campfire. "I don't know where to begin," she said. "I mean, I was expecting something gaudier."

"I wasn't raised to show off."

"Well, at least that would be something. This is what you come up with when you have no vision of life after brain function ceases."

He drew to the edge of his chair. "Now we're getting somewhere."

"What is it that you want to endure for ages?" she asked him.

"That's easy. Some traces of my life."

"What about the world that we live in?"

"What about the cube itself? It's a marvel of contemporary engineering," he said. "The finished product will feature an introductory hologram."

"This will be so five years ago in two years. What else?"

"That's your job," he told her. "I don't need to haggle. I respect you. Name your price."

She finished her scotch. Then she handed the glass to him and stood up. "There are some things you can't buy. One of them is a vision." She liked how that sounded even though she knew it was false.

He followed her as she hurried down the corridor. Each time he tried to catch up with her, she sped up. She was galloping by the time she reached the front door. The driver was playing with his phone. She waved him off.

"I believe in tons of shit," Graham called after her. "Saving the whales. Free market social solutions. *Bitch*. The benefits of learning a second language. But what if you don't think you'll be anything after you die—then what do you do?" Tso didn't look back.

Twenty minutes later, with the nearest bus stop still two kilometres away, she regretted the bravado of turning down the driver. She took a wrong turn that led her farther afield to a beach that had been empty since a metric ton of rats, skunks, and squirrels had died along the jogging path. Gulls circled above her, dismayed by the absence of garbage. The dog walkers, braving infectious disease to allow their pets time to poop and play, broke the desolation. She wished she had that kind of love, everyday and unassailable, for anyone.

She thought she could see her hotel across from English Bay, two empty bus rides away, and took pleasure in knowing where to look. She persuaded herself that she was no longer a tourist in Vancouver; she was a founding citizen of this quarantined city. She ignored her sore feet and resolved to walk home, which took the whole afternoon. Back at the hotel, she showered and sat on the edge of her bed in a hotel bathrobe. She felt tired but unable to sit still. She listened to the air conditioner make a gurgling sound in the room next to hers. Someone was whistling down the hallway while jangling spare change in his pocket. She considered calling her stalker ex. His contact info was on her phone, and her trembling thumb hovered over his name. *Back away slowly*. She put on her sweatpants and headed downstairs where she found Judge Oishi with his daughter, Rose. He welcomed her into the empty seat across from him.

"You made it just before I hit the panic button," Oishi told her.

"I'm having a french fries," Rose announced. Thankfully, she was not the kind of child who needed to be coaxed into acknowledging the existence of an unknown adult. She was that age—three or four, Tso couldn't tell—when a child's speech was half-intelligible. The girl had skin the colour of a pecan, wide-set Asian eyes, and rippling curls. Tso foresaw a lifetime's worth of conversations for her in which she would have to offer her ethnic pedigree or risk being labelled difficult.

While Rose coloured a placemat with crayons, Oishi explained that it was a professional development day at school. His estranged wife needed to work, so he'd agreed to watch Rose for the day only if she could spend the night with him. The hotel staff had set up a cot. Oishi told Tso that his estranged wife hoped he could extend his stress leave to watch Rose during the days through the quarantine. "I see her point. But there's a backlog of cases already," he told her. "I still have another week of this leave. What are the chances things will get better by then?"

Tso stared over his shoulder at the setting sun in a stupor. She suddenly realized she was being asked a question and apologized for not hearing it.

"Are you okay?" Oishi asked.

"I need a glass of wine," she said eventually. "Except for that, I'm fine."

She felt something wither inside her. She had trapped herself within this city to meet with a pompous rich dude. Her own greed had led her to these woeful circumstances. She ordered two glasses of wine. *One for me, and one for me.*

———————

Tso's mind circled back to Yuko. Although Tso had returned her bag, she remembered the meeting on the day planner. Out of curiosity, she decided to keep Yuko's appointment for her. She hoped to learn more about this woman.

She wandered further east than she'd ever gone before in the downtown core to the Annex. The outdated map she had been given at the hotel called the area by a different name. People were always excited to talk about this neighbourhood—the new art gallery and bubble tea shops, the restaurants and cocktail bars—after making all the necessary disclaimers about gentrification and displacement. To longtime residents, the reclaimed area was like having a new room in an old house.

She arrived at a white-tiled coffee shop with gleaming chrome tables and leafy plants. A woman sitting by the window with a single rose put down her phone and stood up.

"Yuko?" she asked.

Tso realized that she bore a passing resemblance to Yuko. Although their mannerisms set them far apart, if you'd only seen one picture on a screen, it would not be blatantly offensive to mistake one of them for the other.

"Gudrun?" Tso answered back.

She was tall with blonde dreadlocks and wore a short top that showed off her tanned and toned midriff. Gudrun stooped down to hug her. "You never confirmed," she told Tso. "But I'm glad I took a chance you'd show up."

There was a chai latte in front of Tso when she took her seat. "That's your favourite drink—did I get that right?" Gudrun asked.

"Yes," Tso said quietly.

Gudrun took over most of the conversation, perhaps because Yuko wasn't a native speaker of English. She announced that she was tired of worrying about the quarantine and disease. Could they agree that those topics were off-limits? Tso nodded. Gudrun was pleased. She told Tso about her training to become a registered massage therapist. She was from Vancouver Island, where everyone hiked. She loved sushi.

Tso's replies were quiet and clipped, and she ducked her head in an ill-informed approximation of a Japanese bow.

"I feel like I've done all the talking," Gudrun said, her eyes wide and teeth flashing. "You mentioned you haven't come out to your parents. What are they like? What are their names?"

Tso prepared a lie. Then her throat clenched. She started to cry.

"I'm sorry," she admitted. "I'm not Yuko. I don't know why I was pretending."

She had known she couldn't maintain her roleplay for long. The more she knew about Yuko, the more difficult it had become to impersonate her. After Gudrun's last questions, she'd instantly imagined a different life for this dead Japanese woman, a life that she had finally begun to control. No more.

10.

Only once Raymond Siddhu was buzzed into the building did he get a key fob from GSSP's managing editor, Harper, a woman who looked exactly twenty-three years old. "You have your own laptop, right?" she asked. "Our IT guys need to do some stuff to it first. They work off-site and they look like lizards. He hides it well, but Elliot's obsessed with security." The space felt more like an oversized home office than he was expecting it to be.

Siddhu had not yet told his wife that he'd quit the newspaper. He didn't want to tell her that he'd left without a severance package. His boss had shuffled some papers and said, "I know it sucks here, everyone's dealing with something. I didn't realize that 'legacy' could be a verb until it was applied to my industry. Don't you want your name on the front page when we run our final edition? Besides, this whole situation has given us a reason to be. Your stories have never been read this much. And now you decide to find work in communications?"

"I've taken a reporting job elsewhere," Siddhu told him.

The editor's phone started to buzz; he looked at it and then pushed it away from him like an emptied dinner plate. Siddhu hadn't liked Curt when he came in two years earlier. He was too managerial and threw around too many buzzwords. But he had taken part in pub trivia nights. He listened to The National, loud, in his corner office on days when he had to deliver termination notices. He knew the names of his workers' spouses and sometimes their children. He'd gained twenty pounds since he started the job; though he kept a treadmill in his corner office, he hung dry-cleaning from the handles. "I'm not going to ask you where," he told Siddhu. "What's gotten into you? Right, you're *feeling stuff*. Have you talked to Uma about your decision?"

Last night, he and Uma had used Skype to attempt video sex fifteen minutes after Siddhu's sons bawled at the sight of their father onscreen. They looked around for him and then wailed in their room until they fell asleep. He could not stop worrying that they would forget who he was. As a result, Uma accused him of looking distracted during their virtual intercourse and ended their call by throwing her smartphone across the room.

"I won't change my mind," he told his editor. In the past week, he had become the paper's disease reporter. At every turn, Horne-Bough's website had beaten them. It was not about intrepid reporting, Siddhu convinced himself, it was Horne-Bough's personality creating a new business model. Maybe it wasn't sustainable or lucrative, perhaps it was something quixotic, but GSSP could still produce the definitive record of this epidemic.

"If you just wait until the end of the next fiscal quarter, there will be another round of cost-cutting," the editor-in-chief told him. "I don't need to let you go empty-handed."

Siddhu shook his head. He had a new job. He offered to give them the next two weeks, but he wanted to leave today. He left escorted by security.

At GSSP, there was a story meeting scheduled at a table crowded with takeout boxes and dirty Ikea silverware. This seemed to be the only raised flat surface in the office. No one except Harper, who was preoccupied by a malfunctioning router, was in attendance for the official 11:00 a.m. meeting time. Siddhu straightened up the table and admired the view of the city's railyard in the distance.

"You can see it even better from our rooftop," Horne-Bough told him when he eventually arrived, throwing his winter coat onto a chair. "If you don't see us here, you can find us upstairs. We've got a gas grill and lawn furniture set up." He was accompanied by the website's other two reporters, including the former intern who had written better, detailed, and timelier versions of Siddhu's own stories that week. The young media mogul looked at the table. "Thanks for cleaning up."

The meeting was brief and uneventful. Each reporter spoke about the stories they were pursuing and how they were spending their days. The actual writing of the pieces, Siddhu seemed to understand, was done in coffee shops. When it was Siddhu's turn to speak, he was relieved that neither of his new co-workers had wanted to cover the anti-immigration and anti-racism rallies being staged concurrently at the old Art Gallery.

"After you get your security software installed, we were hoping you would take that story," Horne-Bough said, eyes gleaming. It occurred to Siddhu that there was likely a vaporizer on the rooftop as well. "You see, we've been spreading ourselves too thin. And I need help to break a big story on a, um, prominent figure."

Siddhu leaned toward the table. "I want in on this."

Horne-Bough centred his index finger on his lips. "Who knows if we're being bugged? That's why I prefer the rooftop." He and the former intern, who had been given the original tip, had been sworn to confidentiality.

"Negotiations are ongoing—we might need to crowdfund. Thankfully, we'll be bringing in someone who's good at passing around the hat."

"You're not going to pay a source, are you?" Siddhu asked.

"Not if we don't have to," Horne-Bough replied. He noted Siddhu's dismay and added, "We are attempting to do things differently. If it burns us in the ass, you can blame the no-longer-rich white kid."

The meeting was adjourned seventeen minutes after it commenced. Siddhu puttered around before asking Harper, on the phone with the company's internet provider, about his payment information. The managing editor, once she was placed on hold by customer service, produced a wad of hundreds and asked him if he needed some cash to "blow off steam." Siddhu hadn't even bothered to negotiate a salary or his potential ownership share—he didn't even know if he had dental coverage. At some point, if this all fell apart, he told himself he'd go into business with his brother Bobby, a contractor who tore down perfectly good houses to build new ones for a profit.

Siddhu had more than thirty minutes to make it to the rally, so to kill some time he got a coffee. Thankfully, it was still considered an essential food item by authorities. He stood in line at the business—coffee shop sounded too homely, café too romantic—that Bernard Rieux had introduced him to; it was the closest to his new office. He took note of the tables and outlets; this might be his new workplace. He looked over his interview notes with the anti-racism protest organizer. The organization for "European-Canadian rights" had sent him a press release that advocated an immediate deportation of all residents of Canada who'd been born outside the country and were of non-European descent.

As he ordered his Americano, he caught sight of Dr Rieux wearing a neon-orange cycling jacket. On their first meeting, Rieux had not smiled once. Today, his teeth were movie-star white and he seemed friendlier, more relaxed.

"You got me hooked on this place," Siddhu told him.

"As I am with your news coverage," Rieux answered brightly. "I read your farewell column. I'm sad to hear you'll be leaving journalism."

Siddhu explained that he'd found a new job. He wanted to write better stories, more timely stories. "And my old workplace had become a graveyard," he told the physician. He lifted his face mask to take his first sip of the Americano. "I wanted something novel."

Siddhu waited for Rieux to get his coffee. "Seems like there's a lot of freedom in your new position," the doctor told him. He seemed to pick his words carefully. "It must be exciting."

"It was an impulse decision," Siddhu said, as they both stepped outside. "How has business been in your clinic?"

"Surprisingly, nothing much has changed."

Before they parted ways, Siddhu mentioned his next stop. "It's going to get ugly," Rieux warned him. He shook his head. "Everyone wants to make this health issue political. Infectious disease doesn't check your party affiliation. Suffering is universal."

It had been a cold, damp fall, but the first week of the quarantine offered glimpses of sunlight. Siddhu passed into Gastown and the business district and could see crowds forming on the other side of a police roadblock. As those with any familiarity with Vancouver's outbreak might remember, the first week of the quarantine concluded with its only large-scale public conflict. For most locals, it felt inevitable, predictable, and tiresome. People were relieved that the rioting was limited and that there was only one during this period of protracted misery. Siddhu himself wouldn't have predicted a riot that day, but he wouldn't have ruled it out. He attended the protest knowing that the turnout would be high—that in itself was newsworthy. Tensions had risen and anxieties had culminated in a march by the city's racist organizations (both its suits and its boots) and a concurrent counter-demonstration.

Several years prior to the epidemic, the city experienced a violent riot when the professional ice hockey team lost a championship final game. Drunken hockey fans, more inflamed by the catharsis of frenzy than any disappointment, trashed downtown businesses and set fire to a police car. On the morning after, Siddhu spent several hours with the newspaper's archivist going through clippings. He interviewed some local historians and academics. They all concluded that the city's first riots had been caused by racial resentments and economic anxiety. The 1907 Anti-Oriental Riots stemmed from an influx of Chinese railway workers undercutting the bargaining power of white labour. Two riots in the Depression era originated, respectively, from a fight for longshoreman's rights and disgruntled unemployed men cut off from government relief.

In the last half-century, the motivations for and conditions that precipitated rioting, said the experts, became less overtly political. The Gastown riots in 1971 arose from a heavy-handed police response to a marijuana-rights protest. People rioted outside a Rolling Stones concert in 1972. The first hockey riot in 1994 seemed to result from genuine sports-induced nihilism. (Vancouver Police blamed the mass disruption and property damage on a short-lived alternative publication. In that free weekly, a columnist offered the cheeky suggestion of looting as a means to alleviating class envy.) These latter-day riots dramatized the struggle between personal freedom—to smoke, to rock out, to throw a tantrum—and state power. Some argued that they illustrated generational divides rather than friction between economic stratas. These were the types of riots reserved for a sleepy provincial city in an economically developed country.

At its outset, the riot that Vancouver experienced during the period of this narrative had the markers of the city's earlier scenarios in that there was an existential crisis that flushed out base resentments. As Siddhu progressed through the crowds, he had trouble finding the original European-Canadian rights group. The sign-bearing anti-racist crowd was far more prominent and formed a throng around the fencing and line of police security along Robson Street leading to the south side of the old Art Gallery.

Food carts were stationed at the outskirts of the demonstration, lending a festive atmosphere to this political event. A majority of the crowd consisted of people who might otherwise describe themselves as bystanders. Siddhu assumed—hoped—they might be anti-racist. Their ethnic make-up was varied, although their identities were largely concealed. Face masks were effective in obscuring identities. Protestors covered their heads in toques and hooded sweatshirts, and as it was also unseasonably sunny, many wore mirrored sunglasses. A number wore backpacks, although Siddhu could not discern whether there were more backpacks than usual.

The active demonstrators began to jeer as the small parade came from an indeterminate point west toward the Art Gallery. He recognized the old Red Ensign flag, the one with the Union Jack in the top-left corner, slung over the shoulders of two young men in black bomber jackets and bleached blond hair who marched beside some older men holding up a banner with the name and URL of their European-Canadian rights group.

He heard the explosion first and then a burst of flame in front of the marchers. It was like thunder and lightning. Later he would realize that the sound had come from a Molotov cocktail that had been launched at the rear of the parade. This sound was, in his memory, like a starter's pistol at a sprint. The chanting stopped behind the metal gates. The young marchers in black formed a defensive circle around the men carrying the banner. The fences gave way and the police line cracked. Siddhu stood behind a VPD officer who shouted at him to move back. The officer distracted him. Siddhu couldn't see who threw the first punch, but soon limbs had been extended and were in motion.

The police buffered the two groups, minimizing the violence between them. The crowd of non-protestors seemed to disperse during this confrontation. Siddhu realized that it had merely moved down Robson Street, away from the police detail, and toward the shops. Siddhu was too far away to hear the glass smashing. Cellphone photos posted that day showed people in face masks stuffing their backpacks with electronics and handbags, others carrying stolen clothes by the rackful. For this seg-ment of the crowd, the demonstration was a pretext to steal, a distraction from the spectre of death. Siddhu asserted his size and jostled himself out of the crowd as the air began to smell like gasoline and burning plastic. He succeeded in turning away from Robson Street, heading back toward Gastown, where he would find a place to write his story. He would piece it together from his own observations and the firsthand reports that he skimmed from social media.

Longtime Vancouverites felt as though they were following a script as the images and self-congratulating police press conferences ensued. But there were significant divergences from the previously established tem-plate. Many have noted that, unlike the previous riot, Vancouverites could not blame this embarrassing event on the "Bridge and Tunnel" elements. They owned this: the racists, the counter-protestors, the onlookers. More importantly, in previous iterations, the riot served to cap off tensions or, at the very least, acted as a release valve. From violence rippled sobriety, introspection, and remorse. Even as they watched homemade firebombs going off—relieved, this time, that no police cars were burned to charred hulls, and that the extent of the rioting was limited to two square blocks—they knew that this did not signal the final throes of turmoil. The rancor in our city had not been discharged; it festered. It made the people of this city sicker.

The day after the riot, Romeo Parsons gave his first televised speech since his election. It was broadcast on television and radio and streamed live. Vancouverites watched it with the single-mindedness of previous generations who'd been limited to only print and broadcast media. They saw Parsons' response as the definitive, official reaction to recent events. On a provincial and federal level, politicians had already expressed concern; some called for a redoubling of medical resources and additional relief funds. But Vancouverites regarded their comments with indifference. They felt second-hand, patronizing. Parsons, whatever his political powers might be, was trapped with the rest of the citizenry. They regarded him as their leader and he still radiated the optimistic feeling that had given him a landslide victory.

The remarks came from within the mayor's cherry-panelled office on the third floor of City Hall. The video had an impromptu air. The mayor sat behind his desk, which was cluttered with stamps, files, and souvenir flags. One of the venetian blinds behind him was unevenly half-lowered. Parsons wore a white dress shirt with a creamy blue tie, slightly loosened. His jacket was slung around the back of his chair. His eyes looked puffy, as though he had been crying, but he was otherwise well-composed, and before he launched into his speech, he flashed his white teeth at someone off camera. The mayor read from his text, his eyes bobbing up regularly from the page as though he was a swimmer doing the breaststroke.

"First off, I want to thank the people of our city for their time," he began after the land acknowledgment. "As always, it's my privilege to serve you, even under these extraordinary circumstances. Yesterday's incident was troubling for all of us who take pride in our city's friendliness, its inclusiveness, its safety. Last night, after watching images from Robson Street and speaking to the chief of police, I could not sleep. I got out of bed and put together some thoughts. Please forgive me if my language is not as polished as I would like.

"It would be foolish not to address the anxiety that served as the subtext for yesterday's violence and property damage. We are undergoing an immensely stressful time. Many Vancouverites are worried about death and illness. Others have found their livelihoods and routines affected by this illness. Many businesses have shut down or have reduced hours. To all of you affected, I want to say that we have not stopped working to find solutions since this health crisis first came to notice.

"We are committed to putting to justice the most grievous offenders from last night," he continued after sipping water from a plastic bottle. "The incidents yesterday struck many Vancouverites as a gesture of hopelessness. People who see no future see no reason not to break a window and steal a pair of sneakers. Our hearts are broken like yours. After the last riot, there was a great up-swell in civic pride as people helped repair broken windows. Kind messages were scrawled on the plywood boards that covered up broken shopfront exteriors. The messages all boiled down to this: 'Not all Vancouverites are vandals—not all of us are rioters.'"

He took another sip of water and a deep breath. "I am going to suggest the opposite: we are all complicit in the tensions and inequities exposed, not created, by the outbreak. We see the illness as an exceptional situation. In reality, it was our founding condition. As many people know, our city takes its name from an English officer of the Royal Navy. When he entered what's now known as the Strait of Juan de Fuca in the early 1890s, he'd already been at sea for a year and had visited Australia, Hawaii, and South Africa on his quest to claim land on behalf of the British Empire. When he came to our region, though, Captain George Vancouver did not see wealth and abundance but devastation. He found abandoned villages and beaches lined with decaying bodies. He saw canoes placed in the trees, which upon closer inspection, held skeletons inside them.

"Amid this devastation, Captain Vancouver was greeted by only a few Indigenous people, many of whom bore terrible scars and were blind. Vancouver saw evidence that there had been a far greater population here in the past—village sites and clearings that would have contained thousands of inhabitants. Some historians now estimate that there were a hundred thousand original inhabitants in this unceded land we now call home. The Coast Salish people of this region were seafaring peoples whose canoes covered the water. Imagine great numbers of them against the first white settlers. History would surely be different.

"What caused such devastation? Smallpox, brought first to the other end of the continent by English soldiers during the American War of Independence. The disease had already struck the area in 1782 when David Thompson visited. He was asked then by Indigenous people whether smallpox was a weapon of the white man brought to destroy them.

"Now, conspiracy theorists have suggested that this epidemic is a foreign plot to destabilize our economy and real-estate market. You don't need to wear a tinfoil hat to see how disease disproportionately affects our most marginalized people, the poorest, the least privileged.

"I came to office promising change while at the same time appealing to a broad electorate. People were disheartened by the Annex project and the previous mayor's tone-deaf self-congratulations over reduced drug fatalities. And yet there has been little appetite to follow through on the consequences of such uneasiness. I do not take your vote as a blank cheque to enact unpopular policies, but leadership requires tough choices. It requires acting out of principle and not in the service of a focus group."

The remainder of the mayor's speech outlined a more severe version of his anti-poverty and environmental policies. City land earmarked for mixed use would be designated only for social housing. Anti-gentrification zones would be created. In the last weeks of his election campaign, the mayor had stepped back from his market-hostile ideas. Now he behaved as though the disease was his own chance to smash a window.

Siddhu watched the speech from a pub, his laptop opened in front of him. He wasn't sure how a story about it would work on Horne-Bough's website. His riot article was received indifferently by his boss, who did not even bother to offer it first to his subscribers. "I'm glad you're here to round out our coverage," he said. "No one can call us mere gossip-mongers."

Siddhu had finished half his article when he was called in by Horne-Bough. His young employer was dressed in a cream hoodie that made his soft skin look like bleached paper. "We got the story we've been hunting down—and, before you ask, it wasn't cheap," he said. "The lawyers have looked at it. Now we need an extra set of eyes on this to make sure we haven't split any infinitives."

According to this report, released only to subscribers, a twenty-eight-year-old woman claiming to be Parsons' biological daughter (her existence had been concealed from Parsons by her birth mother, who died when she was a child) described having sexual contact with the mayor earlier that year. The story would be shared with non-subscribers an hour later.

"Guess who we want to contact the mayor for comment?" Horne-Bough said with a smile. He handed him his flip phone. It was already ringing.

Part Three

KEVIN CHONG

11.

This section of the story takes place over a long, cold winter. Lifelong Vancouverites tolerated snow once a year as long as the rains flushed it away by nightfall. This year, the first of several snowfalls came over three days in late November, the flakes thick like candlewax, and stuck to the ground. In the evenings that followed it turned to ice in sub-zero temperatures before being recoated in snow. As usual, cars fishtailed on the road. Reactions to the weather were even more drastic than usual. Sidewalks went unshovelled. Road salt became scarce. People no longer took pleasure in venting about the city's inadequate road-clearing strategies. Some welcomed the snow as another excuse to remain housebound. They saw the cold as a disease killer and only wished it was colder. Others took it in stride as yet another burden to carry.

The death toll rose sharply as Vancouverites neared the end of the first month of quarantine. There were fifteen and then twenty-five recorded deaths in the first two weeks of the quarantine. By its fifth week, as we entered the first week of December, there were a hundred and twelve deaths. None of these figures were available at the time to the general public, as officials obfuscated and hedged. But we became aware of the steep rise in fatalities by the numbers of friends of friends, then friends, who began to display symptoms. We noticed the silence of acquaintances who were otherwise vocal on social media. New faces ran our scant groceries through the register.

People who were admitted to the hospital were placed in a special unit that became, by the end of that first month, overwhelmed and crowded. They were treated by nurses and doctors in full-body protective gear. Reports about the drastic procedures in place to contain the disease frightened many locals, even when they didn't exhibit symptoms. Those who were admitted to the hospital were isolated. Asymptomatic Vancouverites who shared homes with patients infected with the disease were told to remain housebound for a week until they were in the clear.

Authorities, including Dr Bernard Rieux's friend Dr Orla Castello, did not know what to make of this outbreak and took extreme measures. If they knew the rate at which infection would spread, they might not have been so scrupulous. Having read articles about the efficiency of quarantine, Rieux decided that any effort to seal plague patients from the outside world was ineffective and a violation of personal freedom. He did not share this opinion widely, but perhaps it was revealed in his manner. To outsiders, he seemed aloof and awkward but also independent-minded. Perhaps this explained why he found himself paying unofficial house calls.

The first request came from Megan Tso. Rieux was brushing his teeth before bed when his phone rang. "You're the only person I could think of," she told him. She was calling on behalf of a friend whose father had been feeling unwell.

Rieux later admitted that he found Tso amusing. On the phone, he merely grunted and asked for the patient's address. He told his mother that he was seeing a patient (without mentioning she was the woman from the airport). He got dressed, slipped on a pair of hiking boots, and walked thirty minutes through another flurry. The fresh powder provided traction on the unshovelled sidewalks and icy patches along the side streets. With road salt in short supply, people had begun stealing beach sand to line the roads.

Tso, shivering in a black leather jacket, was waiting for him outside the door of an older house next to a papered-over storefront. She led him to the ground-floor suite where Isaac "Izzy" Grossman lived. The old man wore a bathrobe and lay on a lime-green tweed couch. Tso introduced Rieux to him and to his daughter Janice. Izzy looked at Rieux, who was preoccupied with his gloves and face mask, and then to his daughter. He groaned as he planted one foot on the chipped hardwood floor, then the other, exposing his genitalia.

Rieux discussed Mr Grossman's symptoms with his daughter. He'd been weak and feverish since the morning and said that he was tired. Janice Grossman called Tso when her father began to spit up blood. "He needs to go to the hospital and get put on antibiotics," Rieux said. "They haven't proven as effective as usual. But the chances that he will die without them are near certain."

Mr Grossman shook his head. "It's a butcher shop there," he croaked.

"There must be another way," Tso suggested. "Can we just get the antibiotics from the drug store and give them to him?"

Rieux shook his head. "He has to be monitored closely."

"We can do that," Grossman insisted. "I'm out of work. What else am I going to do? Please, doctor. There's a reason why we called you."

Rieux said he would wait until the ambulance arrived. When he saw the red lights of the vehicle outside, Mr Grossman began to weep. His daughter was in his bedroom, opening drawers and closets in a flurry of motion in an attempt to gather his things. Mr Grossman dropped to the floor in a fetal position. Two paramedics, dressed from head to toe in protective gear, picked him up under each arm, lifted him onto a stretcher, and carried him out the door. Rieux identified himself to one paramedic, whose eyes seemed small within an oversized face mask, and offered a rundown of Mr Grossman's symptoms.

When Janice Grossman followed Rieux with some of her father's possessions in a reusable shopping bag, Izzy raised his arm.

"Don't come with me," Mr Grossman told her. "Don't visit me."

She became immobile. Was he upset at her? Was he trying to save her? Rieux could not tell. Grossman looked to her friend. "Of course you should go," Tso told her. She took her by the arm and hurried her in the direction of the ambulance. Rieux moved ahead of them. From the door, he yelled at one of the paramedics to wait for her.

Rieux and Tso stood in the snow and watched the ambulance disappear. After some careful hand washing with the sanitizer he brought with him, Rieux exchanged his mask for a toque. Tso was already wearing her jacket as she held open the door. She thanked him for coming on short notice. "Which way are you going?" she asked.

He pointed in one direction; she was going in the other. She'd walk with him anyhow. Under a streetlight, he noticed the freckles on her nose and her wide cheekbones. She seemed to him like someone who was tired of being pretty, who downplayed her looks—an attitude and behaviour that served as an erotic dog whistle to a particular kind of person. "I've got nothing better to do," she said. "It's funny how time works. We're all worried about our lives being dramatically shortened, but in the meanwhile, we just wait, playing video games."

"I wish I could take a break," he said.

"But you're not someone who takes vacations, am I right?"

"Not true," he blurted out. "My wife and I cycled through the Swiss Alps two years ago. The year before that we hiked the West Coast Trail."

She laughed. "How many calories did you burn?"

Along Main Street, there seemed to be more people but less traffic than usual at this time of night. Some businesses had posted signs apologizing, in neighbourly language, for temporarily closing. Others kept their doors open, despite a lack of customer interest or inventory, to maintain normalcy. They passed a sandwich board outside one restaurant that had this message written in chalk: "We still have wine (for now). Come inside!"

Tso offered to buy Rieux a glass of wine, and he hesitated only for a moment before he followed her inside. The restaurant was full of people still wearing jackets, the ice half-melted on their boots, and the music evoked his idea of a European discotheque in the 1970s. The server, a tall, tanned woman in latex gloves, recognized Tso, who shrieked in surprise and asked her about her massage school training. After they finished chatting, she handed them menus and wine lists with items struck out with black marker. His eyes were drawn to the black lines. The missing text looked like classified information. "I'm sorry," the server, whom Tso introduced as

Gudrun, told her. "But we ran out of the tempranillo yesterday."

"Are you picky about red wine?" Tso asked Rieux. He shook his head. She looked relieved. Tso picked one of the remaining wines and the waitress took their menus.

"Do you come to Vancouver often?" he asked her. "How do you know everyone?"

She told him it was only her second visit to the city. "I don't know *any-one* here. I met Janice when I arrived a month ago. She's become my Vancouver sister—or daughter. And the waitress, I met her the other day—it's a long story. She didn't even tell me she worked here." The server brought a half-carafe of wine and two glasses. Tso poured. "It's actually easy to make friends. We're all going through something momentous and unique. I have no one here who I know well, who understands. I've chatted with my aunt and my friends back home, but it's stilted. They don't know what's going on in this place, and I can't describe it to them."

"It's easy to make friends when strangers want to talk to you," he told her. He regretted that his statement sounded like an accusation. He was tired and would have blown off Tso's request if it had come from anyone else, but her charisma compelled him, in part, because it was the inverse of his. Even as a child, he couldn't make friends, and in university did his lab projects un-partnered. He compensated by joining clubs and playing team sports. He became a general practitioner, not a researcher—a better fit for his solitary temperament and idealism—so he could have the chance to speak to people. "It's a talent I don't have," he admitted.

"It can be a curse," she told him. "You're always promising people—without even promising them—more than you can deliver." She made so much eye contact, it felt like she was showing off.

"But people beg me to make promises—to predict outcomes, to give assurances," he said, turning to his glass. He downed the wine in a gulp. "At least that's how it is in my line of work."

"Are you worried you'll get sick?" she asked.

He shrugged. "I take every precaution. If I get sick, it will be because I am doing my work." Her attention drifted to the candle between them, which allowed him to continue thinking through her question. "I see patients, good people who have led healthy lives, fall ill for no reason other than genetics or bad luck. Dropping dead during this quarantine would at least serve some purpose."

"I'm not worried about dying. I wrote a book about it—"

"I haven't read it. Sorry."

"I'm not book-shaming you. The gist of the book was, dying gives life meaning. We clear space and feed the earth when we pass on."

"That's common sense," he blurted out, then realized how rude he sounded. "Sorry, that didn't—"

"The wine's really gotten to your head," she told him, pouring the rest of the carafe into his glass. "Yes, you're right, the book doesn't reshape the history of thought. But what I was trying to do was shift, in a small way, our collective mindsets. I told readers to start planning their funerals in their thirties, not when they're in their eighties and on their deathbeds. I wanted them to think about the people they leave behind—family, friends—as a gift."

"So you're in good shape for this epidemic?" he asked her.

"No way. Death I can handle, but being sick frightens me. Not having family or anyone who knows me well enough to call a good friend, should I fall mortally ill, scares me. I figure Janice is my only lifeline."

When they'd finished their wine, Rieux paid the bill, despite Tso's protest, and then waited with her until she got into a cab. He didn't remember his walk home but woke up in bed with his hiking boots on. He clomped into the bathroom and vomited. In a panic, he took his own temperature and concluded he was only hungover (without having had much to drink). Remorse washed over him, a feeling that exceeded anything he did or admitted to feeling. In the churning of regret, he was possessed by a need to speak to Elyse. He tried the number she'd given him, but the call didn't go through because he hadn't used the proper country code. When he got a recorded message asking him to try again, he didn't bother to search for the correct number. Instead he dialled the clinic and told the receptionist he was feeling unwell.

Rieux left the house to sidestep his concerned mother. He took his bike out but was forced to choose the roads carefully. A patch of black ice would further strain the medical system. He stopped on Broadway to chug a bottle of water and find something to eat. His ambitions that day were to expend some physical energy. He hoped to ride to the university and back. While in line for his bagel, he received a text from Castello. She wanted to see him at the hospital. "I'm calling in a favour," she wrote. "Actually, I am calling in two."

They had not spoken since her tirade of frantic messages. Rieux replied that he was on his way. The day had opened up like one extended airport layover as soon as he called in sick, so he was relieved by Castello's invitation. He biked along the Seawall, a ride made easier by the absence of tourists, enjoying the burn of the frosty air on his cheeks.

Castello waited outside the doors of the auxiliary hospital—a wing of the unfinished medical centre that would replace St. Paul's Hospital the next year—reserved for patients with the disease. She had a new blunter hairstyle and was wearing makeup. She swiped Rieux in and led him to a room where they both changed into protective clothing. "We are short-staffed in the auxiliary hospital," she told him. "You used to work a day a week in the lung clinic. I was wondering whether I could convince you to work here for a couple of shifts."

She knew he would be curious. And she knew that he never declined her requests. "Someone I know was admitted yesterday," he told her. "May I visit him?"

Castello pointed at a nurse behind the desk who asked for the patient's name. "His last name is Grossman," he told her. "I don't know his first name. He would be in his sixties. He was admitted last night."

The nurse turned to her screen and leaned into it. "There was an Isaac Grossman who passed away last night, two hours after he was admitted. But he was eighty-five years old."

Perhaps he was young-looking for his age, thought Rieux. It seemed unlikely that two people with that name would come in at the same time. His bloody coughing was, in retrospect, a terminal event, a flag of surrender from betrayed lungs.

"Sorry," Castello said. "Come with me. You should take a look at what we have here."

There was a range of suffering here, from those moaning listlessly in agony—fresh admittees—to those who looked content in their disease-racked repose. Castello and Rieux visited the bed of a fifty-one-year-old man who had been one of the first people admitted for the bubonic version of the disease. Within the first day, he had developed disseminated intravascular coagulation—a clotting of the blood followed by organ failure—and was placed in an induced coma. His legs became gangrenous and needed to be amputated.

"He woke up for the first time yesterday and asked the nurse to scratch his toes," Castello said, her dry laugh like a snare beat.

The patient was sleeping. He had the kind of handsome, imperious face that one saw immortalized in stone, on horseback, in a European capital—possibly he was a banker or lawyer. He needed a shave and for someone to run a comb through his silver hair. But this man was one of the lucky ones. The odds of dying of the disease were comparable to winning the lottery; so were the odds of surviving it. He was intact—more or less—and soon he would be transferred to another wing in the hospital for rehabilitation.

"He doesn't look like somebody who should be sick, am I right?" Castello asked. "The disease can strike anybody, but he looks like someone who gets all the breaks in life."

"I don't believe in eugenics," Rieux said. "But I see what you mean."

"Victor thinks his DNA makes him invincible," Castello said. "Do you know that my surname is the Italian word for castle?"

"I didn't, but it makes sense," Rieux replied.

"Victor's family comes from a town two hundred kilometres from Florence. The other day he told me that he's descended from plague survivors. He was bragging. He believes that people with Southern European ancestry have genes that will protect them from this new outbreak."

"I'm glad you're talking to him again," he told her. "His views were always ... provocative."

"It's not entirely fun," she said. "But we still have our secret language. It gets tiring to ask questions no one else can answer."

Rieux offered himself for shifts in the auxiliary hospital whenever they didn't conflict with his duties at the clinic. He dreaded his evenings alone with his mother even as he regretted neglecting her.

"I have one more request," Castello said as they removed their protective gear and washed their hands. "This one is more personal."

The man responsible for her son's death would be having a parole hearing later that week. Castello would be giving a victim's impact statement. Her lawyer had asked for a delay in the hearing given her high-profile role in the disease resistance efforts, but to delay his hearing would affect the killer's rights. She wanted Rieux to attend. "Victor will be there, if you can't make it," she told him. "But even when we were happily married, he was never someone I could lean on."

Rieux knew he would say yes. Castello rarely used to make requests. Now they seemed to burst forth, urgent and irate. He'd thought that, at this point, she would mention the barrage of phone calls and text messages she'd sent him, but then it occurred to him that she might not remember them. "It's much easier for me to administer an injection or set a broken bone," he said. "Why do you ask me to do such hard things?"

"The answer is so obvious, I feel stupid saying it," she said. She had removed all the protective gear except for a face mask. "Because you live to help."

12.

Megan Tso spent three nights on Janice Grossman's couch after her father's sudden death. Three nights was enough time to feel as though she'd given of herself to another without the resentment of martyrdom. Although it wasn't an entire week of sitting *shiva*, she thought seventy-two hours felt like a traditional interval for helping an acquaintance through a tough time; it was like a "minute of silence" or "forty days in the desert."

She remembered something she'd read the other day: The term "quarantine" had been coined by plague-struck Venetians in the fourteenth century. "Quarantinario" was Italian for "forty days." Ships coming into the port city had to wait out that period, while flying a yellow and black flag, before passengers could step foot on the mainland. What Tso wouldn't give to know that this quarantine would last only forty days—even fifty would be okay. As it was, the word had decoupled from its etymology.

When Grossman texted the news of her father's death, Tso had already been out on a run to clear her head after the previous night's boozy outing with Rieux. It was barely eight when she left the hotel. She bought oranges, cereal, and milk at a corner store that had just opened, then took a taxi to Grossman's.

"They took him into the auxiliary hospital," Grossman said. "They told me to go home, but I waited. When I spoke to a doctor after he died, he said I couldn't see the body because of infection, so part of my brain keeps telling me he must've switched wristbands with another elderly white male patient." Her voice was hoarse and emphatic. "I don't know how someone who never left his apartment, never saw anyone, who hired somebody to wash his kitchen floors with bleach every week, could *become infected*. If he could fall sick, I may as well run around licking toilet seats."

Grossman's gaze swam around the room. Tso forced her to sit and placed a bowl of cereal in front of her. Grossman took a bite and pushed it away. "I don't even know what I want. Except to clean my dad's room."

Tso wanted to be like the white people she'd grown up watching on TV; someone who could stroke a friend or acquaintance like a house pet. Instead, she placed her hands in the back pockets of her jeans. "We can do that later," she told her. "You're exhausted."

"Sorry to text you when I did. My first thought was to call Janet, but then I hated myself for thinking of talking to her. I could imagine her saying nice things to me while Happy Dancing at her house. Janet and my father hated each other. Sorry again," she told Tso. Milk dribbled on her chin. "*You* must be exhausted."

Tso was cutting oranges. She had already gone for a run, and her knees were stiff. She said, "A little tired."

"Would you sleep with me?" Grossman asked. "I miss having someone next to me."

Tso stopped cutting oranges. "*Sleep* sleep, right?"

"Of course." She started rubbing her arms nervously. Everything about this house—the blackout curtains, the candles—gave the impression that Grossman was not a morning person. "I wouldn't suggest we do *that*. Just forget I said anything."

"I would like to sleep with you," Tso said slowly, sounding like someone reciting from a script for people learning the English language.

Grossman shook her head, though her gaze drifted toward the bedroom. "It would probably be awkward."

Tso was, in fact, intrigued by the idea of a sleeping partner. For an
entire year after she moved in with her aunt, they would spend an hour in
her bed at night talking about their plans for the next day. The prospect of
being with someone, of feeling someone's warmth—day in, day out—was
something she craved and wanted to be ready for. She refused to take up
more than half the king-sized mattress in her hotel suite.

She waited for Grossman to change into her pyjamas and climb onto
the air mattress. The bed was pushed up against the wall, and Grossman
took the outside half. Tso removed her shoes and jacket but kept the rest
of her clothes on. She lay down next to Grossman, arms across her chest,
elbow brushing against her friend. She felt self-consciously jittery.

Grossman told her that she planned to call the funeral home when
she woke up. Her father had prepaid for his funeral decades earlier and
made detailed arrangements. "He didn't think I could handle it," she told
Tso. "My half-sister lives in Montreal. He always trusted her more. If she
were the daughter living in this city, he wouldn't have preplanned."

Grossman's father was much older than Tso had suspected. Born before World War II, he and his parents crossed the Atlantic—first to Brook-
lyn, then Montreal—before such trips became urgent escapes for Jewish
people. Izzy Grossman left school early and found his first restaurant job
at age thirteen, then he started to work in the entertainment industry. He

moved to Vancouver in 1963, where he met his first wife and started a talent-booking club. He managed a roster of song-and-dance acts. "But he didn't like the direction music was going in," she told Tso. "And my dad had an affair with a chorus girl who would eventually become my mother. Once they married, she didn't approve of his lifestyle." He briefly ran a comedy club until it burned down. "My mother had left him six months earlier for her high-school sweetheart. Let's just say that made him careless about fire safety." With his insurance money, he bought the house and eked out a living through his rental suites and the grocery store. "We're always talking about me," Grossman said. "Why don't you ever talk about yourself?" She lay her head on Tso's shoulder. She gave the appearance of being larger than she actually was, mainly because of her frizzy hair and wide hips.

"I'm the least interesting person I know," Tso told her. It was a practiced response to a common question. "When I reminisce, even about the good things, it makes me sad."

"You talk about your aunt," Grossman observed through a yawn. "What happened to your parents?"

"My mother died in a car accident," she lied. "I never knew my dad. He had always been out of the picture. See? *Sad.*"

Tso felt an urge to talk about how her mother liked to sweep. And how Tso had asked for a child-sized broom to sweep along with her. And how her mother sang under her breath. She would have spoken these thoughts aloud except that Grossman began to snore. Grossman's arm swung over her, like she was used to hugging someone larger in bed, but

Tso decided to let her sleep for another twenty minutes before she wriggled out of the bed. She felt Grossman's hot breath beat on her shoulders. A puddle of drool collected on her neck.

It would have been a long twenty minutes if Farhad Khan had not knocked. It seemed like he was still singing the same song to himself in Persian as the last time Tso had seen him, three weeks earlier.

"My friend! My saviour!" he said, pulling off his earphones. His skin was the colour of clay and he had a precise beard that looked drawn onto his face. In each ear he wore diamond studs and sported a Lionel Messi soccer jersey. He held a bottle of vodka and a package wrapped in brown paper. "I come home. I see the front door open. I see the door of Mr Izzy open. He is not there, so I come up." He held up the bottle of vodka. "This is for Mr Izzy." He held up the brown paper package. "And this is for the daughter, for being my other saviour."

Tso explained the situation, hoping not to alarm Khan. "We're going to clean Mr Grossman's place," she insisted. "Just be careful."

Khan threw his hands up to his cheeks; he seemed unconcerned about infection. "This poor woman. What a good man. And she is a loyal daughter," he told Tso, suddenly sounding older than he was. He moved a little closer toward her and said in a whisper, "If there is anything you need—because right now, there are so many shortages—just ask me. I can help. Anything to return the favour."

He left the bottle of vodka and the brown paper package with Tso. Within the package were two frozen wild salmon steaks.

"I don't know what he's doing—but he's already paid four months of back rent," Grossman explained upon waking. "And I have never seen him happier. He must be the happiest man in the city."

"All it took was an epidemic," Tso replied with a whistle.

"When you think of it, the disease puts everything in perspective," Grossman added before breaking into the first of many teary jags. Tso brought her water and a Benadryl.

Once Grossman was asleep again, Tso left to retrieve her toothbrush from the hotel and returned with vegetables and rice to serve with the salmon steaks. Then she picked the best Netflix indie romantic comedies. She felt useful.

Grossman had an appointment at a funeral parlour for the next day. Tso accompanied her. When they arrived, they were asked to wait in a reception area that was so crowded they needed to stand. They waited forty-five minutes until a funeral services agent, a dewy-faced young woman who shared a surname with the business, welcomed them into her office. She apologized for the delay. "As you can see, we've had a lot of appointments."

Grossman handed over her prepaid policy papers and began listing her specific needs. Her father didn't want a religious funeral; he had disavowed Judaism as a teenager. He wanted laughter. "It should be in a small room, as my dad kept to himself in his later years," she continued. "And I want a cherry oak casket."

The funeral staffer's eyes flitted between the contract that Grossman brought and her computer screen. "I'm afraid we have a problem," she said, turning back from the screen. "At the moment we only have the capacity to do cremation burials." They had run out of caskets; new inventory hadn't yet been brought in. And they had no idea when they might get caskets.

"But my father has a full-sized plot," Grossman said.

"That's wonderful," the agent said matter-of-factly. "You're lucky to have had a parent who planned so well. Dad left you with so many options."

The single plot (purchased, along with the funeral, in a lugubrious period following Izzy Grossman's second divorce) could be subdivided. Some of it could be reserved for Janice or her sister. Or she could sell the land, which had a prime location in the city's only cemetery, Mountain View. The value of the land, mirroring residential property, had grown exponentially in the past year. And then there was the "plague premium." As it stood, with other cemeteries outside the city limits, there were bodies and cremated remains that would not be buried until the quarantine was lifted. Muslim and Jewish families, whose faiths did not allow for cremation, were most grievously affected. Mr Grossman's plot was a prize. "In this market," the agent concluded, "you would make a killing."

Grossman pulled her grey curls over her face and rocked in her chair. Tso leaned into her and asked if she wanted to go. Grossman shook her head. "I just thought this would go more smoothly," she whispered back. "I don't need to turn a profit." She took a breath and asked the funeral agent if they could build their own casket.

"From pine?" the agent asked. Her placid demeanor was suddenly transformed, and she re-clicked her computer mouse as though she could regain her composure through repetition.

"I would have to find a carpenter," Grossman answered. "But we would use better material."

The agent excused herself. "I'm sort of new here," she told them. "I need to consult with my manager." She returned five minutes later, a smile reapplied to her face, and told them that a homemade casket would work.

For Grossman, the job of building a casket offered a diversion from the more mundane tasks of funeral planning and excavating her father's apartment. When they got home, Grossman called a friend, a cabinetmaker, to commission the project. But this friend was preoccupied by the illness of her wife, who had been admitted to the auxiliary hospital the day after Grossman's father. She then called a contractor only to be told that he was booked solid. Since the quarantine, some homeowners had thrown themselves into renovations and other time-consuming improvement projects. They surmised that the city was too preoccupied to notice that this work was being done without permits. And they had nothing better to do.

"That leaves us with one option," Grossman said. She then committed to building her own casket for her father. For half of that day, she was engrossed in the project, following online instructions for a "toe-pincher" style pine coffin. She and Tso went to the hardware store to collect the boards, handsaw, nails, wood glue, clamps, and rope. Grossman put it together in the former grocery store that had once been Janet's art studio. The ice-frosted windows of the store allowed in more light than Tso expected and was reflected in the polished wood floors. On the interior walls, some oil paintings by Grossman's former lover still hung. In those paintings, Grossman was depicted fully clothed—not as a figure of beauty but a dominating presence. In one image, she was pictured as a herder in a field of goats. In another, she leaned into a pool table lining up a shot. "I've been meaning to send those back to Janet," she said once she noticed Tso looking at the paintings. "She wants to burn them. She says the style is too primitive. And that she used Indigenous imagery that might be considered appropriative. She's worried I'll ruin her career," she added, measuring the casket's centre floorboard. "What she should really be worried about is the novel I'm writing. It's in the fantasy genre to avoid defamation, but it's really about her."

By nightfall, Grossman and Tso had put together the pine casket. The website suggested that it could also be used as a stage or Halloween prop. When they were done, they had realized that promise. It looked like something without being that something. Grossman sobbed at the result. "We'll figure out an alternative," Tso told her. She led her upstairs and back to sleep.

That evening, Tso allowed Grossman to spoon her until she began to snore. Once she detached herself, she stepped out of the apartment, across the landing, and knocked on Farhad Khan's door.

"Ah—my saviour!" Khan shouted. He was bare-chested, in a pair of running shorts. "Please, come in."

The front hallway to the apartment was lined with liquor boxes and cartons of cigarettes. Tso walked by the kitchenette where she had found him after his suicide attempt. The upturned chair remained on the checkerboard floor. "You seem to have some new business concerns," she said.

"Yeah, I have some friends who fix me up," he said, flopping into the middle of a couch. She couldn't help noticing that he had the torso of a swimmer: a tanned, hairless inverted triangle. The torsos she'd seen most recently had all been narrow, wiry, and tattooed. Between the couch and a large television playing cable news, she saw a hookah. "You smoke?" he asked.

"Not in a long time," she said, remembering a trip to Istanbul as a backpacker. She sat across from him in a matching armchair that she didn't remember from her last visit. He huffed the hookah pipe, blowing smoke that made his eyes water, and passed it to her.

The water at the bottom of the blue-glass basin bubbled. She held up her hands, staring at the mouthpiece as if it were the barrel of a pistol. "We've got to be careful about infection these days."

He broke out in laughter. His eyes were red and glassy as he took another puff. "Okay, maybe you are right," he said. "But look at Mr Izzy—such a careful man. So proper, so clean. He doesn't want to be around no one. Not even his nice daughter. And he dies. So if I die, I should die with others."

Tso decided she would get to the point. "You said you could help. By that you mean you can get goods through the barricades?"

"Before I got depressed, I used to sell and re-sell. Long time ago, it used to be bad things. It was bad, not so bad." He leaned back into the couch. "The kind of things kids get in trouble selling. When this sickness happened, it was like a wake-up call. I need to get back to business. I need to make money. I need to love life." He pointed his pinched fingertips in the air in emphasis and took another hookah hit to settle himself. "Let us ... jump chase. It's easier to bring things into the city, but I can also take things out."

"You mean like mail?" Tso asked, knowing immediately she'd missed the mark.

He dipped his nose and looked at her with incredulity. "I am saying I can get *you* out. Isn't that what you want? I won't take money from you, but my associates will charge a fee. It won't be cheap."

She shook her head. "No. What I need is a coffin for Mr Grossman."

He laughed again. "Ah, that is easy. I get you one by tomorrow—the day after, at the latest."

When the coffin arrived the next day, Khan waved off any attempts to pay him. "Maybe I ask for a favour back," he told Tso. "Like in *The Godfather*."

Three days had passed, and Tso left Grossman's house knowing that she had done as much as she could for her friend. At the funeral, so many people came to pay their respects to Izzy Grossman that the small room was quickly filled. Latecomers listened to Janice Grossman's eulogy, which was funny enough to earn a standing ovation, from the hallway.

Within two months of the quarantine, when weekly deaths peaked at two hundred and twelve, the scarcity of burial space in Vancouver would become an issue that distracted people with righteous anger. The city crematorium operated seven days a week. City land earmarked for a playground was used for those who needed urgent burial for their loved ones, but even then, bodies and remains were stacked on top of one another. If only Grossman knew this at the time, Tso thought. Her father hadn't really gone too early. He was first in line.

13.

In the first hours of the quarantine, a few Vancouverites managed to side-step the Canadian Armed Forces roadblocks. Before additional Coast Guard patrol boats arrived, they took their private sea vehicles from the Burrard Marina to Richmond or Deep Cove. Others slipped through the wooded pathways of Central Park, carrying their essential belongings in backpacks and rolling luggage to get to Burnaby and beyond. Siddhu had heard stories of semi-organized gangs of twenty or more darting across Boundary Road in a stampede, knowing that the soldiers couldn't catch them all. The soldiers had not yet been instructed to use force, the outer limits of which had still not been established, to contain them. In the early days, the spotlights that rimmed the city borders like neon beams had yet to be installed. The barbed wire had yet to be unfurled. The sentry towers would take another week to be built.

The first escapees evaded not only confinement but that sense of un-reality that choked so many Vancouverites, that made them long for two-zone bus passes and suburban cul-de-sacs. Envy always overcame locals in between moments of panic and fear.

Siddhu pondered the escapees the way he might look at a friend who bought a stock that skyrocketed. It didn't help that his wife regaled him with these success stories in their nightly Skype chats. By then, she knew that he had quit his job at the paper. She looked increasingly pale, her eyes puffier, as she spoke from their brightly lit kitchen, the pile of dishes overgrown in the sink. The boys would still be whimpering out their last waking moments from upstairs when she called. He wouldn't be able to hear them, but she would turn her head and shush them.

Uma needed him to bear witness to her account of the day before she got too tired. People came to help: her mother (whose flight back from Chandigarh had been rerouted to Seattle), his mother, and Uma's sisters and friends. They watched the boys and brought food, so she could get a massage or sit through a movie. "But then, they always leave," she said. "Sometimes they go before I want them to, and sometimes they can't go soon enough." He knew she was talking about his mother. "What I'm left to do—it's too much. I don't blame you. Not when I think about it. But I need to be angry."

In their relationship, he was the one who cried, the one who needed to be calmed down. Now, he held back his own tears as she worked through her displeasure. Afterward she would apologize through her sobs, and he would tell her to get some sleep. The worst way to end a call was when one of the boys started to scream. He would see her leave the kitchen and stare at the video image of his refrigerator for minutes, unsure of her return, before finally ending their call.

Afterward, he trudged through the snow to take his clothes to the laundromat on Davie Street. He was cycling through four sets of Costco-purchased shirts, pants, and undergarments and was careful not to spill anything on them. Unlike other hotel residents, he neither wore a paper bib nor showed up at the restaurant-lounge in stained T-shirts. When he returned from the laundromat, he would stay in the lounge for a drink with Oishi or Tso, both of whom, he noticed, began to look wan and tired in the Christmas lights. Tso had recently helped a friend deal with her father's death. Oishi was negotiating the terms of his divorce as he returned to work. Two drinks later, Siddhu would be in his room in his underwear, practicing the yo-yo for a few minutes until he couldn't keep his eyes open. Then he stretched out on the bed like a snoring starfish.

He had never lived alone, never gone an entire week without seeing his parents or spent more than a couple of nights away from his wife. This should have felt novel. Instead, the absence of these oppressive forces weighed on him. He should have felt lightened. He felt cheated.

A week earlier, a team of paramedics had rushed into his hotel room, led by a night clerk. One paramedic began to pull him out of bed. He screamed until they realized their mistake—they'd been meant to remove an infected hotel guest from the floor above. Ever since, he could not sleep for more than two hours before getting up and vigorously washing his hands.

He often arrived at the GSSP office wishing he could go to sleep, but then his brain perked up at the urgency of the stories he needed to tell. Horne-Bough offered no direction. He was busy speaking to international news outlets about the disease or was in conversation with his lizard-like tech guys. *Why was he so obsessed with being surveilled?* Horne-Bough seemed happy with Siddhu's coverage—and his discretion—and even presented him with a gift: a life-insurance policy should he contract the infection while working. Siddhu had been looking online for coverage the previous week and felt buoyed by the synchronicity.

There were so many stories to tell: Siddhu could write about the disparity of infection rates between income groups that had flattened as the disease spread throughout the city but had since re-emerged. He could unpack the disagreements between provincial and federal agencies that led to delays in relief payments for locals whose incomes were decimated either by illness or quarantine. He tried to touch on these issues. And then there was the silence in City Hall surrounding the Mayor's leave after his personal scandal and his subsequent refusal to resign. He avoided that one, and thankfully a colleague continued to poke at city officials.

As usual, people contacted Siddhu for publicity. Cleaning services touted their effective, environmentally friendly decontamination policies. Therapists wanted to be profiled on their trauma-counselling services. Even Rieux cornered him to write a story.

"In case you didn't read my email, I am starting a sanitation league," the doctor announced at their coffee shop. "Infection rates are too high in this area."

"About that," Siddhu answered, digging into his pocket to pay for his Americano, "I meant to reply. It didn't fly in the story meeting." That last part was a lie. "One question: Isn't that the city's job, sanitation?"

"Everyone in City Hall is preoccupied. Government acts too slowly. It's up to private citizens to respond," Rieux said. Siddhu saw an impatience in his rhetoric that reminded him of the nineteen-year-olds he'd known in university who wore neckties to class and read Ayn Rand. "More people will die than necessary."

Rieux told him that he'd lead his sanitation squad on weekends and evenings and already had two volunteers. Siddhu was tired enough as it was. He thought of people like Rieux—inexhaustible and determined— and believed it must be fear that drove them. Not fear of disease or dying; Rieux was chasing something else away.

Siddhu left it at that and returned to work. His young employer texted him from the rooftop to come up and discuss a story. Siddhu grabbed his coat and scarf and took the two steep flights of stairs with dread. Even the cold and snow hadn't persuaded Horne-Bough to find another place to conduct his private meetings. Instead, he installed a heat lamp under which he huddled in a fur-lined parka and fingerless gloves while vaping. Siddhu stood under the lamp as if it was an umbrella.

"I wanted to discuss your performance," Horne-Bough said.

Siddhu, his boss explained, had been providing comprehensive coverage of the spread of the disease. He had proven himself worthwhile on that end. His contact list and pedigree were also assets. But he hadn't broken any news. He had yet to generate the kind of excitement that drove web traffic and earned subscriptions.

"I've been doing what I thought was best," Siddhu said. "We haven't had any real story meetings."

"We don't do those." Horne-Bough half-shrugged. "You're new here, but I don't want you to get surpassed," he said. "So that's why I've come up with a story idea. I want you to conduct the first interview with Romeo Parsons since his scandal."

Horne-Bough had already been contacted by the PR company that the wealthy mayor had hired privately. "I insisted that you, as our senior writer, be the one to speak to them," he said. "There was push-back, but we kicked the shit out of it." He presented Siddhu with a contact number on a scrap of paper. "Can you set something up?"

Siddhu nodded and took the number. He already had a story to cover that night.

Early in the evening, Siddhu took a car2go to the edge of the Grandview Highway until he reached a set of electronic roadwork signs placed a few blocks before the spotlights, fences, and guard towers. They were typical roadwork signs that warned drivers of a stoppage ahead and asked them to take an alternate route. They were like trigger warnings that cautioned locals who wanted to pretend that nothing had changed to avoid going farther.

He came to the foot of the guard tower. Between the towers, guards with rifles on all-terrain vehicles patrolled the length of the fence. On the other side, coming into the sealed city, was an unloading area where the freight of a fleet of eighteen-wheelers was being inspected by men with machine guns. A Canadian Armed Forces captain, who wore a pair of binoculars around his neck, stepped out of a door. Siddhu held up the lanyard with his ID, but the army captain didn't bother to look.

"You're the reporter," he said. "You missed all the fun."

Siddhu was invited into the guard tower where he was given a bullet-proof vest. The army captain was a reservist who lived outside the city in Chilliwack. He wore light fatigues and stood about as tall as Siddhu—a few inches past six feet—but, when they shook hands, the officer's hand enveloped the reporter's. He told Siddhu he'd been stationed here since the outbreak began.

The eighteen-wheelers brought basic food items, medical supplies, and fuel into the city. The officer's job was to make sure that nothing was being smuggled in or out. Alcohol, hard drugs, and luxury items had been confiscated while he was on duty. "Even in a quarantine zone, some people can't live without their $25,000 watches," he said. "We do a good job catching their middlemen."

"But why has the black market been thriving?" Siddhu asked. "You can still buy all these goods through connections—or online—if you have enough money."

"We have our theories. Smuggling doesn't occur through trucks or trains—we handle that. The airports have been closed. It exists only by boat," he said before he seemed to notice the voice recorder in front of him. "That was off the record."

Siddhu decided not to correct him about what "off the record" meant. He let the officer disparage the work of the coast guard until a truck approached the gate. It had been emptied of its cargo. The driver rolled down the window and presented him with a security card, which the army captain swiped through a tablet encased in a bulky military-looking shell and had a reader attached to it. The inspection process took nearly a quarter of an hour, as the line behind the truck grew. Drivers, by law, were not allowed to step out of their vehicles. Most of them carried piss bottles because they couldn't use the washroom. Soldiers with dogs boarded the cargo holds while others in gas masks fumigated the trucks' exteriors.

Over a period of three hours, dozens of trucks came in and out.

Siddhu chatted with the army captain, who was amiable, and enjoyed his company. When he felt comfortable enough, Siddhu asked him about rumours made about compassionate "exceptions." The soldier's expression remained fixed as though he hadn't heard.

"There are stories in the ether about people who have been let out of the city because there's a relative in another city who's dying," Siddhu added. "I've heard people talking about diplomats who succeeded in getting citizens of their countries airlifted back to their home nations, where they are isolated for a period of time and released. Do you know anything about this?"

The captain's tone became much more officious, even stilted. "The only people who have been in and of the city, as far as I know, have been truck drivers or infectious disease experts," he said. "I get asked that question a lot."

"My family is in the suburbs," Siddhu explained. "I've been living in a hotel. My boys are a year old."

"If you're going to escape," he told him without making eye contact, "the best way would be to go by boat. Find someone who knows what they're doing, someone who has a licensed driver. Now, that's off the record, too."

From their elevated perch, they both looked out onto the highway at the commuter traffic that bypassed the city. Siddhu used to hate traffic. But now he saw the beauty—the order and purpose—in the car lights on the highway. He saw minivans in the High Occupancy Vehicle lane and imagined families returning from a visit to grandparents. In other cars, he pictured lonesome fathers getting home as their kids were being sent to bed.

The trucks came steadily as they watched from the tower. Near the end of Siddhu's evening, a drone appeared in the sky. It was so small at first that the army captain needed to point it out. "We get one every night," he told Siddhu, passing the binoculars. This drone was white with four propellers and a camera on its base. "It's either a single asshole or a bunch of them who think they were the first ones to come up with this idea."

For weeks, people on social media had posted about hearing gunshots at night, but the city denied that any violence had occurred, and no one had mentioned anything about drones. But at the hotel's restaurant a man had been pointed out to Siddhu. He was a permanent resident who used to pilot a drone above crowds of tourists on the beach from a secluded grassy area. The drone, it was said, would drop a water balloon filled with this man's urine, but he had never been caught. Since the quarantine, there were no tourists and few people on the beach. At the restaurant, Siddhu saw the man most mornings, reading over the newspaper contentedly with his toast and coffee.

The army captain came down from the guard tower with a rifle. He knelt, lined up the drone in his scope, and waited a moment in the hope that the drone might turn back before he pulled the trigger. The crack startled Siddhu.

———

Siddhu grew up in a house with an above-ground swimming pool. His parents had two additional properties that they either rented at a discount to extended family or left sitting empty. His mother drove only German cars. His parents spoke of deprivation in their childhoods: too many family members, too little space, bill collectors that had to be evaded. As a young man, he believed that he was fortunate, anointed by fate to live on the crest of his family's rising fortunes.

In his adult life, Siddhu revised that estimate. He saw wealthy foreigners arrive, setting up their children with sports cars, mansions, and clothing budgets. He had wanted to move into the city (and away from his family), but kept waiting for real estate prices to fall to realistic levels. In his self-pity, he considered himself one of the forsaken. He needed only to do his job to realize how wrong he was. In the city he saw desperation and those who lived in chemically blotted consciousness.

The city's visible history was characterized by a series of dramatic demographic reversals. Asian people moved into areas previously inhabited by white people. White people moved into places previously inhabited by Asians. Rich people moved into places where poor people lived. Neighbourhoods once avoided had become hotspots for professionals and the creative class. Other homes, once brought to life by families, sat empty as investment properties.

It should not have sounded so unlikely to Siddhu when he first heard reports about needles found in the city's most prestigious residential neighbourhood, Shaughnessy. He was too distracted to take notice. These tips came the week that he changed jobs. He could not pursue the story for his old paper, and he half-thought the tips would lead to a hoax or a piece of transgressive performance art. But in his first week at GSSP, he heard Horne-Bough mention squatters, dozens of them, in vacant homes and future teardowns.

He spent the Tuesday afternoon walking through Shaughnessy. He scoured Devonshire Park, where needles were allegedly discovered, but found only uncollected dog waste. He knocked on doors, but no one answered.

It was by chance that he saw a man pushing a shopping cart through the gates of a Tudor-style mansion. Its lawn was overgrown and its towering evergreens fenced in orange plastic mesh—a telltale sign of a teardown. Siddhu followed the man up the driveway to an open garage door, where the shopping cart was parked.

He entered the house and walked into the kitchen. There were bottles and lighters and needles on a marble counter-top. Beyond was a carpeted family room in which lawn furniture and the back seat of a car had been set up. Half a dozen men and women in hoodies and baseball caps sat around staring at the unlit fireplace. He did not know these people, but he recognized them. This was the part of the population that many citizens had wished away. They'd gotten their wish; these people were no longer seen—and yet, they were never closer.

Siddhu introduced himself. With glazed expressions, a few called out to him as if he was both welcome and expected. One woman who had been squatting by the fireplace approached him. She had black hair streaked with grey strands cut in a shag and papery skin the colour of burnt sienna. She refused to give Siddhu her name but said that she had lived in the Annex area until water damage from putting out a fire in the storefront next door had prompted her eviction. She'd found this squat at the end of the summer. "There's nothing special about this situation," she told him bluntly. "There are other houses like this one. We try not to come in and out during the day. He told us to stay out of the way and that we'd be fine."

"Who?" Siddhu asked.

She was evasive at first. Siddhu offered her a cigarette from a pack he'd bought in case he needed to ingratiate himself today. She took it and began to tell him about the city inspectors who snooped around the house as her housemates hid in the closets. They were careful to keep the blinds closed.

"One day, he showed up with pizza and bottled water. He wanted to know how we were doing. He said that homes were meant to be lived in."

"Who?"

"He had a nice face, but he wasn't wearing a suit like he was on all those signs. He drank a beer with one of the boys. Then he said he had to go."

"Was this Romeo Parsons who visited?" Siddhu asked. "The mayor?"

She nodded. "I guess he's still the mayor for now."

Siddhu thanked her and offered her another cigarette.

"You don't remember me, do you?"

Siddhu shook his head.

She said that Siddhu had interviewed her a year before in one of his award-winning stories about the Annex—back when people were still fighting it. "You told me my words would make a difference, and I said you were full of shit," she told him. "It doesn't matter anymore, I guess." She tucked the cigarette behind her ear to smoke later.

Siddhu called the number that Horne-Bough had given him. He expected someone from Romeo Parsons' PR company to answer, but it was Parsons himself on a speakerphone in what sounded like a large, empty room. The audible relief in his voice suggested that he'd been waiting for Siddhu's call. He wanted to speak that afternoon, just the two of them.

"I'm done hiding. I can meet you anywhere," Parsons told him. "I'm just glad you've finally agreed to do it. Your boss said you were too busy." Siddhu pocketed this information for later use. "I know from your byline that you have integrity and decency."

Normally, he would have suggested Parsons' home as a place to meet. An interviewer gets a better sense of the subject from their surroundings, and subjects are at their best where they're most comfortable. Besides, the mayor owned a Coal Harbour penthouse with a wraparound view of the city and a Damien Hirst sculpture. But Siddhu worried that the mayor would intimidate him. He was also unsure of Parsons' present situation with his wife. Was he currently banished to some bachelor bungalow? In his own forcibly decoupled state, Siddhu might be too overly sympathetic. He wanted to see the mayor in public, making eye contact with and waving at hip level (the handshake equivalent that had emerged since the quarantine) to locals who had been, by equal measures, magnetized and re-pelled by him. Siddhu suggested the lounge of his hotel, in an hour. Parsons agreed without hesitation.

Siddhu changed into the best of his four dress shirts and immediately staked out a table. He reviewed the story that had come out so far, most of it advanced by his own colleague at GSSP. Parsons had had a relationship with a woman in university in the late 1980s. She learned she was pregnant. She decided against telling Parsons and returned to her hometown in West-ern Ontario, where she lived until she died of leukemia. Their daughter, Cassidy, only three years old at the time of her mother's death, was raised by grandparents.

In her mid-twenties, Cassidy went through her mother's belongings in the attic and learned the identity of her father. "When I saw his picture, I thought I recognized him," she said in a video interview that Horne-Bough had conducted. "I didn't see a family resemblance, but he has that kind of face that made me think he was famous." It was her boyfriend who sug-gested she contact Vancouver's wealthy mayor. (Cassidy's boyfriend, it later emerged, handled the negotiation for the rights to her story.)

So she sent Parsons a letter. When she didn't receive a reply, she as-sumed it had been misplaced by someone at the mayor's office. Two weeks later, a lawyer contacted her, asking for a DNA sample. She complied. Before the results came in, she received a call from Parsons. "It was like I was talking to a voice I'd been hearing in my head my whole life," she told Horne-Bough. "I'd heard it but never knew who it was." Cassidy and her father spoke for hours. They wept together over the phone. He arranged to fly her to Vancouver, which is when the incident, later confirmed by the mayor in a terse statement, took place.

As Siddhu reviewed this information, Romeo Parsons appeared in the hotel lounge. He wore sunglasses, the rest of his face obscured by a mask and a week's worth of beard. His hair was uncombed, his posture bowed. He was dressed in dark jeans and an untucked sports shirt. Out of habit, they forgot not to shake hands. There was something unpracticed about the gesture for each of them. Siddhu apologized for applying hand sanitizer afterward. Parsons removed his sunglasses and mask as he took the seat facing the empty beach. The waitress, who asked Siddhu if he wanted his regular, took the mayor's request for a mint tea without noticing of him.

Siddhu placed his iPhone in the middle of the table. "Why are you talking now?" he asked.

"I thought the people of Vancouver needed some distraction," he joked. "If I can't save lives, I can do that."

"It makes sense for you to clear the air," Siddhu suggested. "If you're going to remain as mayor, you'll need to show your face again. You'll need to address the questions people have, so that you can move on."

Parsons looked over Siddhu's shoulder as their hot beverages arrived. At first, the words fell out of his mouth like broken teeth. "It took me this long to make peace with what you've just laid out." He held his mug with two hands, and Siddhu wasn't sure whether it was because he felt cold or weak. "I haven't been a public figure for long. I used to make money in real estate. I found homes for wealthy people where poor people used to live. I felt indirectly responsible for the Annex, and all the damage that followed because those developers followed my blueprint. I founded a couple of charities to make myself feel better, but they were like Band-Aids on shotgun wounds. I was forty-eight years old, and all of my adult years were spent in the pursuit of wealth. I realized I could spend the remaining half of my adult life as an act of penance."

"Did you have to be the mayor to do it?" Siddhu asked. "With all due respect, your worship, isn't there ego involved in taking on political office?"

A light caught Parson's eye. Siddhu's prickly question had activated his conversational impulses. "There would be if we already had someone capable in the office. Our last mayor allowed the Annex to happen because people like me made him dependent on our chequebooks. I knew how to avoid that. I was the best person for the job because I had the right mix of competence and conscience. My agenda had been watered down during my election campaign, but who else could radically advance equality and affordability in our city? This infection exposed everything that we had wanted to sweep aside. It allowed us to see others—not just the ones who looked like us—it allowed us to see them as equals. The disease levelled us. And after the riot, I had a chance to speak to everyone. And for everyone to hear me."

Siddhu remembered how he'd cringed at the timing of the scandal. People had needed a moment to waft in the idealism of the mayor's speech and unfettered vision. Instead, they pulled down their blinds and watched the mayor dismantled as statements, screenshots from text exchanges, and interview videos hijacked the spotlight, if temporarily, from an unfolding civic catastrophe.

Partisans suggested that the boyfriend of the mayor's daughter was to blame. It was insinuated that he was sneaky, greedy, and cuckolded—an aspiring EDM producer in a town best known for mineral extraction. Horne-Bough had been negotiating with him since Parsons was sworn into office. Siddhu could see the boyfriend and his boss operating on the same frequency of feigned indifference and performative anger. A recording of a phone conversation between Parsons and Cassidy about their sexual contact, produced the day before the riot, brought their negotiations to the necessary friction point.

"I wanted time to clear this with my wife and our kids. They have suffered, too." He searched the room for prying eyes. Finding none, he leaned toward the middle of the table, speaking into the voice recorder. "If you look it up, there's a specific term for what happened between me and Cassidy. It's not the one that everyone used. The other term implies a broken trust between people who belong to the same household. It·suggests that children are involved. Our situation wasn't like that."

"I did look it up, your worship," Siddhu said. "It happens relatively often between adoptees who meet their birth parents as adults or siblings who were separated at birth. There was even a radio documentary—"

"I broke my family's trust. And I hurt Cassidy's feelings by treating her like someone who needed to remain hidden. I could have avoided much of this hurt." He paused. "But I don't know how I could have avoided the act itself. I wasn't ready for it. And I wouldn't have acted on it, if we both weren't feeling such ... things. I never drank excessively or did drugs, but I know people who have struggled with addiction. And what I felt when I saw her for the first time sounded like what they've experienced—a feeling of peace followed by intense panic."

Siddhu wanted to let Parsons unburden himself before he asked for details, a step-by-step recounting of the choices he'd made. The public had already received Cassidy's account of their night together, spent ordering room service and drinking minibar vodka tonics until she felt so dizzy that she could've been tipped over "with a feather." Parsons, thought Siddhu, was a man who could not reconcile personal misfortune in his life, who knew suffering only externally. He would want to minimize this discussion, present it as something that overtook him, before pivoting into his vision of a more equitable city after the infection.

As Parsons gave his responses, his features regained their distinct bearing, and he became animated. Heads started to turn. People were preparing for selfies with him.

"Are you still in contact with Cassidy?" Siddhu asked.

The mayor shook his head. "Why does this matter when people are dying?"

"Do you wish you were?" Siddhu asked.

The question made Parsons fold inwards. He bounced over his sentences, struggling to find enough words needed to bury a lie—an ossuary of rhetoric. Siddhu hated having to ask Parsons how he met cute with his adult child. He wanted to wash his tongue in hand sanitizer, but if he didn't, someone else would ask Parsons the same rude question. Siddhu had no choice. He needed to earn the life insurance policy purchased for him. He pushed the phone closer toward Parsons and asked him about the events that took place months earlier, when people had the time to commit errors. "Don't spare any details," he added.

The interview appeared later that day on GSSP and was widely re-posted, but it achieved the opposite effect to what Parsons had intended. The mayor sounded defensive, annoyed that the public was so interested in his personal life. He implied that Vancouverites took pleasure in his fall because it was a distraction. By contrast, the public felt that Parsons' desire to return to the policy fight against the disease and the underlying inequities it revealed was merely the smokescreen for his personal failures.

14.

Rieux rearranged his schedule at the clinic to allow for night and weekend shifts at the auxiliary hospital. On days when he would have ordinarily slid into spandex to ride to Squamish and back, he donned pea-green hospital scrubs and booties.

The rate of infection had not abated. The patients came from throughout the city like random jury-pool selections. The poor and the elderly who arrived were admitted with more advanced symptoms. Only a fraction of the patients he saw—between a quarter and a third, by Rieux's count—responded to antibiotics. Castello told him that a vaccine was currently being tested on macaque monkeys at the National Microbiology Laboratory in Winnipeg.

He spent most of his shifts watching people die. He had seen deaths during his residency and on his shifts at the lung clinic, but not in this volume, not with this frequency. These patients looked like nothing he'd ever seen before, yet they sparked recognition within him. It took him into his second day, while sitting in front of his laptop, to find the faces he'd been looking at in Medieval paintings.

Where he worked, no saints interceded from the heavens, no demons pulled his patients by their respirator tubes and IV lines into the netherworld. But those Old Masters were not working entirely in the realm of symbolism. In the sixty-year-old man whose body in repose was polka-dotted in buboes, whose face showed agony blanched in listlessness,

Rieux recognized a model for a sixteenth-century woodcut. An orderly turning over a patient, his broad shoulders twisting through his hospital gown, shared the musculature of a worker hauling a plague victim into a wagon in a famous etching.

Rieux saw himself in those paintings too. Haughty and slight, wearing his gown and mask—preserving his own health without saving others—he felt estranged from his own silhouette. He saw illustrations of plague doctors as crow-like bird men wearing black wide-brimmed hats and ankle-length gowns and wondered whether Medieval painters hadn't cryptically represented the unease of the doctors. In the artist's eye, the doctor was no saviour but a scavenger who descended on a field of death and snatched the least doomed specimens for profit. The plague doctors of the sixteenth century wore masks that resembled bird's heads with glass eyeholes and curved beaks stuffed with aromatics like mint and camphor to ward off disease, because before germ theory was introduced, disease had been thought to spread through odours. Plague doctors held staffs so they could point at infection without touching it.

In the end, it was not the images of dying people that made him restless but their cries for help. Some of them asked for things in languages he didn't understand. They moaned, wailed, and sobbed. He heard them all through his mask, the sounds made distant, like reverberations in a seashell. There was no escape to outside. Others withdrew. They sought private oases. But when Rieux turned inward, he saw his wife's face. He felt a steady pulse behind his eyes, an alarm. It reminded him that he was letting everyone down.

When he wasn't at the hospital, he wanted to find other ways to work. He had contacted Tso about starting a group that could offer sanitation classes and support to areas that had been infected at higher-than-average rates. As more fell ill, mistrust of the medical system had grown to the point that people preferred to suffer untreated at home with their families than to be treated at the auxiliary hospital where they would risk dying surrounded by strangers in masks. As a result, he continued to make house calls.

"Aren't public health organizations already offering clinics and handing out sanitizer and masks?" Tso asked while they were having dinner at his condo. Mrs Rieux had made curried beef brisket for dinner when her son told her he'd invited a guest.

"There's too much mistrust of doctors," Rieux said. "As far as some people are concerned, we are putting disease into them."

The planning session alarmed Mrs Rieux. She had grown worried about her son's workload. As a teenager, she told Tso, he had been admitted to the hospital with ulcers. He didn't tell anyone that he'd been shitting blood because he didn't want to fall behind in classes. He didn't know when to stop.

"This is not dinner table conversation, Mom," Rieux told her.

At least she was sitting at the table, if on the edge of her seat. For most of the evening, she had been in the kitchen cooking or bringing dishes to them in the dining area. Rieux felt compelled to mention to Tso that Mrs Rieux was his mother, and that she was visiting—she was not his servant.

"He once passed out during a math exam," Mrs Rieux told Tso. She spoke English at the beginning of the night but had turned to Cantonese. "In the hospital, he made me bring schoolwork to him."

"What drives him so much?" Tso asked Mrs Rieux with a glint of amusement.

Here is the question he wanted to ask them both: Was it because he didn't like to be teased that he was teased so much?

"He has been exactly the same since he was a child," Mrs Rieux insisted. "All his books and toys needed to be back in their place before he could sleep. One night I asked him why he couldn't leave them on the floor. And he said, 'I don't want you to do it, Mama. You work so hard.'"

"I didn't say that," Rieux told Tso. "I just prefer things to be neat."

Tso had spent most of the night listening to them talk. She seemed unflappable no matter what they said. They were all tipsy on the wine that she'd brought, a prized commodity.

"When he was growing up, we were poor," Mrs Rieux continued. "Bernard's father was a doctor, but he died soon after medical school. I was left with two young children. I had no education, no connections. So I cleaned houses for nice people. I would take Bernard and his sister with me. The families would offer them cookies. Bernard's sister would always take them, but Bernard always said no. He would stay sitting in the same place the whole time, reading a book."

The conversation progressed. Rieux drummed his fingers against his leg waiting for his mother to leave the room. When she disappeared to get more hot water for herself, he felt the need to correct her misinformation.

"For the record, I hated visiting those houses. Not all those people were nice. I hated being poor," he told Tso. "I became a doctor for status and money. My father was a doctor, so I assumed it was something I was capable of being."

"I miss having a mother to embarrass me," Tso said. She poured out the last fingers of Gamay. Rieux wondered if she'd lined up that morning outside the liquor store for a rationed amount of beer, wine, and spirits. It didn't seem like her style. The lineups generally went around the block. "Tell me more about your sanitation league," she continued. "We'll probably need a better name for it."

Rieux envisioned himself giving a series of talks on disease and cleanliness that he could deliver in the city's poorer neighbourhoods. He wanted Tso to organize other speakers to discuss the role of art in understanding illness and mortality. Tso thought these high-minded events would be pointless. "You'd be just another doctor pontificating," she told him. "You don't have to leave the house to learn what you'd be telling them."

"I would be more informal."

She dipped her nose and looked at him as though to say, *You?* They agreed to come up with a better idea. Rieux wanted to help the most people possible. He did not know if that meant saving lives. He wasn't having much luck on that end. He would settle for a reduction in suffering. At worst, it meant that they exhausted themselves in futility.

In any other year, about one hundred and fifty people died in Vancouver every week. At the height of the infection, that rate doubled. Not all of those extra fatalities were the direct result of infectious disease. While in terror of fleas and human contact, people were not living healthy lives. They drank and ate too much and indulged in reckless behaviour to dispel their fears of mortality. They argued over insignificant matters, like driving etiquette. The number of patients admitted to hospitals for alcohol poisoning and injuries resulting from physical violence spiked. An already strained medical system experienced further stress. The rate of drug overdoses, for reasons that exceed our capacity to supply plausible explanations, did not change.

Rieux didn't know exactly what damage Dr Orla Castello had brought upon herself. The health emergency seemed to bring new purpose to her life. She lived to work, shuttling between conference calls, broadcast interviews with international news outlets, and visits to hospitals. She no longer seemed preoccupied, and the colour had returned to her face. She quipped and smiled as she hung around for a second cup of coffee with her old student. But this reinvigorated woman wasn't the same person that Rieux had known, nor did she seem to behave like someone who had moved past her son's untimely death.

On the day of the parole hearing, he went directly from the clinic to the downtown courthouse. Castello was waiting for him by the security checkpoint. "This feels like we're going on a trip," she said as she placed her purse in a tray. "Why put yourself through this if you don't get a vacation?" They were led by a uniformed man who identified himself as a parole board employee into a room with a video conference setup on a laptop. The guard closed the door from inside.

The parole hearing was being held outside the city limits, in the

Federal Penitentiary in New Westminster. At the last hearing, she and Victor had both attended in person. "I don't know whether this teleconference makes things better," Castello said to Rieux as she placed her trembling hand in his. "The last time I went, I wanted to look him in the eye. He stared at his lap when I spoke. He only looked up when someone on the parole board asked him a question."

Initially, the laptop screen showed a table in another room. The hearing officer and parole board members entered the room. The hearing officer stepped in front of the camera and introduced herself. The meeting would begin shortly.

The door of the meeting room opened and Victor Castello appeared. He was dressed in the wool suit he'd worn to his law firm that morning. He was a broad-shouldered man with side-swept black hair, olive skin, and small black eyes. Once he pulled off his face mask, he revealed a muzzle of stubble. Victor had once been a member of his university wrestling team, and his thick arms made him look like a construction worker. Years ago, Rieux had helped Victor and Adam build a garden shed on the Castellos' property while sharing a case of beer. Even Adam, who was only sixteen at the time, was allowed a Pilsner.

Victor pulled a chair over next to Rieux, not his ex-wife. He arched a brow at Rieux and grunted. "I didn't have time to write a statement," Victor said to Orla Castello without exchanging a greeting. "I expect you have something prepared."

"Leave it to me," Orla said. "As always."

The man responsible for Adam Castello's death appeared on the laptop. He must have been in his mid-twenties, but he looked like a teenager. Philip Nguyen was slight, with a full, strawberry-red mouth and a messy mop of black hair that fell across his eyes. He took a seat across from the two parole board members and was accompanied by his parole officer.

Rieux noticed that Victor Castello's hands turned into mallets in his lap, and his breathing grew audible.

The hearing officer began with formalities and introductions. She asked Orla Castello whether she wanted to read her victim impact statement at the beginning of the meeting or toward the end. Castello cleared her throat and said she would read the statement near the end.

The two parole board members began to question Nguyen about his background. He grew up without a father, idolizing an older brother who was a member of a gang. He would accompany his brother and a friend as they delivered weed. When the brother was imprisoned for assault, that friend asked if he wanted to take his brother's place. Nguyen became part of a group that shoplifted clothes and electronics. He made dial-a-dope deliveries. One day, his brother's friend gave him a gun and told Nguyen to prove himself. He needed to "seriously hurt" someone who'd double-crossed the friend's boss.

Adam Castello's death was the result of mistaken identity. Rieux already knew this from news reports during the trial that he and Elyse would read to each other at night before they fell asleep. Nguyen was shown the image of the person he needed to hurt. One night, he asked around at a party where his target was rumoured to be. Someone told Nguyen that he was wearing a specific type of sneakers. Adam Castello wore the same sneakers and roughly resembled the image Nguyen had seen. When Nguyen confronted him inside the house, Adam reacted. He was bigger than Nguyen and was also sensitive to slights—not someone who would back down from outbursts of machismo. Adam was likely intoxicated when he punched Nguyen and pushed him over a couch. Nguyen was embarrassed. He waited until Adam stepped outside to piss in the bushes. Nguyen shot him in the back.

"What was going through your mind when it happened?" a parole board member asked.

"You don't have a choice," he answered. "If I didn't do something, people would find out. And then I would be the one who had to pay for it. I knew it was a bad idea."

The Castellos listened as Nguyen expressed his remorse. Victor Castello's face reddened. Orla Castello's expression remained unchanged. Rieux thought, *Were there medieval painters who had already rendered their agony?* Their faces made his fingers itch for his iPhone to check.

Nguyen faltered at times, and in one of these moments the parole officer spoke up about his client's clean record in prison and his ability to calm others. He said that Nguyen had studied plumbing in prison. His older brother, who was already paroled, was now an apprentice plumber and had plans to start a family business. Nguyen wanted to leave prison to join him and help their mother.

"Do you have any final statements to add?" the parole board member asked.

The screen had shown Nguyen's face in profile. He had not looked into the camera at the Castellos, not even when he described his regret. Now he turned from the two parole board members to look at the parents of the man he killed on the laptop screen.

"Being here, unable to go where I please, has made me appreciate what I had taken for granted," he said. "At night I dream about running in a field. Driving a car. Being at the beach. Seeing the stars at night." He shook his head. His voice cracked. "If I get a chance, I won't mess up. I don't want to hurt my mother more than I have."

Rieux watched Castello unclasp a black leather shoulder bag. He saw a bottle of water and a bottle of prescription pills. From an interior compartment, she removed a piece of folded paper. She held the text from her written statement in her hands. As Nguyen concluded his remarks, Rieux caught glimpses of her text. She wrote of depression and anxiety. She wrote about her broken marriage.

The words on the page jittered in Castello's shaking hands. She would not end up reading her statement. Instead, she folded the printed statement and replaced it in her shoulder bag. Its clasp snapped shut. She rose from her chair and went out the door.

The parole board members were stooping toward their own screen in search of her. Rieux followed Castello outside. She was hyperventilating, flapping her hands toward her neck.

"Let's get you outside," Rieux suggested.

She had trouble twisting the cap from her water bottle. "I don't see the point in this anymore," she told him. "He can see the stars at night for all I care."

Victor emerged from the room. He advanced toward them like a bull. "I told them that you decided not to offer your statement. They're deliberating now," he said. "They will call us when a decision has been reached."

"I'm not going back in," his estranged wife said. "How about you?"

"I've already cleared my schedule," Victor told her. He stared at the ground as lawyers in black robes passed them. He didn't want to be recognized by peers when he was here as a victim. He asked his ex, "Are you ready to forgive him?"

Castello shook her head. "No, but I only have time for one prison."

"I don't want to be angry anymore," Victor said. "But if I let this go, then I let our boy go."

The Castellos lingered, drawing closer to each other but never touching. Rieux stepped back to watch them. They looked like two smokers on a deck, their conversation an excuse to stew in each other's stained breath.

Rieux remembered that the two of them had installed a bench on the Seawall with a plaque dedicated to their son's memory. Orla Castello had been there only on the day it was unveiled. She said she was glad to know it existed. Victor visited that park bench weekly, regardless of the weather. He sat with a newspaper and coffee and remained until he was done with both. He liked to imagine strangers from around the world seeing Adam's name on their visits. They would subtract the year of birth from the year of death and feel sad for a moment—not knowing the circumstances of his early demise but still wistful about a foreshortened life—before they turned back to look at the sun on the water or a jogger running by with a dog.

A parole board employee appeared. A verdict had been given and they were allowed back in the room to hear it. Castello stepped away from her husband toward Rieux. Victor continued alone back into the conference room.

15.

From this point on in our story—until the chapters near the end of our narrative—the experiences of the principal figures become more deeply entwined. Many of the events described here were witnessed by at least two of the "characters" detailed in these recollections. For simplicity, the remaining chapters are told through a single perspective but have been verified by others present.

Megan Tso was initially surprised that Rieux would contact her about finding a way for ordinary people to help fight the disease. "You're well connected," he told her over dinner. "I've seen the way people respond to you."

She knew he was withholding something from her. "There are other well-connected people in the city," she said. "People who actually *live* here. Why me?"

Rieux had a way of speaking that was remarkably strident and abstracted; he sounded like a zealot. Even drunk on wine and wearing a baggy T-shirt that engulfed his wiry body, he vibrated with the arrogance of a doctor. *He could be a cult leader*, she thought, *but, thankfully, he runs a charisma deficit*. People simply didn't respond to him. On his best days, he was charisma neutral.

"I see two types of people working for us," he replied without answering her question. "Those who are noble and those who think they're invincible."

"Which one am I?" she asked him with a snicker.

"You're noble. You have no fear of death."

"Yeah, I'm real chill about dying."

He looked almost wounded. "I don't know you very well, but that's my belief. I think you'd be okay with whatever risk might come if you knew it was for a good reason."

"Well, thank you, I guess, for thinking that I have nothing to lose."

What people needed, Rieux and Tso decided together, was not more medical intervention, but help. The Sanitation League of Vancouver (Tso could not convince Rieux to agree on a catchier name for their group) would provide meals and run errands for those affected by the disease.

Until they found more volunteers, Rieux and Tso worked in separate shifts that entailed different demands. Rieux volunteered on weekends and those nights when he wasn't at the auxiliary hospital. Often he would escort callers—who usually lived on their own—to the hospital and admit them personally. Tso worked during the weekdays. She had designed a poster to outline the Sanitation League's mission and distributed it in areas of the city most affected by the disease. The poster advertised a hotline (a burner cellphone that they passed back and forth when one took over duties from the other).

Janice Grossman was excited to join the Sanitation League. As always, she offered herself whenever an opportunity arose. Since she had finished cleaning her father's apartment and completing the paperwork that tailed any death, she had taken stock of her life. In the past year, she had lost both her long-term partner and her father. She was frightened, but she also felt invincible—after all, she'd remained on her feet after the worst had happened, and her new freedom gave her a sense of exhilaration. She no longer needed to take her father to his doctor's appointments. She could sell the house and live comfortably for years. She could also rent her father's apartment and the retail space and have enough income to quit her job. "I'm worried I'll self-sabotage myself and adopt six dogs with special needs," she told Tso. "I tend to complicate things."

"Isn't this a distraction?" Tso asked her.

Grossman swore it wasn't. "I'm helping other people. I'm spending time with a friend."

Until she could collect her windfall, she lived off her credit card and devoted herself to a variety of creative projects. She had plans to turn her former lover's studio into a performance space. She worked on a novel but got stuck on revising the first sentence: "For seven centuries, the rival clans of Mok-Tah fought until the cloudy day Princess Destiny emerged from a dragon-drawn carriage and announced that she would offer herself as the bride to the person or spirit who would join the warring factions."

"The first sentence needs to be perfect," Grossman insisted soon after she'd made her comment about self-sabotage. "But all that sitting has been murder on my back. Delivering meals is the perfect task. I need something to get my blood circulating."

They expected their first few days to be slow, but response to the posters continued to be sluggish even weeks later. Rieux felt that they needed more volunteers and wanted to help more people. It came as no surprise to Tso that he had studied Utilitarianism in high school and read about the lives of people who saw charity in the starkest, most actuarial terms. "Most Utilitarians gave up their own happiness for the sake of others. I think I could do that," Rieux said. "What I can't stomach is how they put strangers ahead of their own loved ones. A Utilitarian would donate their kidney to give a stranger twenty years of extra life over their own mother, if it only gave her another five years. That always struck me as a pathology."

Tso was given the task of recruiting Raymond Siddhu to report on their activities. She joined him in the hotel bar. The hulking reporter was unusually morose and ordered four rye and sodas that evening. (Rye was the only liquor the bar was serving that week.) It was his twin sons' first birthday, but the weak hotel wi-fi signal failed before he could watch them blow out birthday candles on his phone.

"I don't see an end to this," Siddhu complained tearily. Christmas was soon approaching. Moreover, his wife had stopped using antidepressants. She said her mood had picked up from regular workouts. Now she hardly had time to talk with him, and the kids were left to family while she went to the gym.

He also found his workplace challenging, with a puzzling boss more preoccupied with digital security than news. The promise of an ownership stake had also not come up again.

"If he doesn't give you any direction, why don't you write about the Sanitation League?" she asked him.

"It'll get buried."

"Not if you write it well."

He rolled his eyes. "Couldn't you just make a better poster?"

"Touché." They clinked their glasses. Unlike Rieux, Siddhu teased back. He agreed to ride along with her and Grossman the next day.

When she returned to her room that night, she found a bouquet of white anemones on her desk. There was no card. At first, she assumed they had been ordered by Rieux, who was formal enough to send bouquets. Had she told him about her favourite flowers? How would he have the wherewithal to get anemones (a luxury good that would have to be smuggled into the city)? As someone who read widely, he might have known that anemones were once used by European peasants to ward off disease and bad luck. She would text him about the flowers tomorrow; for now, she was too tired to think.

Siddhu was waiting for her by the elevators when she left her room the next morning, playing with his yo-yo. She'd thought his public displays of yo-yo-ing were ploys for attention, but he seemed too engrossed in his activity to engage in conversations during his tricks and too psychically displaced by them to talk much afterward. She decided that he yo-yoed as a social crutch, the way others looked at their smartphones.

At the hotel lobby, the front desk clerk waved at her. "Did you like your gift?" the clerk asked.

Tso nodded. "Who sent it?"

"He said it was from a secret admirer." She added that the person who brought the flowers to the front desk did not look like he worked for a florist. "Not a bad-looking guy, by the way."

Now it struck her as odd that Rieux would describe himself as a secret admirer. As Siddhu waited for her outside, she sent Rieux a text about the flowers.

Siddhu and Tso caught the bus to Grossman's house. In her kitchen, they made a dozen brown bag lunches for people who called the Sanitation League for regular meal delivery. Each lunch contained two turkey and cheese sandwiches, a fruit cup, Oreo cookies, and milk. They climbed into Grossman's car to drop off their meals. They visited old Asian ladies in crumbling bungalows, single men living in rooming houses, and the swanky condo of a young lawyer who could barely open the door. It made no sense to help the lawyer, but Rieux insisted that their job was "not to rank the people on a scale of suffering based on our assumptions." Tso disagreed, and they had one of their ongoing debates about privilege and equality.

Each delivery had allowed the Sanitation League a pretense to check on the client. Many were healthy but frightened to leave their houses. Others lived with people who had been admitted to one of the hospitals. Some felt unwell but had symptoms inconsistent with the bubonic and pneumonic forms of the disease. If Rieux was paying a house call, he would also administer a take-away test for the disease. Even when the results appeared positive, clients were reluctant to call an ambulance. Many preferred to die at home than find themselves alone in a hospital with a faint chance of survival.

Around lunch time, Rieux texted back to say that he knew nothing about flowers. Her hand tightened around the phone.

Siddhu monitored their home visits with a skeptical eye. He entered other's places of residence with mask and gloves and tried to touch as little as possible. "You've spent four hours visiting half a dozen people," he told Tso. "This isn't very efficient. And I mean that as an observation more than as criticism. What are you going to do when more people call your hotline?"

"There are still more healthy folks than sick ones," Tso replied. "I believe there are enough good eggs out there—who can accept some risk, who want to do something—to take care of the ones who don't have anyone else."

"Besides, it's Christmastime," Grossman added. "I don't even celebrate the holiday, but charity is already baked into the calendar."

"Why do *you* want to help people?" Siddhu asked.

"I've tried sitting around, trying not to get infected—and I was suffocating," Tso said. "It's about fulfilling our purpose as social animals. It's like your situation. Look at it: You were doing fine when you were telling the world about what was happening inside the quarantine zone because it served the community. It was only when you were forced to muckrake—to cover the mayor's personal scandal—that you became overwhelmed."

"That's not the whole story," Siddhu insisted.

"It's more than you'd like to admit."

Siddhu tossed his notebook in the air. "Sign me up," he said. "I'll volunteer too."

Tso and Grossman clapped.

"Are you still going to write your article?" Tso asked. "Can you do that if you're a volunteer?"

"It would be a violation of our code of ethics ... except we don't have one."

Their laughter was airy. What strange times they were part of. They behaved with the recklessness of teenagers hunting for new ways to intoxicate themselves.

While waiting for their next call, the burner phone rang, and they recognized the caller: Farhad Khan. Grossman's tenant asked them to meet him at an intersection in south Vancouver. They drove to an industrial area of the city until they reached a block with an auto-detailing business and a storage facility. Khan was waiting for them outside a white cube truck. He was dismayed not to see Rieux but asked them to climb into the cargo hold. "It will be a short ride. This is no way to treat friends, I know," he said with a placating expression. "For your safety and protection, it is better for you to be hidden."

"How well do you know this guy?" Siddhu said as he watched Grossman climb into the van.

"We've seen him at rock bottom. He always leaves you wanting to know more," Grossman said. Khan had started the truck, and she waved at the others to hurry. "Come on, idling creates pollution."

They sat on crates of wine that shifted in the dark. Their ride felt both brief but longer than they wanted it to be. When the door slid open, they found themselves in a warehouse. To one side were pallets loaded with alcohol and cigarettes. Khan led them to an interior office area. On their way, they passed racks of designer clothes, boots, shoes, and purses on shelves. Farther off, they saw antiques and, in a glass cage, a large, live lizard reclining under a heat lamp.

Khan enjoyed the awe they displayed at his collection. "We are going big," he told them. "You never know when this will all end."

Siddhu was the last to follow Khan into the warehouse office. Tso noticed his hands twitching by his sides as he resisted an urge to document this scene.

Inside the office, a man lay shivering under a blanket and was using an oxygen tank to breathe. He attempted to sit up when he saw them, but the exertion tired him so much that he needed to close his eyes.

"This man is my brother," Khan said with such emphasis that Tso decided that he was not asserting a literal truth. "He is sick and needs help." Tso began to speak when Khan raised his hand. "He is in trouble with the law. He is a good man, but he has made a mistake in the past. What is the point if he gets out of hospital only to walk into a jail?"

Khan suggested that Dr Rieux come to care for his so-called brother. Khan would provide whatever medicine or equipment was required. They would find a private nurse. "We just need a good doctor to make my brother healthy," he told them. "You know if you take care of my friend, I will take care of you."

"Do you get your goods by boat?" Siddhu asked. His attention still lay with the warehouse outside—the smuggling operation.

Khan shrugged. "Some of them. What do you need?"

He explained that his family was in Surrey. "What's your price to get me back home?"

"It would be ... significant," Khan said. In his Costco-purchased clothing, Siddhu looked like someone whose wants exceeded his means. "The last time we tried we were almost caught."

"What if Rieux helps with your ... brother?" he whispered.

Khan's nose lifted as though he was taking in the smell of a good idea. "Then it would be our gift to you, my friend."

Grossman's tenant guided them back to the cube truck. They rode in the darkness of the cargo hold again. When the door opened, they grimaced in the daylight and glare of grey ice.

As Grossman drove them back to the hotel, Siddhu remained silent. But his face seemed to glow as he processed the possibility, and risk, of an escape.

"I'll see you tomorrow," Grossman told them outside the hotel. "Once I drop off the phone with Rieux, I'm going to work on my book. I'll sanitize, too. Is it weird to say I had a lot of fun?"

Siddhu suggested to Tso that they get dinner together in the hotel restaurant. The restaurant's meals had deteriorated after a line cook fell ill. Thankfully, he'd gotten sick at home. The restaurant might have closed— although people had become lax with sanitary measures that had seemed ineffectual. They had already eaten every dish on the menu, continually revised and diminished, several times over.

Tso agreed to dinner but first wanted to change into a fresh set of clothes. Siddhu said he'd do the same.

"Do you hate me for wanting to leave?" Siddhu asked as they waited for the elevator. "You've hardly spoken to me."

"I thought you were the one being quiet."

"Who knows if Bernard will agree to help Khan's friend? But I've been away from my family too long." He leaned back against the elevator wall and sighed. "I want to help you guys too. Janice was right. Today was fun."

"I'm not mad at you. I don't think you're wrong. I'll just miss having someone to meet for drinks. And I think the judge has a crush on me, so ... But you need to see your family. I get that."

The elevator opened to their floor. Tso thought about the anemones in her room and felt her heart pulse as she stared down the hallway. Maybe it was the judge. "Would you mind coming to my door?" she asked Siddhu. She briefly explained about the flowers from last night. "It's probably nothing."

They arrived at her door. She inserted her card into the lock and stepped inside. The bed was made, the pile of used bath towels had been whisked from the floor, and the anemones remained on the desk where she left them. Nothing looked askance. She thanked Siddhu and told him to get a table downstairs. "Order me a rye and ginger if the server comes before I get there," she added. "I won't be long."

She washed her hands and changed. Then she sat on the bed. It felt good to elevate her feet. Maybe she was invincible in addition to being noble. She had vanquished the dissatisfaction that had been following her around in the past couple of months and no longer felt too busy to be able to do anything well.

She was looking out the window when she heard buzzing. She'd left her phone on her desk by the flowers.

The Caller ID read "Unknown." She knew better than to answer random callers, but if it was who she feared, she didn't want to avoid him. She could only hope to put him off for so long. The voice was unmistakeable.

"Anemones are flowers for the forsaken," he told her.

"Markus."

"I missed your voice."

"Where are you?" she asked. She needed to look up whether restraining orders could be enforced across countries.

"On your side of the gates," he told her. "I could tell you needed me."

Before he had hung up, she was out the door.

16.

New Year's celebrations in Vancouver were more muted than usual. By year's end, the death rates had fluctuated to the point that some people were optimistic. Although the unusually heavy snowfall had interrupted the plans of many, the holiday season was not without merriment. People who had spent the past two months in their homes eating canned food now went out to see family and take in the Christmas lights. Some went to church. Many of them had put their calendar-watching aside. They'd stopped waiting, if only for a week. In the middle of the night, fireworks were going off again, startling Rieux from sleep.

On Christmas day, the doctor invited his new friends over for Chinese hot pot. The phone rang as the first loads of watercress and beef were placed in the bubbling broth. Mrs Rieux was closest to the phone in the living room. She handed it to her son.

Rieux had not heard his wife's voice in more than two weeks, when she'd left a voicemail. It had been a month since they'd actually spoken. Elyse had then seemed concerned about Rieux, but she also sounded distracted, perhaps drugged. She now sounded certain about the decisions she had made and would make in the future.

"I miss you now," she said. "I never understood people who go on about missing the people they're leaving the minute they step out the door. I used to text 'I miss you already' when I went on a business trip. I was lying. It should take time to miss people. It took me a little longer than I wanted."

"I feel that way, too," he confessed. "I didn't miss you at all. I got caught up with everything."

Elyse could hear Siddhu laughing in the background and Grossman and Tso's voices. Rieux told her who they were and remembered that she didn't know them.

He could have said that he felt guilty, as well, for having forgotten about her for days at a time. For entertaining the idea that her passing in Mexico might make it easier for him to grieve. For thinking of her already in the past tense. For ignoring her system of organizing paper and plastic recycling. For putting her toiletries in a box and placing it in her closet. For thinking of her as a character in a movie he once loved. And for other things he couldn't yet admit to himself.

They stayed on the phone together for a few more minutes but exchanged barely any words. It had been a long time since they'd been silent together. There had been fraught silences, but this was one of their sweet silences. Their wordless conversation felt choreographed, as though they were both following a musical score, waiting for their extended rest to break before they offered their final holiday salutations and returned to their Christmas dinners.

"Are you there?" Tso asked after Rieux returned to his place at the table. She was seated next to him.

"Sorry—what?" he asked.

"I asked you whether you wanted a fish ball."

He smiled. "Always."

———

By the New Year, the Sanitation League had grown to encompass a team of two dozen volunteers, including a few doctors and nurses who admired (and were amused by) Rieux. Our story's nominal protagonist had hoped it would become a city-wide effort spanning age, ethnicity, and income but tried not to reveal his disappointment at its actual scale. Tso would have teased him for wanting to become a disease "disruptor." This was not true. He only wanted to help as many people as possible. It did, however, bother him. He'd thought the League was a good idea.

Befitting their name, the Sanitation League also cleaned houses. Rieux often delegated this non-urgent task to others. On the first day of the New Year, a request to clean was called in and no one else on the team was available. When Mrs Rieux saw her son with a mop and bucket and learned of his task, she volunteered her services.

"You did this for thirty years," Rieux said, waving her aside. "You've earned your rest."

She flung her hand in the air. "Don't waste thirty years of experience!"

"What if you get sick?" Rieux replied. "I would never forgive myself."

Her nose wrinkled so far back into her face that Rieux could see the grey hairs in her nostrils. "I have lived long enough—I feel like I'm already living my second life," she told him. "Don't act as though you are ashamed of me or what I did to feed you and your sister."

She didn't give him a choice. He relented. She giggled as she put on her jacket and slipped on her face mask. "I let you sit in a chair and read when you were a boy. But now you will scrub with me."

They boarded a van that Rieux had rented, filled with biohazard cleaning materials. Mrs Rieux held her phone in her lap, listening to Cantonese opera as they drove.

They turned up at a rooming house five blocks from Rieux's clinic. A familiar face opened the door: Rieux's favourite patient, Walter. He had called in with a pseudonym: Willy Love. He was dressed in a white sleeveless undershirt, a black baseball cap, and cut-off denim jeans. He was barefoot.

"Welcome, welcome!" he said.

"Happy New Year, Walter."

Walter had an attic space in the rooming house. Mrs Rieux pulled the mop and pail out of her son's hands and started right away in the bathroom. "This is going to take a while," she said in a voice that was not displeased. Despite her threats, she seemed content to clean alone.

Walter asked Rieux if he wanted tea. Rieux declined, leaving him to make his own cup. Rieux's patient invited him to sit in his bedroom, which was up a set of stairs. The room was filled with clay sculpture, abstract figures in the shape of bonsai trees but with the texture of sea foam and human musculature. A single bed was pushed up against a wall on which Walter had taped some faded photos. There was only one chair, so Walter sat on his bed. The room itself was too sparsely furnished to be messy, but it did have a smell.

"Everyone else is gone," Walter announced. "They've all died."

The landlady who lived downstairs had fallen ill first; her son started to collect the rent. Then two other longtime tenants were taken away last week. Neither of them returned. In a less dire situation, Rieux would have evacuated him, but there was no place to send Walter. The city had had a vacancy problem before this all started.

Rieux could hear his mother singing Cantonese opera from the bathroom downstairs. Her voice echoed from the empty tub.

"Why haven't you come by the clinic these last couple of months?" Rieux asked. "I used to see you all the time."

"You would never tell me I was sick," he said, "so I went to other doctors. They didn't tell me what I wanted to hear either." As he spoke, he reclined until he was flat on the bed. He traced the edges of the faded photos taped to the wall. "Now it's just me, and I need to stay here alone, remembering everyone."

There were red marks on his arms and feet, possibly from bed bugs. They, like Walter, were indestructible. Rieux would call the landlady's son to ask him to get an exterminator to the property. Walter caught him looking at the red marks. He pointed to a figure in one of his faded pictures.

"This old friend taught me how to tattoo with ink and a sewing needle, and for a while I would give tattoos to lovers and acquaintances. I got pretty good, but I never experimented on myself. I was terrified of needles. And I loved the body God gave me."

"What changed?" Rieux asked. "Was it the disease? The quarantine?"

He nodded. "It felt like old times. I was watching people around me dying—again. These were the people who did nothing wrong the first time. Everyone just stood by. Doctors just like you." He sat up. "Do you know what time it is?"

Before Rieux could answer, Walter said that he'd stopped counting the days. "I can't tell you when, exactly, but I became so sad that I couldn't bear time passing," he continued. "I saw the Christmas trees, but I don't know what day of the month it is unless someone makes me sign a cheque or wishes me a happy new year. My assistance payments come electronically."

The day the barricades went up, Walter continued, he thought about his old friends again. He remembered, in particular, the friend who taught him how to tattoo. This friend had thrown himself in front of a train.

Rieux stared at Walter's relatively unblemished body and thought that it didn't look the way the body of someone who suffered from serious illness might look.

"I got out a sewing needle. I only had red ink. And I marked myself. The day after that I marked myself again. Now I use it to keep track of the days we have been locked up together. If I want to know how long everyone has been suffering the way I have, I just need to roll up my sleeve."

Rieux's mother popped her head into the room. "Finished!" she said. "Would it be alright if I cleaned the kitchen?"

As they waited, Walter asked if he could listen to music. "You can wait with me," he told Rieux. "But I have talked enough." He found an AM station that played Top 40 songs. The room was warm, which somehow made Rieux's eyes burn. In the past few weeks, the doctor had shuffled between various types of fatigue—double-blinking tired, tired in the feet, tired in the shoulders, emotional exhaustion, tired from being around people. On top of this, he experienced a state of being submerged. In this frame of mind, he imagined himself as a sea mammal that could hold his breath indefinitely but became increasingly fixated with that undetermined moment when he would have to break the surface.

In these middle days of the quarantine, any word of stemming the disease was shushed away as false hope. Rieux wanted to be impervious to these vagaries of feeling. If he did all he could, he wouldn't ever need to regret his decisions.

He could have altered his wife's prognosis if he had more forcefully urged an aggressive treatment strategy. She had initially chosen to revamp her diet and seek alternative treatments before she visited an oncologist, but he could have overruled her. He pushed away these thoughts by working so hard that sleep, when he gave in to it, obliterated him.

Rieux craved exercise and air. He daydreamed about taking a forest hike. But he was worried about what might come when he stopped working. It could be physical collapse. It could be listlessness. It could be some insight that he was trying to evade.

———

When Raymond Siddhu came to him with his plan, Rieux did not hesitate. Farhad Khan's nameless friend might have been in trouble with the law, but he did not deserve to die. Rieux asked Khan to secure antibiotics and ensured that they were administered correctly. He checked on the patient daily. The man's recovery was atypically prompt. Within a week, he was back on his feet and working again in the smuggling trade.

"Are you lonely, doctor?" Khan asked Rieux after his friend was given his last check-up. Siddhu had accompanied him.

"I have my mother to keep me company," Rieux said. "Otherwise I'm too busy to feel lonely."

Khan slapped Rieux's arm. "No, don't play stupid with me, okay? I can introduce you to friends of mine. Lovely girls. They have heard about your hero stuff and would like to meet you."

Rieux shook his head. "I'm married."

"Let me repay you," Khan said. His chin kept bobbing as he offered him alcohol, drugs, weapons. He seemed agitated that Rieux acted without need for reciprocation.

"I'm just glad your associate is doing well," Rieux answered. "But if you want to do anything, you might consider volunteering for the Sanitation League."

This prompted laughter from Khan. "I'm sorry. I am just too busy." His attention turned to Siddhu, who seemed on the verge of speaking. "My friend, I have not forgotten you. Are you ready to go home? And when? Tonight?"

Siddhu's eyes widened. "I might need another day," he said. "I want to talk to my boss. I should pack."

It became clear to Rieux that Siddhu had been biding his time. The reporter wanted to know about the type of boat they would use, whether he needed to swim, what he should bring, and the potential risks involved. Siddhu started to mop his brow with a McDonald's paper napkin. He was so eager that he crowded Khan's space, forcing him to step back with a nervous smile.

Khan told him that he could not provide the answers yet. He would call tomorrow. "It will be in the middle of the night. Get your rest."

They were placed in the back of the cube truck again. "By now," Siddhu said in the dark, "I think I could find the warehouse. I know the turns he takes by heart. He even adds an extra loop in the Best Buy parking lot as misdirection."

"I'm not positive Khan's associate was all that sick," Rieux observed. "If he had what everyone else had, he'd still be recovering. That guy was practically bouncing off the walls."

"He was probably tired from smuggling," Siddhu suggested. "Caught the flu. Everybody either under-reacts or over-reacts."

When the truck's doors opened again, the sky had already given way to the night's scowl, even though it was only four o'clock in the afternoon. They were on the street by Rieux's car, opposite an auto-body shop.

"Do you mind if I drive?" Siddhu asked cheerfully. "It's been two months."

Rieux handed him the keys. They sat in the car waiting for the windows to de-fog. Siddhu seemed disfigured by his giddiness. It made Rieux's skin crawl. And yet he had known about Siddhu's scheme all along and even sympathized with him. But when he imagined Siddhu on the other side of the gates, he became enraged.

Siddhu drove the car to the Best Buy parking lot. Rieux already knew that the reporter was trying to find Khan's warehouse. The doctor found Siddhu's curiosity obnoxious.

"Where do you think the boat leaves from?" Siddhu asked. "All the marinas are under lock and key."

"I don't think you should go," Rieux said. "You've been a good addition to our brigade. I would be disappointed in you if you left."

Siddhu stopped the car. His hands tightened on the steering wheel. "My family needs me."

"I understand your emotional wants. But people are dying, and we can help them. Escaping would be cowardice."

Something seemed to back up inside Siddhu's eyes. Then that thing hurtled up against his face.

"I always thought the Sanitation League was a modest initiative by someone with heroic impulses," he told Rieux. "And yet we are risking our own lives by going into so many infected homes. You made your volunteers sign waivers. At the end of the day, we could be saving more lives if we all stayed at our sinks washing our hands."

Rieux did not reply. Siddhu started the car again and turned the radio up loud. "And I know the real reason why you don't want me to go," he shouted over the music.

"What's that?" Rieux asked.

"You need me as a chaperone. You don't want to be alone with

Megan. Because you don't understand your own *emotional wants*."

It took Rieux longer than necessary to absorb his friend's insinuation. "That's not true."

"You can deny it if you like. In any case, you still have your mother and Janice to keep you two apart."

He blinked twice. He felt both shame and relief. "Does she know?"

Siddhu shook his head. "She's got other things on her plate." They stopped outside the city transfer station where garbage normally sat before it was relayed to the landfill in Delta. Presently, excess waste was collecting on a barge in the Fraser River. "I guess Farhad did a better job in hiding his tracks than I thought he did," he said. He took a breath, then added: "I cheated on my wife before. I don't recommend it."

"You did?"

"We had just gotten married at the time, the kids weren't born yet. But I did. With the woman my parents didn't want me to marry."

"Was she non-Indian?" Rieux asked.

Siddhu's eyelids quivered. "Why does it matter? Just because I'm from an Indian immigrant background doesn't mean my family is interchangeable with, like, say, the family in a magazine article you read on a plane."

"I'm sorry."

"But yes, she was white. And she was older and already had a kid. And she didn't finish high school. What I'm saying is that there were other things that a non-immigrant, non-Asian family would also object to."

"*I'm sorry.*"

"Forget about it. As I was saying, Uma and I were not getting along. She was visiting family in Ontario. It was always easier with this other woman. We fought all the time, but when we fought, everything got said and then it was done. With Uma, an argument from the week before can flitter around you like a swarm of gnats. And so I called this old flame up when her kid was with his dad. I wanted to see what it was like to be with her again. I'd always done the right thing until I didn't. I remember waking up, going to her bathroom. She had dug up my old toothbrush. I started brushing my teeth. I kept looking at myself and thinking about my toothbrush at home. I thought about how the bed at home was still unmade on one side."

The last half of Siddhu's story was told through choked sobs. Rieux was uncomfortable with his friend's display. He patted him on the arm, but soon found himself pulled into the reporter's damp embrace.

"I don't want to leave you all. And part of me is afraid of seeing Uma," Siddhu admitted. "I feel so bad."

Rieux felt like a marsupial in his mother's pouch.

"I do, too," he said into Siddhu's chest. "Look, when Elyse got sick, I tried to find the best oncologist and walk her through the stages of treatment. Her friends told me to visit handicraft websites so I could make her an advent calendar she could use to count down her treatments. That's how hard I tried. I wanted to do all this because I didn't want to feel what she was feeling. I wanted to help her to ignore her suffering."

The authors of this account debated the inclusion of this passage. They were mindful of the hurt it might induce. What swayed them was the underlying principles of this story: to describe, honestly and fully, life during this moment in our city's history. We wanted to show how this calamitous intervention reconfigured our decisions and values. And so any changes in behaviour that arose from our reactions to the disease and the subsequent quarantine were to be included. Even those who never so much as coughed during this period—and that would be the majority of the citizens—felt themselves deformed by the disease.

17.

As the city's funeral parlour and crematorium staff worked at full capacity, the demand for funeral services prompted them to become creative. Churches offered after-dinner funeral services, for example, and some funeral-home chapels either overlooked the presence of alcohol at their evening services or offered their own cash bars for whatever booze they could find and mark up. Families of the bereaved also utilized unusual venues.

Raymond Siddhu's experience of the deaths of others felt like a time-delayed bomb. For the first two months, he'd witnessed only the collateral damage wrought by the disease. Since the holidays, there had been funerals galore. The week before, he'd attended three funerals of former co-workers at his old newspaper. All of them were held at the city's old pressman's bar. The cartoon renderings of old editors, reporters, and photographers had been taken down years ago when the bar became a live-music venue and then a Belgian beer bar. But the faces—more lined, greying, and voluminous than before—were their own caricatures. There would have been more people at each service-cum-wake, but so many of Siddhu's former colleagues had already retired to the suburbs or islands.

"I keep expecting him to jump out from behind a curtain and yell *surprise*!" one ex-journalist, whose cubicle was adjacent to Siddhu in his first two years at the paper, told him.

"The living wake is all the rage these days," Siddhu observed. "People don't know when they're going to go, and they get fed up with hiding at home, so they invite everyone over for drinks."

"I go out in the evenings more than I have in the past ten years. The city has never been livelier since the night funerals started."

"That would be a great pull quote," Siddhu said. "Can I use it?"

"For you, anything," he said. "But make sure you note that I was on my fourth drink." The man spilled his rum and Coke as he was caught up in a fit of coughing. Siddhu stepped back and slipped his face mask on. This, like many other things, was no longer considered an impolite gesture.

Siddhu went to bed with a happy buzz. He knew that the next day would be his last in Vancouver. If nothing went wrong. He checked out of his hotel room in the morning, after having packed his Costco clothes in a duffle bag left on his bed with a note saying they could be donated or destroyed.

The call from Khan was to come that night. A more logical person would have waited to check out then and have someplace to rest until leaving in the middle of night. But Siddhu knew he wouldn't be able to rest. This way, he could depart on a moment's notice, and he would save money on a day's accommodation. He needed to start thinking about money again.

The idea of his last breakfast made him nostalgic. Judge Jeffrey Oishi saw him enter the lobby restaurant and invited him over to the table he shared with his daughter Rose, who was colouring a menu in crayon.

"Her school has closed indefinitely after two kids in grade seven got sick," the judge said. "Her mother and I are trying to make do. You're acting jumpy. What's the matter?"

Siddhu leaned across the table and whispered, "I am getting smuggled out of the city."

Oishi shook his head. "I've heard of this scam before. A friend of a friend tried it. He was told to go through a tunnel in the basement of a house near the gates to Burnaby. At the other end, there were soldiers in uniform. This sap paid $20,000. I hope they didn't soak you for as much."

"I cashed in my Air Miles," Siddhu joked. He'd heard the legend of the tunnel too. It sounded like a bad joke from someone who'd binge-watched TV shows about Mexican drug cartels. "Sorry to leave, but the food here is getting to me."

"I know. You miss your kids." Oishi tilted his head toward his daughter. "I'm not used to seeing her only half the week. I get up on my mornings without her and panic for a second. I think I lost her. I think she's under the bed, the way my phone sometimes is."

Oishi told his daughter to wish Siddhu luck. She was uncommonly beautiful in a way that made Siddhu envy women for their ability to fawn over young children without becoming criminally suspect. This yearning had only come recently. Before his twins were born, babies were as interchangeable to him as eggs in a carton.

Oishi's daughter looked up from her menu and smiled at him. "Can you Walk the Dog?" she asked.

If only children would ask me for more complicated tricks, he thought. But he complied, smiling when she asked for another trick. When he was done, he gave his yo-yo to her. "You can teach your daddy," he told her.

Siddhu decided to skip breakfast. He didn't want to linger and wallow in goodbyes. He got a bagel around the corner and started for Horne-Bough's loft. He knew that he would get there later than usual if he went by foot. Would people even notice he was late or had quit? There were no rules at his office, only expectations that he'd brought from other workplaces. Perhaps he shouldn't feel so guilty about his resignation without notice. This job had always been a pit stop on his way out of journalism. He'd given himself a year before he'd start to write political speeches or press releases for energy companies. For that reason, he wrote with the aim of reaching a breaking point.

When he showed up at his nominal workplace, it was empty except for the managing editor. Harper was eating buttered pasta while watching a stand-up comedy special on Netflix. She told him that Horne-Bough had slept in. "He has his Do Not Disturb sign up," she told him. When he asked about the other staffers, she paused the laptop. Two reporters had quit the day before, she told him. One cited stress, another, the former intern that Siddhu once mentored, stormed off after a rooftop shouting match that she could hear from the long table downstairs. A third employee had been admitted to the hospital yesterday after feeling nauseated and feverish.

"Elliot had a soju bender last night," she told him in a stage whisper. "He's not happy about the turnover. Were you looking for him?"

"I was, but I'll check back later," Siddhu whispered.

He realized that he could just leave. He didn't need to explain himself. It had become a phenomenon in this city—occasioned by illness, death, and confinement—for people to ghost. If a friend stood you up for a walk in the park, you were left to wonder whether they were gravely ill or terrified of the outdoors. Horne-Bough, thought Siddhu, would be a lousy job reference anyhow.

Siddhu was turning toward the door when he heard Horne-Bough call out for him. "I've been waiting for you," he said from the steps to the rooftop. "Why did you turn up late?"

Horne-Bough was wearing a vintage bathrobe over an undershirt and pyjama pants. As usual, he suggested that he and Siddhu confer on the rooftop. The managing editor had made him a cup of tea that he took with him. For once, Siddhu was glad to be outside. It was a clear day, and the cold was on the right side of bracing. The rooftop allowed a view of the city from its ugly side: post-war buildings, railyards, and none of the cranes that imposed themselves on the skyline elsewhere. In this light, it seemed like a place that refused to be pulled under.

Horne-Bough shivered, teacup rattling in the saucer, as the heat lamp started to wake. "I was hoping to sleep off my disappointment," he admitted. "For me, this site was a vehicle. I wanted to make a profit and redefine news. But I also wanted influence. We succeeded for a while—we had the best coverage, hits from around the world. We showed how news could be effective if we harnessed connections and dirtied our hands. But that turned out be the easy part. I don't know how people can handle the *disloyalty*." According to Horne-Bough, the other reporters had resigned over money. "They dressed it in procedural stuff, but it all boiled down to the bucks."

Siddhu asked him about his sick colleague, expecting a remark about how put-upon he felt that an underling faced death.

"I was allowed to visit him," Horne-Bough said, eyes shadowed in sadness. "We're permitted to do that now."

"I reported about that," Siddhu said. Hospital administration had relaxed their policy on visitors because infection rates weren't being reduced. They also wanted to encourage the infected who were afraid to die alone to seek treatment. Siddhu had noticed a complacency settle in on Vancouverites since late-November. Some of them decided not to wear their face masks. They were returning to buses and other indoor public spaces as the weather had become more unfriendly. He couldn't tell whether they were being fatalistic about infection or whether they thought themselves, having survived this far, impervious to the disease.

"He doesn't look too good," Horne-Bough said about the sick employee. "I was there for five minutes, but he could barely acknowledge me. The kid's parents were crying. I couldn't get out of the hospital quickly enough. When I got out and into a taxi, I wanted to tell the cabbie to turn onto the highway and drive. It was the first time I wanted to leave. If there was only a way to get out of here."

Siddhu interrupted him. "I might have an idea," he said. He proposed a story: He would document, wearing a body camera, going through (or under or over) the barricades and patrols. "I met this guy who says he's gotten people outside."

"And are you going to turn back?" Horne-Bough asked slyly. He could see Siddhu's end game. "Are you going to stop when freedom is in hand?"

Siddhu thought about it for a moment. "I don't think so."

"Is this your resignation?"

"Who knows if I get across?" Siddhu asked. He had been ready to quit. Now it seemed like he could delay. "Maybe I'll get stopped. I'm going to write this story however it turns out. I could still write about the quarantine from the other side."

Horne-Bough threw his hands in the air. "You're the only reporter I have left. Do I have a choice?"

They went in search of a video recorder he could use on his trip, something that could be concealed from publicity-shy smugglers. They decided that Siddhu would have to buy one.

The rest of the day felt like a dream. He filed his piece about the advent of the late-night funerals. Occasionally he would emerge from his daze to panic. Crossing the streets, he worried he might get hit by a car before he could see his family again. Wouldn't that be the crowning absurdity in his life story?

He went to a local store that specialized in surveillance equipment to buy a covert video camera. The store seemed busy that day, full of people looking for GPS trackers, night-vision goggles, and cameras hidden in lamps and grandfather clocks. Siddhu settled on a camera that was built into a pair of fake reading glasses.

Outsiders might presume that living in a quarantined city with a more visible police and military presence would have amplified security. How much theft occurs in an airport? In fact, the city had enough pockets for would-be criminals to hide. Confinement and idleness drove some

Vancouverites into criminality—they were normally law-abiding people who, at worst, stole unattended goods and bought fenced items. The disease made other people desperate. They raised online donation campaigns for friends immobilized by grief and then pocketed the proceeds. The rate of infection was overshot by the rate at which people robbed and stabbed one another. These people were roughly equalled in number by do-gooders like Rieux.

In the evening, he Skyped with his wife from a coffee shop. "Why aren't you in your hotel room?" Uma asked him as she rushed their sons through dinner. She seemed annoyed. He noticed that she was also wearing makeup for the first time in weeks. "Why are you calling so early?"

He lied and said that he was on his way to another funeral. He didn't want to tell her about his escape. That would scare her. He asked to see the boys, but they were too preoccupied with their chicken and rice to notice him. He asked Uma to leave the phone on the table so he could just watch them eat for a few minutes.

Then he found a more comfortable armchair in the centrally located coffee shop favoured by international students studying in front of textbooks and glowing laptops that displayed web pages in foreign languages. He was prepared to wait.

The call from Khan came at ten. He gave his address and was told that "an associate" would pick him up in five minutes. Siddhu stood outside and shivered for half an hour until the white cube truck appeared. The driver had a stringy beard and looked Southeast Asian. He didn't speak, but pointed to the cargo hold, which was empty. Siddhu climbed inside.

He sat on the floor. He typed a note for his wife, one for her to read in case something happened on the way home. He admitted to his affair. He told her the combination to the safe in the basement rec room where he kept three-thousand dollars in cash and some of his grandmother's jewellery. When he was finished writing, he left the note in his drafts folder. She would find it eventually if he didn't survive.

The car stopped, and the cargo-hold door rolled up. Before his eyes could adjust to the light outside, he could smell the trash in the transfer station. The odour that came at him was first sweet, then stomach-churning.

A garbage truck was idling at the gate of the transfer station. His driver stood outside the cube truck talking to the driver, who was sitting behind the wheel. Siddhu's phone rang. "My friend will give you a suit to wear. Put it on," Khan told him. "Then climb into the garbage truck. By then you will know what will come next."

Siddhu checked the camera in his glasses to make sure it still functioned and donned the mask. When he slung the heavy messenger bag over his shoulder, he wished he'd left his laptop with Oishi. The driver of the cube truck gave him a hazmat suit, then pulled out a grey garbage bin. He told Siddhu to don the suit and climb inside the bin.

What he feared happened next. The garbage truck driver extended the vehicle's forked arms to pick up the trash bin. Siddhu found himself thrust into the air and then upended into bags of trash. He could see a slice of moon above him. And then one yellow canvas bag and then another was tossed into the truck. They landed on either side of him.

The garbage truck started to move. He felt something crawling on him. When he grabbed the rat, it squealed and bit the glove of his suit. He flung the rat over the side of the truck bed. Siddhu checked the glove and was relieved to see it wasn't punctured. Another rat crawled onto him, then another. He imagined himself falling ill the second he got home. He fought the rodents off until the truck approached a checkpoint at the Knight Street bridge, then let the rats crawl over him until the truck was allowed to pass.

They approached an even fouler smell. He raised his head and could see a barge. The truck backed up in front of it. He could hear the sound of hydraulic pistons. Then he was tilting and started to slide. The rats squealed. He needed to dig himself out of the trash bags. Up above he could see the crows and seagulls circling. The trash was heaped in a hill toward the river-facing end of the barge. He climbed on his hands and knees up to the top of the pile. His was one of a flotilla of trash barges. In the distance, further up the Fraser River, he could see a Coast Guard patrol vessel.

He waited about half an hour, batting away vermin and swallowing his bile. Then a fishing boat pulled up to the lip of the barge. He climbed down the pile of garbage and took the pilot's hand. The pilot climbed onto the barge and retrieved the two canvas bags.

"Do you mind sitting behind me?" the pilot asked when they climbed onto his boat. Siddhu became aware that he was radiating his stench.

On both sides of the river floodlights were trained to catch escapees. Their boat traversed a narrow bend in the river as soon as the Coast Guard was out of sight, and the pilot dropped Siddhu off at a shipyard.

"Welcome back to the world," the pilot said. "You're on your own now."

Siddhu tossed his hazmat suit in a dumpster. He should set it on fire, he thought. He threw away the messenger bag that held his laptop and carried it with him as he walked up a road in an industrial part of Richmond. He would have called a cab if it didn't mean waiting for half an hour. He wanted to move, to savour his freedom. He turned onto a road that opened up to farmland on both sides. The air was streaked with the scent of manure. Siddhu's adrenalin tapered, and he started to feel cold.

Nothing had changed on the other side of the river. He walked until he reached a gas station where he could wash his face and buy a piece of beef jerky and waited there until a cab arrived. Siddhu spoke to the driver in Punjabi as they took an on-ramp onto the highway.

He double-tipped the final driver in the night's succession of chauffeurs, then felt for the keys in his pocket—he'd kept them there the whole time he'd been at the hotel. The lights were out in the house, so he opened the door quietly. He wanted to wake up his wife and kiss his kids, but first he wanted to be clean from infection and not smelly. He threw his clothes in a garbage bag and placed them in a bin. After removing the spy store reading glasses, he climbed into the shower. He'd been imagining this shower—in this own bathroom—in the cab. The shower head spurted water on him, as it always did. The pressure was terrible. It would be heaven.

Through a crack in the shower curtain, he caught sight of Uma, entering the bathroom sleepy-eyed. When he pulled back the curtain, she screamed at the sight of her naked husband. They looked at each other in disbelief. For the last several months, they'd existed for each other only on screens. When he placed his hands on her face, she began to sob.

He tried to explain how he'd returned home with the compression of a haiku. "Made a deal with a smuggler," he began. "Then a garbage truck, boat, taxi. Needed to shower first."

"You smell terrible," she said, laughing and crying.

18.

For six months after grad school, Megan Tso volunteered at a hospice. She interviewed three dozen people as part of the program and collected the raw data of their lives. Most of these patients—even the teenagers— grew excited to name their childhood addresses and elementary schools. For some people, the act of reciting their parents' names was enough to prompt tears. Soon afterward, they would open up about forgotten pets, long-suppressed traumas, old resentments.

From this experience, Tso honed that talent for getting people to reveal their interior lives to her. The dying spoke with no fear of consequences. She, in turn, knew that some of them wanted an exchange of personal information, and because they would carry her secrets to their graves, she freely shared her own story with them. She grew close to several people at the hospice and attended their funerals. At these services, family members approached her warily, treating her as an interloper. But in a matter of weeks, she'd learned more about their spouse or parent than they had ever dared learn, and soon family members brought her into conversation, wanting to know whether they had been bad-mouthed by the deceased.

In Vancouver, circumspection came easily for Tso. Everyone hid behind their masks but spoke candidly from behind them about their nightmare scenarios and theories, their sexual prospects, their survival strategies.

Her best friends in Vancouver were Grossman, Siddhu, and Rieux. When her ex-fiancé Markus re-entered her life, she had no desire to confide in them. She liked that they knew her in this vacuum. They were not acquainted with the jittery, self-loathing version of herself. She spoke to a friend in Los Angeles about Markus, who advised her to call the police. She was reluctant to do so. Markus had never threatened her with violence directly, but he trailed her and made it impossible to get beyond him. He would back off for months at a time if she seemed distressed enough by his stalking behaviour. He'd found a line to toe.

After he called, Tso messaged Grossman for permission to stay with her. She was invited over immediately, gathered her things, and threw her iPhone in the trash. The last time Markus found her, he had hacked her phone's location settings.

Grossman, it turned out, was eager for company. While she had been resilient in the weeks following her father's death, she experienced a setback after receiving a letter from Janet's lawyer demanding the return of her work. This led to an angry phone call in which Grossman's ex-lover denounced her as a parasite. "I was making such progress on the first sentence of my novel," Grossman said, taking fresh towels into the ground-floor suite, "but now I just want to drink scotch and eat ramen."

Her current plan was to focus on a new project: a performance space in Janet's old studio, a tribute to her father. It was one of a spate of new businesses that had opened since the quarantine went into effect and people began a new age of soft lawlessness. This underground economy had been prompted by the run-up in prices, a quarantine-related reduction of the workforce, and an implicit relaxation of licensing requirements. People were working as amateur massage therapists and running restaurants from their dining rooms.

Tso entered Izzy Grossman's old apartment and saw that most of his personal effects had not yet been removed. Black-and-white photos taken in Europe at the turn of the twentieth century still hung on the walls. The appliances, cupboards, and cookware in the kitchen were from the 1970s and were mustard-yellow and fake walnut. On a bookcase she found the collected novels of Leon Uris and James Clavell. She tried to sleep on his waterbed but found herself seasick.

She laid her blanket on the couch, remembering that he had fallen ill there. On a side table was a picture of Mr Grossman with his two daughters—Grossman's half-sister as a teenager, Grossman as a toddler. She didn't want a dead person staring at her, so she turned the picture face-down before she fell asleep.

In the morning, Rieux appeared at the front door. He'd taken the day off from the clinic and wanted to accompany her on her Sanitation League shift. He wondered why she'd gotten rid of her phone and checked out of the hotel room. She could have dodged the question today, but not indefinitely.

"My ex-fiancé has come to Vancouver," she told him. "He's been giving me trouble since we split a year ago."

Rieux's expression remain unchanged.

"It must be easier to come into the city than to leave it," Rieux said. He waited a moment. Then he added, "Do you want to talk about it?"

She shook her head. "Maybe later."

They spent their morning delivering meals. The last one had to be taken to a woman who lived on a houseboat on Granville Island. She was caring for her mother who had fallen ill but refused treatment. Tso had seen the old woman a couple of times in the past month, groaning from within her daughter's bedroom.

The houseboat was clad in corrugated aluminum. The windows facing the icy-slick boardwalk were portholes. On the rooftop was a weather vane. The daughter welcomed them inside. "She passed away this morning," she told them.

The houseboat had polished hardwood floors, a granite kitchen island, and a baby grand piano. The old woman's body was still in the room behind a closed door. Her death was not unexpected, but it had been sudden.

"I guess you don't have to come by tomorrow—to help us," she told Rieux, who nodded gravely. Tso looked at the doctor but he offered no explanations. Then the idea of what "help" might have entailed fluttered against her mind. She fought back her reaction.

The daughter asked them to wait with her until her mother's body was taken away. She conformed to the expectations one might have about a woman who lived on a houseboat. In her forties, she was sensible in practice, eccentric in outlook. Her face was sun-creased but finely featured. She probably had a source of wealth that allowed her to project comfort. It surprised Tso that this woman would call the Sanitation League for help with cleaning and lunches instead of hiring a maid. Tso offered to make her tea. She felt the need to serve her.

"My mother was a remarkable woman," the woman told them at her kitchen table. "She had lost my older brother in a swimming accident before I was born. Then my father died when I was still a toddler. She had to raise me alone. I once asked her how she got through it. She said she went to church every week. I think that's where she must have caught the disease. She wrote letters every day to friends around the world. She always tried to remember the happy moments—suffering was the other side of the coin. And all of it was like a grain of sand on a beach. She used those exact words. In the last hour, she no longer seemed to be in pain. I played her favourite Sinatra records and everything within her quieted."

From this woman's table they had a view of the deck and the ocean kayak tied to its railing like a leashed pet. Beyond it was False Creek and the grey, ever-churning water. On the other side of False Creek were the glass condo towers of the downtown peninsula. Two paddleboarders came into view. They caught sight of the woman at the table and waved to her.

"You think you're alone, and then the paddleboarders appear," the woman said. "Sometimes they seem to be looking for me. I'm a little disappointed when they float by without a hello."

The old woman's body was collected. Rieux and Tso bid farewell to her daughter. Afterward, they walked to the market for lunch. Most of the vendor stalls, the ones that sold chocolates and salmon jerky to tourists, were empty. They got clam chowder and half sandwiches and sat outside with the seagulls.

"Did we accomplish anything?" Tso asked.

"We tried," Rieux said. "We accomplished an attempt."

He threw the crust of his bread for the seagulls. She knew him well enough to know that he did not like bread crust. But not well enough to know the name of his wife.

They watched the seagulls gather around the crust and he threw them another piece. "I was supposed to administer a lethal injection for her mother tomorrow," he admitted to Tso. "They had someone else in place to do it. They had the official approval and documentation for medical assistance in dying. But the doctor they had picked fell ill, and not every doctor will do it. They asked me because they couldn't find anyone else."

"I gathered," she said. "I thought you were opposed to people dying. Don't you want people to fight?"

"My choice for the woman's mother would have been for her to go to the hospital. Her choice was to die in her daughter's bed. It's her choice— by law."

"I know the law in this country. It's relatively new. But what about you? Isn't your job to prolong life?" she asked him. "Isn't that the oath you took?"

His grip on the paper cup of tea tightened. "I took on this job for status to avenge my mother's poverty. I'm no saint. But I developed my own appreciation for medicine as I practiced it. Why am I setting a broken bone? Or why do I prescribe medication for cholesterol? It's not about healing. I don't have a view of life in an abstract sense. I don't care when it begins or how precious it is compared to a gorilla's. I just want to help people."

She liked how his eyes caught light in mid-speech. He became engrossed when he spoke like that, searching for arguments from a book-case in his mind.

"I read somewhere that the ability to take your own life is the kind of escape clause that makes anything bearable," Tso suggested.

"Only if you don't have strict religious beliefs."

"Was that woman religious? Maybe it was an act of God that allowed her to die on her own, without a doctor's assistance. She got her wish without committing a mortal sin."

"Are you religious?" he asked.

"I think of myself as agnostic."

"There's no such thing. Either you believe or you don't."

"My aunt took me to Sunday school, and I cannot get those stories out of my head. Isn't it possible not to believe in God but still feel his influence?"

"Dostoyevsky would agree with you." He sighed. "Anyhow, I'm glad I didn't have to give a lethal injection. I wasn't looking forward to it."

The paddleboarders came into view from under the Granville Street Bridge. "I used to think people who were into paddleboarding looked stupid. Are you surfing or are you canoeing? Pick a lane," Tso said. "Now they seem different. They look brave: 'We won't let a pandemic interfere with our indecisive recreational activity.'"

Rieux waved to the paddleboarders. They waved back. "I've always wanted to try it out," he said, looking at her with a raised eyebrow.

They found the aqua-sports rental facility. Lessons were two hours long but not being offered in the winter. Rieux lied and said they'd paddleboarded before. The person behind the counter looked at Tso's skinny jeans and leather boots, but he didn't say anything. He slid the two waiver forms toward them.

Rieux paid for the rental of two paddleboards, paddles, and wetsuits. They changed at the rental place and left their clothes there. She watched him carry his paddleboard. *This is a bad idea.* He didn't look like he knew how to carry it. They headed toward the marina and walked to the end of a boardwalk where Rieux stopped to look at his phone. He had Googled "how to paddleboard."

"It's simple," he announced afterward, snapping his lifejacket in place. "Let me try it first." He lay his board down on the water. Then he picked it up and pointed it in the opposite direction. He reached for a springy leash attached to the board and cuffed it around his ankle. Dropping to his knees on the boardwalk, he crawled over to the board.

Rieux's features and manner were, if not exactly WASP-y, then de-ethnicized. It took this attempt at water sports to remind Tso that he had to cultivate his whiteness, that he took pains to behave as though he hadn't been raised by a poorly educated Chinese woman.

Still on his knees, he paddled away from the dock. He looked like he was impaling the water, and the loop that he took was awkward. Eventually, though, he stood, wobbly at first, then confident. He looked the way a boy does before he learns to draw the curtains on his face.

"Now it's your turn," he told her. "It's easy."

She dropped her board into the water but couldn't get over its bobbing. She had gone surfing before, she'd ziplined. And now she was stuck in an infectious disease zone, and her maniacal ex-fiancé had just come into town. *Why am I afraid of this?* she thought. She pulled her board back in.

"I don't think I want to," she said. "I've done enough that scares me."

He nodded, but stayed in the water, looping. "What part of it scares you?"

"Standing."

He brought his board alongside the dock, steadying it with his paddle. "Let me give you a ride. You don't have to, but ..."

She cautiously climbed aboard his paddleboard, facing forward in front of him and kneeling. He paddled away from the sailboats and yachts and toward the Burrard Street bridge, but soon they doubled back and under the shadow of the Granville Street Bridge. Still on her knees, she lowered herself to get as close as she could to being eye-level with the water.

"Imagine how nice this would be if we were doing it in July," he said. "How are you faring?"

"Up and down," she admitted.

And then she told him about a doomed relationship with someone whose violence was made worse because he'd never physically hurt her. In the rambling voicemails he'd leave in the past year, he talked about wanting to put them out of pain with the compassionate tones of a veterinarian used to reasoning with besotted dog owners. Every time she said "I," he would say "we." Markus told her she was pushing him away because of what happened to her own family. And while it was true she pushed people away for that reason, her friends needed to tell her that leaving him was still the right thing to do.

Tso could confide in Rieux because she was on the water, and she sat in front of him, not making eye contact. He was the gondolier she'd hired on a lark, in a town she was finished visiting. And because she was in the water, and the water knew everyone's secrets. She stopped short of telling him about her mother and brother; she'd never even told the hospice patients about that. To give up her entire life story, she would need to be conversing with an ancient mariner.

Then she imagined Rieux plunging a needle into Markus and putting him out of her misery.

On the shore, a child in a face mask waved at her. Soon they were passing the houseboats. The woman they'd visited was on her deck, leaning against the rail. She called out something they couldn't quite understand, something along the lines of, "I should have expected to see you."

And yet Tso didn't expect to see her. She was surprised to see a familiar face. Tso had been thinking about how unlikely it was that she was here, on the water. *You think to yourself, who would ever do something like this? Then you think, what if I do this? Just to play a role. Then you're passing by someone. And that person thinks, who would do something like this?*

They were on the water for half an hour, tops, before Rieux needed to turn back. He admitted that paddleboarding was a test of his core strength. In the last stretch, Tso could feel the strain in his strokes. She wished she could take over.

"Shall we get back to our work?" he asked her. They had just stepped onto the dock. The water in False Creek had returned the softness to his face. The tone of his voice had changed. There had been only duty and determination in it two hours before, mustered with scalding tea on his tongue. Now he seemed to be speaking with the water under his feet. He asked his question as though it were the answer itself.

"Shall we get back to our work?" she asked back.

And so they did.

19.

Rieux was working at the auxiliary hospital when the announcement about the vaccine came. His job here was not only monotonous, but it forced him to see suffering as a collective process. He'd become accustomed to the old and weak dying, followed by healthy adults, and finally children with faces aged by pain. There were categories of patients, types of death. He needed to tell himself to speak to each one as though he would see them the next day. He administered the ineffective antibiotics as if he was pretending to be a child waving a magic wand.

Orla Castello asked him to be one of the doctors standing in the background on camera when she delivered the news about the vaccine. Rieux took his break early, disinfected himself, changed into his street clothes, and stepped outside. A communications officer from the Coastal Health Authority asked him to wear an ill-fitting set of scrubs.

"Thanks for being an extra in our production," Castello told him. "I'm just the warm-up act. Our headliner is waiting in the wings. We need star power for this."

A small crowd of news media had been assembled, though most of the news figures here looked at Castello skeptically. Not even Siddhu's nerd-chic employer had bothered to bring his Polaroid camera. If the vaccine had been released a month earlier, there would have been spontaneous street parties. In that time, though, Castello had made announcements about positive but temporary shifts in infection and mortality rates. Her office had issued press releases that did nothing but reiterate the devotion of the city's medical staff. Any residual excitement about the vaccine had been eaten away by timed leaks about its imminence.

As promised, Castello's prepared statement about the vaccine was brief, with no time given for questions. She introduced another speaker to talk about the city's plan to encourage vaccination.

It took Rieux a split second to recognize the mayor when he emerged from behind a door. There were gasps among the news media and some of the medical staff in their scrubs when Parsons made this first public appearance since the scandal, after his poorly received interview with Siddhu. Photos of Parsons had been posted on social media from time to time. He had grown a beard and started to wear a baseball cap. In some photos, he'd looked gaunt. Now, he looked like a close replica of the version of himself that had won the election.

According to Parsons, the vaccine would be freely distributed not only at hospitals, but also at community centres and libraries. Under Canadian law, immunization was not mandatory. An awareness campaign was being launched with print, internet, and billboard advertising. Door-to-door canvassing was an option still under consideration.

A question period followed. One reporter asked him whether he would go through with his anti-poverty measures. He said he would risk his remaining political capital on it. He refused to answer a single question about the scandal but shook his head briskly and said, "I've apologized to the city in a press release and to my family in private, but I'll also do it now. I am sorry. The thing I've learned through my own personal downfall is how little it matters in a larger context. I hid in shame for the first months of this disease because of these reports. I should have snapped out of it earlier and helped. I should have used my power and privilege to help the people of Vancouver instead of wallowing in my own misery. Suffering is not equally distributed. Some people—namely, the oppressed—have suffered more than others. And I will fight for them. Next question."

Castello leaned over to Rieux and spoke in a whisper. "It was his idea to do this press conference," she said.

"The people who hate him will continue to feel that way," Rieux said. "And the people who lost faith in him—do they care?"

"He wants to talk to you—about what, I can't tell you. Do you have a minute?"

Rieux had to wait while Romeo Parsons offered his cheekbones for selfies. Even after his misconduct, he was still wanted in photos. The mayor noticed Rieux's impatience and made his last photo quick. He then pulled the doctor aside and thanked him for his efforts with the Sanitation League. "I want to be a volunteer," he told Rieux, then immediately added, "and this isn't a publicity stunt."

Rieux did not habitually turn away volunteers, but he felt a strong urge to break from this practice now. "I want to like you," he said. "And I didn't vote for the other guy. I didn't vote at all." Parsons began to speak, but Rieux held up his hand. "This is not about your personal business," the doctor told him. "It's because I don't think your idea of suffering is grounded in reality." Rieux added that he believed the mayor's intentions were good but that his remarks betrayed an intellectual superficiality. "It's hard for me to explain," he said. "Let me show you."

Before he took Parsons into the ward, they had to change into hazmat suits. Parsons stepped into the gear tentatively. He seemed more worried about leaving his handmade Italian shoes in the change area than what he would see next.

Rieux could only admit afterward to his cruelty. He had taken a dislike to Parsons after the speech he gave following the riots. To Rieux, his remarks had been divisive. By claiming that the disease had somehow enacted karmic payback on the rich, he was saying that some people deserved to die. By contrast, the mayor's own downfall, the consequence of a poor personal decision, he'd attributed to a rare psychological phenomenon, which allowed him to sidestep blame.

The mayor, Rieux believed, had also invoked the history of smallpox in the region gratuitously. He had invoked *au courant* ideology to explain an unprecedented event because he wanted to blame the affluent ones for their disease instead of considering its randomness. (The authors of this chronicle do not necessarily agree with Rieux's interpretation of the mayor's intent.) The doctor had somewhat blunted himself from feeling, but he knew about the types of suffering that hobbled bystanders. And he felt a pain dig into his own side whenever he stopped working; it opened its mouth and spat misery. He knew what he was doing to Parsons.

Rieux led the mayor down a corridor of partitions. The ward resembled a tent city—or a peculiar art class. Each partition contained another student artist's slightly different take on the same scene.

Tucked away in one room were ten hospital beds set aside for infected children. There was extra room for parents. Some slept on mats beside their child's bed. Rieux and Parsons reached the bed of a four-year-old girl. Her parents sat slumped over in chairs on opposite sides of the bed. The mother slept soundly. The father, who looked like he was tasting something bitter as he slept, briefly stirred and opened his eyes at the sound of his child's whimpering. He closed them again.

"She was brought in twenty-four hours ago by her mother," Rieux said quietly. "Her father came in shortly afterward. She has not responded to treatment."

The doctor pulled over an empty chair from another partition. "If you want to understand what's going on in this city that you lead, I want you to stay in this seat until it's over," he instructed the mayor. "If you still think you want to volunteer after this, then we will be pleased to take you on." Rieux did not tell Parsons that he was the only volunteer who had to undergo this test.

The doctor had witnessed the deaths of children since he began work in the auxiliary hospital. He mentioned this facet of his job only once to his friends, saying it was the most difficult part. But Rieux minimized his own distress by de-particularizing those deaths, slotting them into a category—"the worst ones," the patients who were the most "emotionally taxing." He used those words as stoppers for his bottled emotions.

Last year, he'd reread parts of *The Brothers Karamazov*. He didn't have the energy to go through the whole book, which he'd first consumed one vacant winter as an undergrad. Now he summoned his own memory of the

Grand Inquisitor section, just before Ivan's allegorical tale in conversation with his sensitive brother Alyosha. Ivan insisted something to the effect that he could not accept the harmony of God and the universe if it included the torture of children. What remained in Rieux's mind was that he did not go so far as to deny God by insisting on disharmony. Rieux himself didn't want to accept pointlessness—and the ensuing pursuit of gratified appetites—because of a child's pain.

The authors of this piece (who shall be revealed soon) have, up until now, refrained from describing the deaths of children. They were not consequential to the stories of the figures we've followed. We are aware that the suffering of children can be acutely difficult and may prompt, among readers of this history, their own troubling memories. For some parents it might incite a painful consideration of their own worst fears.

We feel that the following episode merited inclusion. We are aware that the suffering can't be entirely glossed over. We agonized over how best to describe this material. One of the authors suggested leaving a blank page in place of an account, which another dismissed as a "trite gimmick." We decided, in the end, to neither dwell on nor gloss over this child's death.

We therefore kindly invite those who might feel most sensitively about this material to either skip the remainder of this chapter or read it at arm's length.

///
///
///
///

The mayor agreed not to leave his place at the foot of the girl's bed until she died. He made a call to his assistant to clear his schedule and then turned off his phone.

The little girl had roused herself awake. Her arms were folded across her chest, one hand over a fist. She started shaking wildly. Rieux held the child down by the arms while he hushed her. He and Parsons heard a clunk as something rolled onto the floor. Parsons reached down and picked up a metal yo-yo. He rolled the thread back into the axle.

First the father, then the mother stood as the child continued to convulse. They were surprised to see Parsons with them but accepted his explanation. He realized that the mother and father were on opposite sides of the bed intentionally. Neither of them spoke to Rieux. When he'd offered his prognosis, they looked at him as if they'd been slapped.

The child did not seem calmed by the presence of her parents. She did not seem aware of them. Her eyes did figure eights in the chalky light. Then she shut her eyes, relaxed her arms, and fell into an agitated half-sleep. Her jaw remained clenched, and she periodically grimaced.

Both of Rose's parents understood that their child was gravely ill, that she was likely to perish. They had fallen into a trance of pre-mourning and panic—a state that many Vancouverites experienced in those days. The child's calmer state briefly snapped them out of that condition.

"What have you been doing for the last couple of months?" the mother, Lisa Randall-Oishi, asked Parsons during one of these lulls.

"I was still working but not in public," he said. "There was personal stuff too. I had to move."

"Are you in a hotel?" Jeffrey Oishi asked.

"The townhouse version of a sad bachelor apartment," he said. "The assistant city manager loaned it to me. She's living with her boyfriend. It forced him to commit"

This was perhaps the only moment of levity that day.

Rieux left Parsons for a couple of hours as he attended to other patients. When he returned, Parsons was alone with the child, holding her hand as she tossed her head from side to side on the pillow. Her parents had gone for dinner during a lull, but a new wave of fever was striking her. Her mouth opened as though she wanted to swallow something in front of her. Then it moved as though she wanted to speak, but no sound came. She gritted her teeth again and her body stiffened. She threw her arms and legs out like she was fighting a phantom.

The mayor looked to Rieux in disbelief. It was not only hard to watch—it was too much to watch. This girl's frantic movements and voiceless moans did not correspond with his expectations of death, even a painful hospital death.

The wave of fever subsided, and the child rolled to one side of the bed. She clutched her yo-yo and a stuffed Arctic seal. She pushed away her blanket. Parsons pulled it back, and the smell of her sticky sweat filled their noses.

Rieux knew the wait wouldn't be much longer. He left to eat a muffin. When he returned, Rose Oishi's bed was surrounded. Her parents had rejoined Parsons, and Dr Orla Castello was now there too. Rieux did not want to think poorly of her presence around grieving parents. She could empathize with them, but there was also a part of her that eagerly greeted newly bereaved parents to her own state of brokenness. She would talk them through the first few moments so she could relive them herself.

Elyse sometimes accused him of being cynical, and this was another moment when he wished she was wrong. And yet, he was not self-aware enough to understand that his own motivations with Parsons—to prove him wrong in the most devastating fashion possible—were the same.

He looked at Castello and saw that the time was approaching. Rose struggled under her covers again, then tossed them away from her. She turned over and drew her knees to her face in a fetal position. She raised her head, her neck stretched, and started to move her eyes. New tears had filled them. Suddenly, she screamed.

The parents said something to Rieux, but he couldn't remember what they said or what he said back. They moved around pointlessly, taking turns sobbing on one another. A nurse came into the room and they calmed themselves again.

Rose Oishi was quiet through most of the evening. Throughout this time, there had been a din of groaning and sobbing from other rooms that regular visitors had to ignore. Rose Oishi's scream was clear as glass and had the effect of dishes crashing onto the floor of a busy restaurant and silencing the room.

When she finished screaming, she turned onto her back. It was now a little past one in the morning. Her eyes sharpened into focus and she looked at her mother and father for a handful of hollow breaths. Her fingers clutched the railing of the bed before they slipped. She arched her back, then slumped onto the bed.

It seemed like everyone around that bed and in that room had waited for her scream to end. The din in the room returned. The parents, who had braced themselves against her bed, commenced their wailing. Castello poised herself to console them.

Rieux watched Romeo Parsons, who looked up into the fluorescent lights and then back at the body of the newly deceased child. He was like Leontius in Plato's *Republic*, who could not resist the urge to gape at recently executed bodies by a wall. "There, ye wretches," he says, addressing his own two eyes, "take your fill of the fine spectacle!" Each time Parsons' eyes returned to the dead girl, the more they dimmed. Rieux did not need to tell him that this child was not responsible for her own death.

The doctor realized what it meant to have never had children. He had wanted them with Elyse and knew they would consume his life. But the love parents had for their defenceless children was still an abstraction for him. Parsons, by contrast, had children. Rieux already knew that. But he would have known just by looking at Parsons' face then.

The mayor turned to Rieux and spoke in a froggy voice. "I've passed your test," he said. "Let me know when the first shift begins."

Part
Four

KEVIN   CHONG

20.

The vaccine was introduced to the public through a stubbornly icy last half of January. It was heralded by health officials as a turning point, and in the end statistical evidence would support the claim. In the meantime, confusion ensued after its release. Death counts spiked in that period. Half the citizens thought the inoculation wouldn't work. They believed it would hasten their deaths or that it was a part of one of many conspiracies. The other half of the population, who submitted to vaccination, viewed it as the end of their troubles. They found themselves in four-hour lineups and got visibly upset when clinics began their days without supplies.

Raymond Siddhu watched these developments from home in his pilled bathrobe. He subscribed to his old newspaper and tried not to read their articles like a former employee or a competitor would. Opening the door each morning to get the paper from his front step was his only exposure to the world outside his house in the three weeks since he'd returned home.

He had become, as he feared, a stranger to his own sons. When they were reunited at last, Ranjeet bawled at the sight of him and Ravinder did not make eye contact. When Uma went out to the gym or the mall, he watched the boys until they were tired of being watched. He'd turn his back to get more blueberries from the refrigerator and they would burble back to life. He wished he hadn't given his yo-yo away.

Siddhu traded bowls of ice cream for smiles and hugs. He let them watch TV beyond the rationed time allowed by Uma and stood in front of it until they spoke to him. By the end of the third day, they responded to him, shrieking and tumbling into his arms. They wrestled on the couch after he delayed bedtime.

"It's harder with the kids now that you're back," Uma fumed. "We had a structure."

While the boys napped, he laboured slowly on his escape story for GSSP. Horne-Bough wanted it badly and sent Siddhu texts twice a day to inquire about its progress. "Our readers want this," he said. "You swam in garbage, you wrestled with rats, then you busted out of the city. You're a fucking hero." Siddhu felt an obligation to finish the story but worried about the scrutiny his illegal act would invite.

"Once you publish that story, the cops will come for you and take you right back to the city gates," Uma said. "Are you sick of us already?" She had been jittery since his return. She wanted him to fix the running toilet and screamed at him when he couldn't leave the house to buy the parts. Then she tearfully stroked his arm. "Why have you become so cold?" she asked. She had become so hot.

He hadn't gotten used to sleeping on only half the bed again. He lay there, coiled, worried he'd spring if he dropped his guard. His body may have left the barricades, but his mind had not escaped. He did not, of course, want to return. And yet, he'd not been ready to leave.

One night, he attempted to have a video chat with Megan Tso. She didn't accept his call. When she called back, he was already in bed. Uma was drifting off and was startled by the incoming call. He took his tablet into the kitchen.

"Is it too late?" Tso asked from Janice Grossman's apartment. She was drinking wine and eating Triscuits with slivers of apple and cheese.

"A little," Siddhu admitted. "But I'm glad you called. Still hiding out, I see. What's the latest on your stalker?"

"You don't want to know," she told him. Her expression was more resigned than fearful. "Let's just say he's still looking for me."

He heard someone say from offscreen, "Is that *Rrrrrrrrrr*aymundo?" Tso nodded. Grossman appeared onscreen in pyjama pants and a tank top. On one of her bare arms she wore a bandage. She had been vaccinated. "We miss you, buddy. And not just because you had the best yo-yo tricks. The quality of news coverage has dropped. Where am I going to learn the truth about City Hall?"

"We could ask the mayor himself," Tso suggested. "We just spent eight hours with him, scrubbing bathrooms and driving old people to clinics."

Siddhu pinched the bridge of his nose. He felt an acute nostalgia for the drudgery of the Sanitation League. "I feel like I'm in two places," he confessed. "The whole time I was in that hotel room by myself, I'd fantasize about being beamed home, like on *Star Trek*. Now I'm home, but it doesn't feel right. It's like I'm still being beamed back, like I'm transparent and there's sparkly light coursing through my body, and I'm not quite here yet. Does that make sense?"

"*Star Trek* is with the Vulcans, right?"

He could normally tell when she was being sarcastic. This time he wasn't so sure. "Yeah, it was set in the twenty-third century, when humankind had to leave earth to find problems," he said. "Am I crazy for missing my old life? This whole thing has been terrible, but I felt like I was in a community for the first time."

"It's true. I've seen people risk their lives for strangers, people who would otherwise be unheroic. Being at home surrounded by family, in safety, must be a comedown."

He knew that was sarcasm.

They chatted about Judge Oishi and Tso told Siddhu about his daughter. Siddhu asked her about Rieux, but she only mentioned that he looked tired. Then she yawned and said good night.

He returned to bed. Uma was now awake, lying on her side, scrolling through her social media feed on her phone. Her face was pinched. "Sorry," he told her. "It was a call from a friend."

"Is that why you've been so off?" Uma asked. "I have noticed."

Siddhu wanted to say the same to her, but he started to weep. Uma wrapped her arms around his shoulders and held him for the first time since the night of his return. He felt her own tears on his arm.

"I need to tell you something," Uma admitted after he had quieted. "I've been seeing someone."

They both remained still long enough to notice each other's wet breathing.

"How did you find the time?" he finally asked her.

She sat up on the bed. "Is that really what you want to know?"

"Are you still having an affair?" he asked.

"Yes. But it's not anyone you know. We met online."

"Are you in love with him?"

"I don't know where it's going. I thought you wouldn't be back for a while. And then, there you were in the shower one night."

"Do you still love me?"

She hesitated. "Yes."

He felt a warmth pooling from separate directions, the sadness in his head and the despair in his body.

They agreed to talk about it the next day, and Uma started to snore within five minutes. Siddhu found himself braced against his edge of the bed. He got up and made the pullout in the spare room, then fell into the middle of the thin mattress like a skydiver and plummeted from the waking world.

In the morning, he heard Uma feeding the kids. Their laughter was brighter around their mother. It was laughter that hadn't been coaxed.

Siddhu changed in the master bedroom. This was the day Uma's mother came over from the other side of the duplex to watch the kids. Sometimes she took them to the park so Uma could nap or read a book. Probably Uma used that time to meet her lover. The thought of it made him sob as he ran a toothbrush across his teeth. He took his laptop and grabbed the car keys from the table by the stairs.

At the McDonald's drive-through he ordered an Egg McMuffin and coffee. He turned off the engine in the parking lot, opened his laptop, and reviewed the latest draft of his story. Once he completed his read-through, he sent it to Horne-Bough along with edited video clips from his hidden camera. He felt the satisfaction, the dread, the relief, of doing something he couldn't take back. Horne-Bough instantly replied that he would release it in an hour. "This is the story I've been waiting for—and you did it all on your own," he wrote. "Prepare to have your name on the tip of everyone's tongue."

Earlier in his life, this would have been a dream realized. Now he dreaded the idea. He did not want his phone to light up. He had seen what happened to Romeo Parsons. The mayor had fallen more quickly than he had risen. Siddhu wanted his daily bread, his daily practice. He wanted all the time available to watch his boys grow up.

He drove to the hardware store and bought a new flapper for the toilet. In the hardware store parking lot, he sent a text to Uma to tell her where he'd gone. "I hope you didn't need the car," he wrote. He sent another text to say his story would be posted.

How did they drive into this ditch in their relationship? Uma had attended the same high-school as Siddhu, two grades below him. Her older brother played basketball with him. As a teenager, Siddhu spent an evening on a couch with her watching a Batman movie. He had forgotten about that night until she mentioned it to him seven years later when they found themselves seated next to each other in a banquette of a lounge bar. They were at the birthday party of a mutual friend and he'd had to work to make her laugh. He used to be popular with women, now he couldn't remember how.

He couldn't imagine dating again at his age. He felt like a blob.

He checked his phone. Uma wanted to know if he was doing okay.

His article still had not appeared. No one would come for him in a patrol car, not yet.

He hated killing time, but he ended up at Guildford Town Centre Mall in Surrey. In the mall, he bought some Duplo blocks and Play-Doh for the boys. He looked at his watch and decided he had enough time to buy himself two new shirts. He had lost weight in quarantine, despite eating at greasy restaurants once or twice a day. It must have been all the walking.

He checked his phone again. The article still hadn't appeared.

He checked his phone again.

He checked his phone again.

He checked his phone again.

He checked his phone again.

He checked his phone again. This time the website was down.

Then came a text from Uma. "Read this," she wrote. She'd included a link.

It was from his old newspaper. An image of Horne-Bough loaded onto the screen, a photo taken a few years ago. Horne-Bough was wearing a fedora and an eyebrow ring. The headline loaded afterward: "Media Entrepreneur Charged with Hacking." The breaking news item was brief. More details were to follow.

An anonymous tip and a cache of information led the RCMP to the arrest. Mostly, staffers within City Hall had been hacked. The mayor's private email address as well as his web-search history had been hacked. Siddhu figured the whistleblower was one of the disgruntled GSSP staffers who'd left in December. It made so much sense to him now. His own email had probably been compromised. Hadn't Horne-Bough anticipated his needs well?

Siddhu felt his anticipation dissipate. He was on a hot air balloon that began drifting back to the ground soon after its ascent.

"I guess my story has nowhere to go," he wrote to Uma. "I'm coming home."

But all he wanted to do was keep walking around the mall. He had no reason to hurry. And the world had opened its door to him once more.

21.

In the third week of January, as Megan Tso and Jeffrey Oishi were finishing a shift with the Sanitation League, she saw her face on a telephone pole in Strathcona; an image from a vacation she'd taken three years earlier in Berlin, standing against a spray-painted section of its Wall, was placed on a poster under the words, "MISSING SINCE SEPTEMBER 24TH." It listed her full name, age, height, and weight, and a description of the butterfly tattooed on her ankle. An email address and a cellphone number were given at the bottom of the poster.

Was that why she had gotten those funny looks in the last few days? Were people inspecting her? She tore the poster from the telephone pole and climbed into Oishi's Audi. As the judge drove, she noticed another poster a block up on Princess Avenue. "Stop the car," she said. The car caught black ice and slid along the street before coming to a halt.

"What is it?" Oishi asked.

"The hell I escaped."

They had spent the morning and afternoon taking seniors to get vaccinated. This was his third day riding along with her and he'd held up well. The judge was on leave from work, and his hands shook periodically, but he insisted that this was better than sitting in his hotel room with a bottle of rye and his daughter's stuffed Arctic seal, scrolling through his iPhone photo album. He was helping people who had gone through this. It made him feel less alone.

Within an hour, both Grossman and Rieux texted her images of the poster in separate neighbourhoods. Each of them told her to call the police. She knew they could do nothing. She had grown accustomed to Markus's unyielding insistence on her life.

As a criminal judge, Oishi was aware of the extent that the law protected Markus more than it did her. He suggested that she get a black-market taser.

"Did you dump him because he was possessive?" he asked.

"He dumped *me*," Tso said. "He hated how messy I was. But then I moved on with my life. He no longer had me to blame for his own failures. So he insisted on harassing me."

"What's his end goal?"

"I don't think it's to get back together with me. His end goal is just to make me miserable."

Oishi looked out the passenger window and pointed to one more poster. Tso told him to continue driving. "I wish my wife and I hated each other less. We have so many other things in common," he said.

The other night, he'd tried to kiss her in the restaurant lounge. He wasn't her type, but she let him kiss her long enough to entertain but reject the idea of doing more. She missed physical contact. Her body felt like a callous, and she wanted to be touched to regain sensitivity to the world. She imagined herself with Oishi and how it would be afterward, and she could only picture the kind of mutual regret that made former lovers hide behind trees to avoid each other. He knew that, too. When she told him it wouldn't be a good idea, his apology followed a hot sigh of relief.

They met Grossman at her apartment. Outside, on the sidewalk, she'd placed a sandwich board. In chalk she had written: "Izzy's Storytelling Night: Come *Laugh & Cry* at the Plague." Grossman had cooked a roast with Yorkshire pudding before the performance at her club, and the smell of the meat rendered Tso wobbly with hunger. And Grossman was making real gravy.

Afterward, they helped her get ready for the event. Grossman had reimagined the ground-floor studio as a performance space that she named "Izzy's" after her father. She had commissioned a neon-style LED sign with the name and an illustration of her father's face—younger, eyes a-twinkle in a way that Tso never saw firsthand—that hung outside the front door. Inside was a small stage. A vintage bar had been installed.

It took Tso a moment to notice the bare walls. "What did you do with all of Janet's paintings?" she asked Grossman. "Did you return them to her?"

"Sort of," Grossman said. "Janet believed that I was in wrongful possession of her creative work. She was right. But those paintings all featured my image. At no time did she ask me whether I wanted to be in her paintings. So I returned them to her with my likeness cut out with an X-Acto knife. I'd always felt invisible in our relationship and even when Janet painted me, she painted me the way she wanted other people to see me. The holes I made in her work make it more honest." She filled Tso and Oishi's respective wine glasses before filling her own. "What do you think? Does that sound psycho?"

Tso removed the torn poster from the back pocket of her jeans and held it up. "You'll have to up your game."

Grossman nodded at the poster. "Why don't we get Khan to take care of that nuisance?" she asked.

Oishi looked puzzled. Tso quickly explained the situation with Grossman's tenant and his role as a fixer and procurer. They had called on him recently to acquire additional vaccine, and it came through the next day.

"What could Khan do?" Tso replied. "Send him off on the garbage barge? He'd only end up back here."

Grossman stared up at the ceiling. "He could do other things." When Tso didn't respond to the insinuation, she added: "I bet Khan could find someone burly and unscrupulous to take care of your ex."

"I already caught your hint."

They took their places as the event's start time approached. Oishi stood at the door, taking the cover charge. Fifty folding chairs had been rented for the event, which had only been advertised on social media and in a few local culture blogs. In the first ten minutes after the doors opened only two people had come. Grossman and her friends waited nervously as show time approached. Just before eight o'clock, people came in a cluster, and a line formed outside as Oishi fumbled with change. Grossman poured her guests plastic glasses of red and white wine and offered pre-mixed highballs from cups. A few of the attendees recognized Tso, who worried they had seen her ex's poster, but they had met her at the after party that followed her book event in October. They thought she'd made it out of the city. Tso's memory of her first days here felt like keepsakes from another era and world. But only three months had passed since she'd first come to this big house.

The start time needed to be pushed back. Every chair was occupied and they scrambled to find more. People had come out of curiosity. They saw friends they hadn't spoken to since autumn. The room, initially draughty, was warm with body heat and the air electrified with the smell of booze. Grossman was starting to grow out of her tinted grey hair, and its black roots were showing. She had changed out of her apron and old jeans into a black tuxedo shirt and jacket over hot pants and fishnets. It was the first time Tso had seen her friend looking so femme. She resembled the photos Tso had seen of Grossman's mother, the dancer. And then she understood her friend's look to be a salute to both her parents.

As Grossman took the stage, Tso remembered how jittery she'd behaved at the book event and then her pudding-smooth delivery on the tour bus. Her preamble before introducing the first speaker in her roster of storytellers—friends, social-media acquaintances, volunteers for the Sanitation League—was delivered in a confident but off-the-cuff manner.

"This space was created by a cataclysm," she said shortly after giving the land acknowledgment. "Everyone here has seen a friend or family member or co-worker fall ill. Some of us have lost our livelihoods. Some of us no longer have reasons to get out of bed. When this crisis is done, the city will hire a world-famous artist to build a monument to those who perished. It'll be fucking beautiful. And I will drive my tour bus around it and talk about how difficult this period was. But who will pay tribute to the rest of us who lived and are still searching for new reasons to get out of bed? Only we can do it. We pay tribute to each other. Tonight, I pay tribute to you."

The speakers varied in quality. Some spoke with notes and stumbled over their own sentences. Others came off as too polished. One speaker, a professional comedian, made light of his maniacal devotion toward cleanliness that led him to develop a crack addiction to offset the stress. Another storyteller, a florist by trade, spoke of giving birth alone, right after her husband had been hospitalized with the disease. He had been one of the lucky ones, but both she and her partner had felt alone during their respective hospitalizations. As the night continued, Tso realized how far off she had been about Grossman. When they first met, Grossman seemed to her like a professional devotee. She let others take advantage of her to blot out her own thwarted ambitions. But bringing people together—Rieux had incorrectly ascribed this ability to Tso—was her genius. She magnified the talents of others. She (literally) gave them the stage on which they could shine.

Tso and Oishi allowed their friend to play host as they stacked the chairs and collected empty plastic wine glasses. Tso watched the judge throughout the performance. For the first half of the show, he reacted to every comment or laugh line a beat too late. Then he seemed in sync with the rest of the audience. Near the end, he filled his plastic cup to the brim with wine and leaned against the wall.

They finished cleaning and headed to the after-party upstairs. On their way up, they saw Farhad Khan. The smuggler rarely stayed in his apartment, only returning to change his clothes or to move boxes in and out with his associates. He stood at the top of the stairs, ready to fist bump Tso.

His eyes stopped smiling first. When they reached the top landing, he hung his head down, nodded hello, and then dashed down the stairs.

Before Tso could wonder aloud about Khan's peculiar behaviour, Oishi told them that they knew each other. "I thought his name sounded familiar," he said.

Oishi explained that he had met Khan during a trial. Khan had had run-ins with the law since he was a teenager and served time in youth detention centres for drug offences and stolen property. When he came into Oishi's courtroom, he was charged with possession for the purpose of trafficking over half a million dollars of cocaine. Crown prosecutors offered him a lower sentence—one that meant he was out the door with time served—in exchange for testimony that led to the arrest of his boss.

"We're not talking about high-level gang leaders, but a bunch of kids who were in over their heads," Oishi explained. "If this boss was a pro, Khan would have been dead years ago. There'd be bullet holes in his windshield, and no one would care—because he deserved it." Instead, a young wannabe was given the task of killing him soon after his release. He was supposed to be at a party. "This so-called hitman shot someone who happened to be wearing the same shoes," he said. "What a waste. He was innocent. He was someone's kid."

Tso didn't spend much time at Grossman's after-party. There were too many sad stories swirling in her head. She returned to Izzy Grossman's apartment and tried to fall asleep on the couch.

In her book she'd written about the need to ascribe meaning to death. She had come to the conclusion that only heroic firefighters and villainous terrorists authored their own meaningful demises. For everyone else, a full, well-lived life could be undermined by a painful or abrupt exit. Survivors scrambled to give meaning in these moments. They would say that someone who died after a long struggle with terminal cancer used their end of life to demonstrate grace and courage. If a ninety-year-old man died while rock-climbing, loved ones could speak about his passion for the sport. But in the past three months, Vancouverites had faced deaths that resisted meaning. People died prematurely, painfully, and for no reason. At least this suffering happened collectively, and survivors could take comfort in one another. But even in this ocean of collective anguish, there were people who felt lonely in their pain.

Megan was woken early the next day by two police officers. She was asked to identify the body of a man who was killed the previous night in a traffic accident on Denman Street. The victim was described as a Caucasian male in his late twenties or early thirties with light brown hair and blue eyes and a "trumpet-like symbol" tattooed on his right bicep—Markus was a Thomas Pynchon fan. He died without identification. Among his possessions was an address book with her name and the hotel that she had checked out of weeks earlier. The front-desk clerk at the hotel who knew that Tso had often shared meals with Oishi called the judge in his room. She didn't hear the voicemail that Oishi had left for her until she grabbed her phone on the way out the door.

"Did he run into traffic?" Tso asked the police officer. She had never taken Markus's talk of suicide seriously. It felt like a scare tactic.

"I don't know the details," the officer replied. "But there were witnesses at the intersection. And the death is being treated as accidental."

Tso wanted time to clear her head. The police officers insisted on driving her to the morgue at Vancouver General Hospital. She threw on her coat over her pyjamas and stepped into the back of the police cruiser. The morgue, one officer explained, was functioning at full capacity, so the city was doing its best to dispatch bodies.

The night before, she had dreamed that she'd seen Markus on the street and run after him on the icy sidewalks near the hotel. The faster she ran after him, calling out his name, the more desperate he seemed to evade her. The dream ended with the policeman's knock on the door. If it hadn't, would she have chased him blindly into traffic?

At the morgue, she was taken to a room decked out with Haida art and boxes of Kleenex on a coffee table. A grief counsellor entered the room and explained that Tso would not need to see the body herself. "This isn't like TV shows," she explained. She held a clipboard with a picture of the deceased and placed the picture on the table face down. Tso turned the picture over immediately and saw that half of his face was swollen and bloodied. The other half—the right side—was the one she had seen for the better part of two years, snoring peacefully, when she woke first.

"Do you recognize this face?" the grief counsellor asked.

"I do," she told her. "We lived together in California. We were engaged. He was used to driving. He was a lousy pedestrian. Like me."

How did this happen? He had spent so much time torturing her.

Just yesterday he was postering the city in search of her. And then he was gone—like that. Suddenly, ambiguously, randomly. She was released from him. She didn't know whether she now felt broken or had already been broken. She had broken herself to keep from being irreparably destroyed.

She last saw Markus alive at a reading in West Hollywood, a year earlier. He interrupted the event with his accusations and she had to stop making public appearances in Los Angeles for that reason. Still he had no trouble finding her; they had friends in common. Tso didn't move out of the city. He would find out where she lived but stop short of confronting her.

He preferred to leave reminders instead. This was his final reminder.

And this was how Tso overlaid meaning onto a traffic-accident casualty amid a pandemic.

22.

When Romeo Parsons joined the Sanitation League, three of its volunteers had already contracted the illness. One died as a result. Parsons was well aware of the risks involved. But when he started to exhibit symptoms in February, he didn't believe that he was ill. He had taken the vaccine, which had been remarkably effective. The drop in new infections and fatalities in the last week dispelled any notions that the disease was merely having an "off" week. The disease had finally been throttled. Knowing that, Parsons didn't feel he could have contracted anything worse than a cold. He continued his work as usual.

Parsons put in tireless shifts for the Sanitation League. He mopped vomit from the floors of infected homes. He rocked to sleep a colicky infant whose mother was ill. He did his work as quietly as possible. He kept his face mask on and wore contact lenses instead of his signature glasses. When he was recognized, he posed in selfies and offered hugs to those who wanted them—they often did. Many of these admirers wanted to absolve Parsons of his transgressions. *You're a good person. It wasn't your fault. You had a sickness. It wasn't your fault like it wasn't my fault I got bitten by a diseased flea.*

"It was a set-up," one woman said, after insisting to Parsons and Rieux that they eat her cookies. She had lost her husband right before the New Year and needed help donating his clothes to the Salvation Army. "Your enemies put her up to it."

The mayor accepted these kind but patronizing words stoically, like a donkey accepting lashes to his hide.

Parsons was outside this woman's house when he told Rieux that he needed to sit down. The woman lived near Commercial Drive, and her house faced a park that was filled with men playing bocce ball in the summer. Rieux pulled the mayor's arm over his shoulder and led him to a park bench. Parson's face was hollowed and clammy. Only minutes earlier, he had been joking with the woman, whom he'd started to called "Cookie." He was a nicknamer. He had pet names for his staff and people he was comfortable around. He hadn't given many nicknames out since his scandal. He still addressed Rieux as "Doctor."

Rieux placed his hand on Parson's forehead. He was feverish.

"You need to go to the hospital," Rieux told him.

"I will do no such thing," Parsons answered in his gravelly baritone. "You can drop me off at home."

Rieux told him to wait as he collected his car and pulled up by the park bench. As the car moved, Parsons slumped against the side window and began to shiver. Rieux insisted on taking him back to his condo.

Mrs Rieux was displeased to see a sick man brought into their home. She fumed outside on her son's deck, cleaning the gas grill.

Rieux set the mayor up in his own bed. He called Tso and asked her to go to Parsons' temporary digs and collect his clothes and other personal items. She arrived with Grossman that evening. They each took turns watching Parsons, who waved off requests to speak to any of his estranged family members.

The disease advanced quickly. His cheeks were papery and his cough was severe. Parsons' forehead was shiny with sweat. At times, he howled like a cornered animal.

"I need you to do me a favour," Parsons asked Rieux during a lull in the pain. "If I am in too much pain, I want you to kill me. I'm afraid I can't bear it."

Rieux said he would. But he said it knowing he was unlikely to carry out the request. Parsons would have to be lucid to agree to medical assistance in dying right before any lethal injection. In his present state, he would probably become delirious, howling for death but unable to give his consent. He would then die in one quaking shudder.

Grossman kept watch over Parsons after he fell asleep. In a supine position, Parsons looked like a handsome mannequin, but he'd aged severely in the past six months.

Mrs Rieux had regained her equilibrium, offering Tso hot water and cookies. She chatted with her briefly before returning to her room to listen to Cantonese opera.

"Your mother reminds me of my own mother," Tso told Rieux as they sat at his dining room table. "They had different faces, but there are times when I catch your mom from the corner of my eye and see mine. They were built alike. My mother also smelled like sandalwood and wore jade bracelets around her slender wrists."

Over the past two months, since the Sanitation League had been founded, she and Rieux found themselves exhausted but not willing to be alone (or without the other). Sometimes Grossman or Siddhu would join them. Most of the time it was just the two of them. They walked from Rieux's apartment to Ken Lum's East Van Cross or to the Olympic Village. They stopped for tea or a glass of wine. They talked about books, films, TV, travel, food, work, and relationships. In all that time, Rieux never heard Tso refer to her family. He remembered only a passing mention of an aunt. He knew better than to ask her about the subject. She always deflected.

She stared at her hands as she told her story. To Rieux's ears, it sounded as if she had not told this story often—if at all. It came out in fragments. She backed up a few times in her narrative to correct an earlier point in her account. The following story is an edited, condensed version.

"My mother died when I was six. I only have a few memories of her. In one of them, I'm running toward her on the beach. She's wearing sunglasses. I fall in the sand and start crying. She picks me up. For many years, I tried to suppress every reminder of her. I had an older brother, too. He was eight. His name was Paul. He had Down's. He was born in China. I can hardly remember him now.

"My father had come to the United States to do a PhD in physics. My mother arrived in his second year with my brother and studied part-time to be a nurse. First we lived in Pennsylvania where I was born. Then my father dropped out of grad school. He told my mother that another student had made a complaint about stolen research. He claimed that he was falsely accused. The university sided with my father's colleague because he had more influence. The West was not as different from China as my parents had hoped it would be.

"If I was born with an ability to handle social situations, then it came from my father. He was a great talker. He was confident. I don't remember anything he said, only the way people gathered around him. He was short so he wore platform shoes. It was his charm that allowed him to get a job as the manager of a seafood restaurant in Flushing, Queens—where we'd moved—without any previous experience in restaurants or as a manager.

"In public, he was the star of any room. In private, he fumed about slights. He imagined my mother was having an affair. He would beat her regularly. He hoped to interrupt her training as a nurse by relocating, but she was able to transfer her credits to a school in New York. He screamed at my brother for having Down's. He never screamed at me, though. Even when I got between him and the rest of the family, he simply took me by my shoulders and led me to the room I shared with my brother and closed the door on me. Then he'd start to shout again.

"I don't actually remember any of this—it was all told and retold to me, in bits and pieces, by my mother's sister—the woman who raised me. I'd blocked it out.

"I don't remember New York at all. I don't remember my father losing his job. And I can't recall the accusations of embezzling from the restaurant. Or the night we left our apartment in Queens with only our clothes and a few photo albums and got into a car. We drove to California in three nights and four days. My father had a friend there who put us up until we found our own place. He had a lead on a job with an import-export company. California is where the memories of my family start. I was nine years old. There was the beach and Disneyland.

"My mother might have left my father in New York if he had chosen any other destination. She had already completed her training as a nurse. She had friends in Queens. But her sister, my Aunt LiLi, lived in Los Angeles. And while my mother would have to learn to drive, she liked the idea of a winter without snow.

"She got a job as a nurse, and my father found work too. We had a nice house with a yard. My father purchased a convertible. My mother started playing Mahjong again. My brother was placed in a special school that he liked. The arguments stopped for a while. But then my father lost his job. He was stealing from work. My mother was planning to leave him. The arguments started again.

"I don't remember much about my first year without my mother and brother. I know I must have gone to school. I remember the room I had in my aunt's apartment. I remember a new school where everyone walked around me and talked very slowly. Aunt LiLi worked as a secretary for a Chinese-language church. At night, we knelt at my bed and prayed to God to watch over my mother's and brother's souls. She kept photos of my mother and brother in her room, above the dresser. There were no pictures of my family that didn't also include my father. I hated going into her room because I had to see their faces.

"I just recalled another memory of my mother waiting for my dad to leave the apartment. She asked me to pick out my favourite doll, my favourite dress, and my favourite book. She packed them into a suit-case along with my brother's action figures. I saw her outside, stowing the suitcase in the trunk of her car.

"Here are other things I have no memory of: the shooting itself. The police coming. Leaving the house that night. The first few days after the shooting. The interview with the police officers and the child therapist. But all of that happened to me.

"My father had forged the signature of his boss to obtain lines of credit that he used to play Blackjack. His boss wanted to see him in jail. My mother may have known this. In his note, he indicated that he would take his entire family away before he could erase the shame of his own life. I have long wondered why he changed his mind. Why did he spare me?

" 'God saved you,' " Aunt LiLi told me. " 'It was a miracle.' " In truth, I was my father's favourite. This is my opinion: I was the one possession of his that didn't arouse shame. He was simply too vain to kill me.

"I have hardly anything of my mother's. She left a tube of lipstick at my aunt's house when she was visiting the week before her death. For years, I slept with it in my hand. Even when I couldn't bear to look at her picture. Even during the time I was telling my friends in high-school that I never knew my mother.

"A year after my mother and brother were killed, Aunt LiLi in-sisted I get baptised. I didn't resist her. She was a good woman. The church we attended—the one my aunt worked for—had a wading pool built into the stage. I was baptised with a few other new members. Each of them had their head dunked into water. I began weeping as I stepped toward the priest. I was upset because I had an irrational fear that the priest would drown me. I was upset, too, that I was sinful. And I was upset that the water would wash away my mother from me.

"When Markus died, some memories of my family were cracked open. I saw everyone afresh.

"Why did Markus choose to obsess over me? Did I choose Markus because he reminded me of my father?

"Some people have gleaned my family story. They pried into my silences for my own good. They asked well-meaning questions. I answered them as briefly as I could. You're the only person I have told this story—the most complete version—to. I'm going to tell Janice too." She looked up at him. She was done. "This felt good."

Rieux sat with this story once it was complete. It was three in the morning, and he could not account for how much time had passed. They must have talked about other things. Throughout Tso's account, he had asked questions and sought clarifications. Tso had cried, but not as much as he would have thought. At that time, everyone cried; tears had been as omnipresent as face masks and hand sanitizer since the outbreak and quarantine. The economical choice would be to describe the times nobody wept.

He worried throughout her telling of the story that he was not reacting to it properly. He wanted to convey his empathy. But he was allergic to expressiveness by disposition and profession. He could not touch her.

"I want you to know I appreciate learning everything about you," he told her finally.

"You don't know everything," she said.

"The rest is trivia."

Tso looked at him, then the table. She nodded.

Grossman interrupted them, flapping her hands as though they were aflame. "He's awake." She removed a glass from a cupboard and filled it with filtered water from Rieux's refrigerator.

The mayor was sitting upright in bed. His hair was matted to his forehead with dried sweat. He swallowed the water in a gulp and asked for more. Rieux examined him. The fever had passed. The doctor did not have any extra "dipsticks"—the white plastic devices that could detect the bacterium in a blood or urine sample without a laboratory test—on hand. Now he thought that Parsons might not have had the disease. Perhaps it was a flu brought on by exhaustion. It may have been a coincidence, too, that patients brought in during the final weeks of the quarantine responded better to treatment. Their recovery rates were a reversal of the dismal results witnessed near the beginning of the outbreak.

Grossman returned with another glass of water. Parsons drained it and asked for yet another. Midway through the third serving, he put the glass on the nightstand. "I've finally had my fill," he told them, wiping his wet chin with his hand.

Rieux and Tso exchanged looks of disbelief. For each of them, Parsons' recovery was their first pleasant surprise in months.

He turned in the bed and drew his legs to the floor. He became aware that he had been stripped down to his boxer briefs and undershirt. Grossman sat next to him and patted him on the knee.

"We were almost finished writing your obituary," she told him. "Thanks for nothing."

"You can save it for later," he told her. "Maybe you'll need to add a couple of new paragraphs at the bottom. I don't like the way it ends right now."

Part Five

KEVIN CHONG

23.

By early February, optimism and anxiety coursed throughout the city. For the first time since the outbreak began, Coastal Health Authority officials reported steep drops in both infections and fatalities. The success was attributed to the vaccine, and the anti-vaxxers or those who'd found excuses to avoid a needle rushed to the various clinic sites. During this wave, supplies correctly anticipated the surge of demand.

With good news came opportunities to call as many press conferences as possible. In the second week of February, one media event was arranged by Dr Orla Castello to announce the imminent closure of the auxiliary hospital. In the ensuing question period, Castello admitted that discussions about lifting the quarantine had begun. "There will be another press conference when we have a firm date in mind," she added.

Romeo Parsons kicked off a full return to his role as mayor by announcing a date in late May for a referendum on his anti-poverty plan. "It's also a referendum on my leadership," he said. If the people voted "No," he would resign. He acknowledged again his personal troubles, blaming them on hubris and an "outdated sense of a private life" that had not considered digital security. In a separate press conference with Canada's Prime Minister (onscreen through a satellite connection), he also announced details of a federal stimulus package that included infrastructure improvements like free wi-fi in the downtown core.

The tentative date in mid-March for the reopening of the city was made known two weeks in advance. The barricade gates would be removed and the airport would open if the infection rate continued to drop. "It's not unusual for these epidemics to lobtail," Castello said. "We expect to see the last gasp of disease before the reopening." Her tone implied that the reopening was conditional on our good behaviour.

This caution was not heeded. Strangers waltzed cheek-to-cheek, mask-to-mask, on Robson Street. Cyclists on the icy bicycle lanes rang their bells cheerfully as they passed one another. Restaurants and bars gave away celebratory rounds of smuggled, premium-priced alcohol. Parents took their children out of school for ice cream and Go-Kart rides.

To survive, Vancouverites had adopted a measured approach to the privations of the quarantine. They could not waste the energy needed to stay alert to infection. Their tears were reserved only for the suffering of those closest to them. With the deadline in sight, they lost their composure. Like long-distance runners with the finish line in sight, they began to notice their ragged lungs, sore joints, and aching muscles. They bawled and wailed in agony and relief.

During those two weeks, people started to wonder about the future. Some of them used that transitional period to ready themselves, while others booked vacations to their "bucket list" destinations. Some romantic relationships crystallized in this period, and many more dissolved in anticipation of freedom and possibility.

Not everyone prepared for their new life, but no one expected to return to their old one.

———

Janice Grossman had been offered her previous job as a tour-bus operator, at reduced hours. She declined to return. She hoped to continue hosting performances at her unlicensed space. "I mean, *I know the fucking mayor*," she told Tso. "I nursed him back from the grave." To make up for lost income, she rented her downstairs apartment to Jeffrey Oishi.

In the process of preparing the apartment for rental, she cleared some of her own space. She found Janet's unopened letters and read them for the first time. There were three separate letters written three months apart in the first three months after their split. The first letter was the longest and most conciliatory. The final one was cold and brief. The second one fell in the middle of those extremes.

"She basically wrote the same letter three different ways," she told Tso. "The third letter was the clearest one." In her unanswered correspondence, she explained that she felt guilty for mistreating Grossman and that she could not repay her. She would never be happy trying to repay her. She chose instead to live with her guilt and move on.

The admission of fault moved Grossman. "It means more to me than her saying she would always love me," she said. "Because love fades. It's guilt that lasts."

To celebrate the city's reopening, Grossman reactivated another "long-dormant thing," her internet dating profile. She invited Tso over for tea so that she could share her initial impressions about her romantic prospects. Hanging on a clothes line from the wall over the kitchen table was what at first seemed to be a chain of paper dolls. Upon closer inspection, Tso realized that the dolls, held to the clothesline with binder clips, were pictures of Grossman. They were the cut-out images of herself from Janet's paintings.

Grossman noticed the figures had caught Tso's attention. "I'm not sure I'll keep the cut-outs like that," she said. "I might put them all in a scrapbook." She had arranged the paper dolls from the youngest-looking one—Grossman wearing her Gertrude Stein T-shirt—to depictions of her from later in their relationship. Each figure, stripped from its tableaux, was finely detailed. As the paper dolls danced across the clothesline, the depictions of Grossman's features gained wrinkles and the tint of her hair mutated. Her expression grew lighter, less like a horny satyr and more restful and content, as she collected experience. At the end of the line, Tso saw her friend.

———

From outside the quarantine zone, Raymond Siddhu sent out resumes for various communications jobs in the public and private sector.

As he waited for a response, he continued the couples therapy that he and Uma had begun in late January. During their sessions, Siddhu revealed his previous infidelity to his wife. Although she had long suspected the incident, she felt its sting, but she also appreciated his confession as an attempt to reduce her own sense of guilt over her affair. Siddhu realized that the schism in their marriage had been exacerbated by the strain of separation; it was a fissure that had been growing since their sons were born.

They each wrote a list of their daily childcare tasks. He'd known she did more work around the house, but this chart was striking. "The list is skewed," Siddhu insisted at first. "She's been on maternity leave."

Now out of work, Siddhu began to take his sons to the park. He did their laundry and cooked dinner on the days when Uma, whose internet fling had ended, did the books in the office of her brother's Honda dealership. Uma texted him during the day to check on his emotional temperature. Saturday nights alternated between date nights and "me" nights—when either Siddhu or Uma were free to do what they wanted.

He followed the coverage around Elliot Horne-Bough's arrest for invasion of privacy and began to craft a proposal for a true-crime book. Out on bail, Horne-Bough remained an enigma worthy of study, but Siddhu had found his erratic leadership style to be exhausting. Writing about him, especially if he were to cooperate, would return Siddhu to his mercy for an indefinite period of time.

That's when he received a call from the mayor's office for an interview as a communications director. They set up an appointment for the Monday after the city gates opened. "The mayor obviously knows your work," his aide told Siddhu. "He wants you on his team."

Siddhu knew he didn't want to be on the team of any person or party or company. As a journalist, he had aligned himself with the objective truth. At least he strived to do so beyond any of his inherent biases and the limitations imposed on him by deadlines and access. He also knew he had to feed his family. And he liked Parsons. Given a choice between Horne-Bough and Parsons, he'd work for Parsons.

———

Orla Castello completed paperwork for early retirement. When she met with Rieux for coffee, she had already made plans with a nonprofit to help coordinate the founding of a hospital in Sierra Leone. A new wave of the Ebola virus had decimated the medical system, taking down ten percent of its doctors and nurses. She would leave in the spring.

"I want to get out of here before they start handing out medals—not that I expect to get any," Castello said.

"You'd be the first in line," Rieux told her.

"I have a feeling that the wrong people will get those medals. They'll be the ones who come out of it talking about 'lessons learned.' They'll talk about innovation and say it was simple. It was actually complicated. People suffered no matter what we decided to do."

She asked Rieux about his wife.

"Elyse has made a remarkable recovery—I shouldn't have called her treatment quackery," Rieux said. "But we've grown too far apart. She's leaving Mexico but has no plans to come home."

She leaned across the table toward him. "I'm sorry," she told him. "I love both of you."

He squeezed her hands.

This was the first time he'd admitted out loud that his marriage was over, something he hadn't even told his mother. He felt like he'd stabbed himself.

"I didn't know how poorly I cared for her—until all this happened," Rieux said. "Things might be different if I'd understood her pain."

"You always tried, Bernard. She knew that," Castello said. "You're too hardworking. When are you going to take a vacation?"

"In about two weeks," he said with a smile. "I still have patients to see and paperwork to put together."

The bill came to the table. She snatched it from the plate like a cat swatting at a bird. "Go on holiday earlier," she told him. "People are going to live and die whatever you do."

———

The Sanitation League met an unceremonious demise as calls to its hotlines and emailed requests plummeted more drastically than the rate of infection. Tso and Rieux personally thanked every volunteer for their service. They talked about throwing a party after the quarantine was over, but neither could manage to do anything. Besides, Tso needed to leave.

Through the US consulate Tso purchased a ticket home. The time in Vancouver had drained her savings—the consulate would reimburse her, but the lag in processing meant that she pushed up against her credit-card limit. She needed to make money soon, and her old job had opened up. A friend in Los Angeles emailed to say that she was moving in with her boyfriend. Tso had always loved her apartment. Did she want it? Tso could take over her lease in March.

She decided that a sudden return to her old life would be the best cure for any hangover that came from her experience in Vancouver. Leaving these new friends behind would be bittersweet, but there was no point in staying in one place when everyone else's lives were being reordered. *You either leave people, or you're being left behind*, she told herself.

At the US consulate, she was given an envelope. It had been couriered from their Japanese counterparts. The note was written on tissue-thin writing paper in a frail hand.

Dear Megan Tso,

I apologize for our late reply. I apologize also for our simple English.

Thank you so much for sending to us the passport of our daughter, Yuko. The consulate official said you tried to help her when she became sick.

We thought you might want to know more about Yuko.

Yuko was our only daughter. She was twenty-two years old. She studied English for a year in the United Kingdom. She wanted to work for an airline and travel. She loved dogs.

We are very sad since she died. But we know that she lived a life that made her happy.

Thank you for reading this letter about our daughter.

Yuko's Mother (and Father)

Tso's hands trembled as she reread the note. She saw a girl running down the beach into the embrace of the person who made her.

———

After being released on bail, Elliott Horne-Bough announced his latest venture with philanthropist and family friend Frederick Graham. Evermark™ would create luxury monuments for the ultra-rich, built to last a thousand years.

———

"I think we should keep an eye on Farhad," Grossman told Tso a few days after the reopening was announced. She had heard him screaming into the phone in his apartment.

The smuggling trade had not yet been affected. As inspection protocols remained in place, contraband was still required to meet the city's more celebratory appetites for foie gras, champagne, and Atlantic lobster. But within a few weeks, his services would no longer be in demand.

It was Oishi's move into Izzy Grossman's apartment that prompted Khan's next outburst. When he saw the judge outside the house with the moving van, he ran up to Grossman's apartment, pounded his fists against her door, and demanded that she open it.

Tso, who had moved to Grossman's couch until she left the city, was wearing her pyjamas when she cracked open the door. Khan slipped his foot in the crack and pried it open.

"What message are you trying to send to me, eh?" Khan asked. "Have I not been your friend? Why do you rent to that judge?" he asked. "Is there a reason why you're torturing me?"

Grossman appeared a moment afterward. Khan shouted to her over Tso's shoulder. He kept thumping his bare chest like an over-emotive singer.

Grossman didn't know about Oishi's connection to Khan. "He needed a place to stay," she said.

He threw his hands in the air. "A man needs to feel like he's at home. Not like he's on trial."

He stomped back into his apartment. When they heard glass breaking and other noises, Grossman called the police. Khan stormed out before they arrived. Grossman prepared an eviction notice for him, but he never bothered to pick it up. He never returned to the apartment.

A few days before the quarantine was lifted, one of Gastown Annex's newest condo projects, set to cast the rest of the block in its shadow, was set ablaze. Police and firefighters found Khan sitting on the curb with two tanks of gasoline.

The damages to the stone and steel foundations were superficial, yet the developers wanted Khan punished severely. Later that year, when Khan stood in the courtroom for his sentencing, he swayed back and forth until his lawyer asked him to stop. He dutifully answered the questions that the judge asked him but otherwise looked swept up in his own private music. He seemed disappointed that his prison sentence wasn't longer.

24.

When the reopening was announced, Rieux booked a ticket back to Hong Kong for his mother. Mrs Rieux had begun to sigh at the pictures of her growing grandchildren recently sent by his sister. She had been here too long. "I imagine Elyse will be home soon," she told him. "I don't want to get in her way."

Rieux resolved to spend more time with his mother now that an end-date to her visit came into sight. She was at the age when any visit could be her last and he would only be able to see her in Hong Kong, where he found it difficult to breathe in the smog and heat.

He received two tickets from the Cantonese Opera troupe. The actress whom Rieux had attended to had recovered and regained her strength. To celebrate their imminent departure and to show their appreciation to the city, the company would stage a farewell performance before they travelled home to China. Rieux and his mother were invited backstage afterward.

"Once was enough," Mrs Rieux said. "You don't even like the opera!"

"It was my fault. I didn't put in the time to understand it," he explained. "I read about this one."

She nodded. She wanted to go. "Thank you, Bernard," she said.

The performance took place in the same theatre, but this time the house was full. Since the reopening had been announced, pedestrians filled the streets to the curb and passengers on buses stood shoulder-to-shoulder. People behaved as though they were already free. Rieux was reminded of visiting less temperate Canadian cities in the spring and seeing shirt-less joggers running alongside towering snowbanks that had only begun to thaw. Vancouverites would have looked the same way to outsiders: like maniacs.

He flipped through the program. The original version of *The Peony Pavilion*, written at the end of the sixteenth century, consisted of fifty-five scenes and took days to perform. This popular adaptation, which featured eight scenes, lasted only for an evening.

The lights dimmed on a stage that was made to look like a garden. The actress he had treated stood in the green light. Her cheekbones seemed to jut out more noticeably, but it was hard to tell in her makeup. She played the lead character, a young woman named Du Liniang, and was followed onto the stage by another woman, who played her maid. To Rieux's relief, this performance was subtitled.

Du Liniang comes from a wealthy family, which confines her to the estate and the manicured gardens that surround it to preserve her inno-cence. In her boredom and sadness, she wanders outside and falls asleep. In a dream she meets a man named Liu Mengmei, who convinces her that they are destined to fall in love. She wakes up from her dream, dismayed it wasn't real. In her despair, she wastes away and dies.

Three years later, a scholar stops at a temple to get away from a snow-storm. He presents an offering to a painting of a young woman. He sees his own name, Liu Mengmei, within the poem that accompanies the portrait.

Du Liniang's ghost appears. She tells him about their fated love and instructs him to unearth her tomb. The god of the underworld has allowed her to return to life and re-unite with her lover. Since it is a comic opera, they must succeed in proving to everyone—the cemetery custodians, her parents, the Emperor—that he is not a graverobber and she is not a ghost. And that they belong together.

Rieux's mother was again stirred and delighted. The story was a comedy along Renaissance lines: not a lot of yuks, but an expression of vitality. *Life has more good parts than bad ones ... let's end this story on a high note.*

Mrs Rieux sang along to the songs—audibly. She did not even feign resistance when he suggested they go backstage. Once there, she clung to her son's side as they waited to congratulate the performers. She offered the same crooked smiled she used when she'd met the parents of Rieux's classmates and was embarrassed to speak in English. One actress noticed a trace of an accent in her Cantonese and asked her about her family's hometown. "We come from the same village!" the actress gasped.

The doctor's mother sighed contentedly during the drive home. As a child, Rieux often discovered her asleep on the couch, her arms cinched around a pillow that he always imagined to be a stand-in for his father. It was a fanciful notion. His mother hardly talked about her husband. It seemed difficult to imagine how deeply his parents had fallen in love when they could barely speak the same language.

Rieux was pleased by her reaction to *The Peony Pavilion*. While he found himself drifting in and out of the performance, it would not be fair to say that it had left him unaffected. Throughout the opera and the ride home, his mind latched onto the idea of lovers existing outside of time and space. Wasn't it simply a fanciful notion rooted in anguish?

People fell in love at the wrong time, all the time.

People fell in love out of time, all the time.

The city was full of people still in love with ghosts. Always, but now more than ever. And ghosts waiting to be reborn and reunited.

––––––––

For Rieux, his days at the clinic swung so far back in the direction of normalcy that it felt like another type of abnormal. During the quarantine, Rieux had noticed not only a drop in volume, but an outright reluctance in patients with everyday ailments and chronic conditions to come in. No one wanted to go to the doctor unless they feared their lives were at risk. With the reopening of the city in sight, his office was crowded with patients with asthma or hepatitis C.

Rieux completed one day at the clinic with his favourite patient, Walter, whom he saw for the first time since Rieux had visited his home. He noticed that Walter had added another band of red marks to his arm as the days of quarantine continued. As idle chatter during the exam, the doctor asked Walter whether he had any trips planned for after the reopening. Walter told him that he'd had been evicted from his apartment. He had a week to find a new home at a fixed price range or stay in a shelter.

"Things were better when everyone was afraid—they were too busy to hurt me," Walter said. "Now that everyone is returning to normal, it's back to survival mode."

Rieux didn't know what to say. He placed one hand on Walter's arm and held it. Afterwards, he renewed his prescription for medication to treat hypertension. He would take more time with Walter if he needed it. Rieux had gotten behind with waiting patients a few times that day, which cut into his break and lunch. He blamed the end-of-day fatigue on his lack of rest and food.

"You look pale," Walter told the doctor when he uncuffed the blood pressure monitor. "Drink some milk."

Back home, he told Mrs Rieux that he was tired from his work day and she shouldn't worry. He admitted later that he had been feeling weak for the past several days, but Tso and Grossman were expected for dinner that night. They needed to distribute leftover money that had been donated to the Sanitation League, and there were several options to be discussed. Rieux remained in bed until woken by his mother, then changed back into his clothes and sat slumped on the couch, a cup of warm water in his hands, while his mother prepared the meal.

His guests arrived. Grossman yelped upon encountering Rieux and his ashy complexion. "Doc, you're not looking good," she told him. "Let me show you." She took his flash photo on her Samsung Galaxy and presented him with the image. "We need to take you to the hospital."

Even as Rieux suggested that it could be "just the flu," he realized how he sounded. When he stood up, he felt dizzy. He saw his bag by the door and staggered toward it. He removed a white plastic stick that looked like a home pregnancy test. Grossman helped him to the bathroom.

"We'll know for sure in fifteen minutes," he said when he returned to the living room.

He held the stick in both hands. Everyone watched the clock, repeating the same thought, *It has to be the flu. It doesn't make sense to get it now.* A red line appeared over the positive sign. His eyes lidded, and he began to blink erratically.

"It's true," he said. "It's true."

———

An ambulance was called. Tso accompanied Mrs Rieux, who remained in her son's field of vision at all times, to the hospital. He was sent directly from the Emergency Room to the Intensive Care Unit, where he was given the new antibiotics that were more effective in treating patients during the recent rounds of the disease. He slowly took in the room, the monitors, the lines attached to him. Seeing that everything was in place allowed him to relax.

"What's my prognosis?" he asked Tso.

Mrs Rieux looked to Tso.

"I'm not a doctor," Tso said.

"That's why I like you."

He closed his eyes and slept. It was past ten o'clock. Tso told Mrs Rieux to go home. She assured her that she would remain by her son's side. Who knew how long it would last? Tso called Grossman and asked her to drive the doctor's mother home. She knew Mrs Rieux needed to rest.

Tso pulled up her chair and scrolled through social media on her iPhone. She needed to save battery life in case Mrs Rieux called. Rieux slept with his head to the side. His legs were almost hairless. They were strong and lean, like statuary—his arms, too. Her eyes darted past the egg-shaped lumps that had formed on the sides of his neck. He had a scar under his eyebrow, a white horizontal line. She'd never gotten around to asking him about it.

Nurses came and went. She was too worried to ask the doctors anything. Dr Castello stopped by—as a visitor—and told Tso that Rieux was being treated for both the bubonic and pneumonic versions of the disease. He had been exposed to the illness for months. *Why now? Was it possible for his body to have resisted it until he completed his work?* Tso wondered.

Castello said she would visit again and left. She seemed uncomfortable with Rieux as a patient. An hour passed. Tso closed her eyes. By the time they fluttered open, another three hours had vanished.

Rieux had been making a whimpering sound. People afflicted with the disease typically flailed and screamed. Rieux suffered the way he lived: he was reserved, still, stoic. He kept his arms by his side and his jaw set.

His eyes remained fixed ahead as though he were a tightrope walker unwilling to look at the ground. Tso moved to the side of the bed and leaned over so he could see her face. His pupils slowly adjusted. With great effort, he wrenched his mouth out of a pained wince. If he couldn't force a smile, he was able to create an unflappable expression.

"Where's my mother?" he asked.

"Janice drove her home. I told her to get some rest."

He closed his eyes. "That's good. I'm thirsty."

She offered him water from a cup, guiding the straw onto his colourless bottom lip. He thanked her. He began to say something but let out a moan. He tried again, with the same result. She realized that he only wanted to talk so he could hear other voices. She pulled up her chair and began to speak. First, she related the plotline of a TV show she'd watched the other night. One character reminded her of Siddhu. She relayed details of her last conversation with the reporter. She wished she had a book she could read to Rieux.

He fell asleep. She drifted off too and woke up when Mrs Rieux arrived. Grossman followed her into the room with a bag that contained family photos and the iPhone charger that Tso had requested. Rieux was awake and looked comfortable. He had adjusted the bed so he was sitting upright.

"It's just a lull," he told them.

Rieux spoke as though he were holding an invisible stopwatch as he raced through his instructions. He explained that he wanted to be cremated and his ashes scattered into the water at Locarno Beach. He did not want a funeral service. His will was located in a safety deposit box at his bank. He left some money for his mother's care, but the rest would go to Elyse. There was also a small life insurance policy.

He plowed through these orders, ignoring Tso and Mrs Rieux's repeated pleas to relax. Rieux glared at Tso and told her she needed to write down his instructions. He could still make people do things. She removed her pen and some scrap paper from her bag. Finally, Rieux added, he needed Tso to contact Elyse.

After the instructions were recorded, he relaxed. He asked his mother for water, then sipped it slowly from a straw.

Tso's iPhone was giving out. Grossman handed her the cellphone charger in a bag that also contained a notebook along with other hastily gathered items. Tso had seen Rieux jotting in the notebook in his car, and she'd noticed it on his dining-room table but had never been curious about its contents until she held it in her hands.

She flipped it open and saw their names. "What is this?" Tso asked Rieux.

He grimaced. "A hobby."

"Why do you refer to everyone by their last name?" she asked.

"To be impartial."

She shook her head. "It doesn't work."

Rieux told her not to read it. He was not done yet. He feared that he wouldn't ever be done. "Someone needs to tell it," he told her. "Otherwise it will recede in memory. The way we forget everything. You should write it."

She frowned in dismay. "I would turn it into something else. Raymond would want to look at it too." He reached for the notebook, trying to take it back. In doing so, he dragged one of the lines from the machine. "This part with Siddhu, for instance—"

Mrs Rieux had a way of innocently interrupting others. Since her command of English was basic, she often tuned out conversations and forgot to wait for a proper break in a chat before voicing a thought.

"Megan," she said in Cantonese, "you should go home and rest." She took the notebook from her. "I will keep this for now."

Tso walked back to Grossman's house. She was relieved to have shed her latex gloves, which irritated her skin. She removed her face mask and took in the moist air. A heavy rain had fallen the night before, warming the ground. At Grossman's, she showered, changed, and ate a sandwich. She had never gotten around to charging her phone. When she returned to the hospital, Rieux's face was obscured by a respirator. His eyes widened when he saw her. She saw his lips moving. He began to cough. She went to the bed and took his hand.

His fingers looked as though they'd been powdered in coal dust.

"He started babbling shortly after you left," Grossman explained. Her eyes were swollen. "Then he started coughing. There was blood."

He looked like someone riding a roller coaster. His other hand was by his side, balled into a fist. He looked ahead into the distance, beyond the room's glass partition, as though he was gaping at some great drop that he was inching toward.

They tried their best to soothe him. Mrs Rieux wiped his brow with a towel. Tso held her hand over his on the railing. Grossman played music from his iPhone: singer-songwriters with acoustic guitars and harmonicas—Bob Dylan and the Band, Richie Havens, the McGarrigle sisters, Hayden, and Gillian Welch.

Tso had researched end-of-life ceremonies for her book, and during her stint with the Sanitation League, she'd joined hands with family members and priests in prayers and last rites for the dying. She wished that they, if not Rieux himself, could have taken comfort in these rituals. She knew they would be an affront to him.

A doctor came and consulted with a nurse. They decided that Rieux required heavy sedation. His medication was increased, and soon he slumped in rest. She looked at one monitor. She needed a nurse to explain that his blood pressure was dangerously low.

Tso and Grossman decided they should eat. They made salad bar plates and bought bottled water in the cafeteria, then sat by the windows that looked out on a set of grey concrete apartment buildings.

"I don't think he's going to make it," Grossman said.

Tso looked down at her lap. "He's fighting. I wish I were more optimistic."

"This is triggering memories of my dad. Only this is worse. Maybe it's worse because it's happening now."

Rieux spent the rest of the day unconscious. His hands grew as dark as eggplants as the infection grew.

"We need to let him pass," Castello said when she came at ten. "He knew what the risks were. I don't think he expected to last through it all."

Grossman took Mrs Rieux back home. Tso remained in a chair. She was supposed to call them should his condition take its final turn.

Tso was woken up by a howling sound. Rieux's eyes were open but unfocused. She rose and took his blackened hand, but he did not respond to her presence. He shrugged away from her and rolled to his side. He made a noise that grew thinner as the air left his watery lungs for the last time. And then the noise stopped, like a string on a musical instrument that had snapped.

———

Tso called Grossman, who had stayed with Mrs Rieux. They arrived quickly, as though they had been waiting in another room. It was not yet six o'clock in the morning and still dark outside. The three women wept over Rieux with all the energy they had reserved. They knew this would be the last person they needed to mourn. There was nothing to hold back. Mrs Rieux addressed him by all his childhood pet names, stroking his hair. With all the regret of someone who had withheld a desire until the opportunity had passed, Tso yearned to embrace Mrs Rieux.

She remembered her own mother's funeral for the first time in a quarter century. Her mother lay in an open casket, eyes closed, and Tso saw with a surprise that she was wearing makeup. This was not her mother, and yet when they closed the casket, Tso needed to be held back from it.

Rieux's body was already starting to stiffen, but Tso ran her latex-covered fingers over his knee. She cupped his upper arm and brushed his cheek.

And then Tso kissed him through her face mask. A nurse walked in and screamed at her to stop.

25.

Given these hints, some might have already suspected the true identities of our authors. With this story coming to an end, it is time to tear away our masks.

Megan Tso and Raymond Siddhu, the two of us, collaborated on the completion of the project based largely upon the notebooks of Bernard Rieux.

We discussed many different approaches to this chronicle. That we settled on telling our respective stories, along with Rieux's, in one braided narrative by no means suggests that it has been a seamless process. As the reader can tell from our authorial interjections, disputes arose as we stitched together this book in separate cities between other obligations.

We also felt inclined to openly disagree with or contextualize some of the statements that Rieux made, as his views—though he shied away as much from the term "libertarian" as he did from any other label—could offend readers who might otherwise find him sympathetic. Rieux's beliefs never hardened into dogma, and he was always receptive to our thoughts on social justice even if he never fully accepted them.

Rieux's writing style was clinical and based only on his firsthand experience. We chose to honour (for the most part) his formal constructions and his arm's-length treatment of his characters. His notebook effectively formed the skeleton of this book.

The late doctor wrote about his reflections during the outbreak and quarantine but refused to speculate on what the other figures in his story felt or thought. We decided that we could deepen the impact of this chronicle if we each brought to the story our own personal moments and excavated inner lives. As Rieux wrote between exhausting double shifts, we also suspect that—given the time—he might have infused more of his own interior life to the story upon revision.

Since some of Rieux's accounts are only fragmentary, we each tried to fill in the gaps in his narrative using our own specific skills. Siddhu brought to the story his reporting background as he interviewed the minor figures in this piece and checked details. Tso pored over the literary works that Rieux was reading and quoting from in his notebooks. She overlaid scenes that were originally written in an objective voice with some of Rieux's more philosophical ruminations. The omission of most medical details was Rieux's choice, as he found his own work the least interesting (and possibly, the most dispiriting) aspect of this period.

Any history contains contradictions. This one had relatively few of them. And this was entirely the result of Dr Bernard Rieux and his steadfast eye. We attempted to honour him in our efforts.

We only resist calling him a hero because Rieux loathed the term. He would say that he could have acted in no other way.

We are bound to the objective truth: he was a doctor, a son, a husband, and our friend.

Many histories benefit from distance. Our collaboration to complete this book, while written in spurts, began shortly after the quarantine was lifted.

The end occurred on the third Sunday that March. When the gates opened at midnight, fireworks were lit across the city—above Coal Harbour, from its highest point in Queen Elizabeth Park, and in backyards, alleys, and unlit parks. Tso was reminded of how loud it was when she'd first arrived in Vancouver that past October.

Siddhu rode in on the SkyTrain on the following Monday. He kept his gaze fixed on the list of stops, even though he could recite them from memory, eyes closed, backwards and forwards. He walked to the coffee bar by the Art Gallery. In only a couple of days, the city had already returned to normal. There were neither too many nor too few people.

Tso was waiting for him with a latte. She put down our coffees and we embraced with the gusto of people who no longer worried that physical contact could kill us.

"How much time do you have?" Tso asked.

Siddhu's interview with the mayor wasn't until the afternoon. Tso would fly out that night. She walked with her coffee in one hand, dragging her suitcase with the other. She suggested an ambitious jaunt, and Siddhu agreed to it after some hesitation. He looked forward to stretching his legs but admitted to being in terrible physical condition.

She had seen the news alert on her phone as she waited for our coffees. We strolled up Robson Street. Storefronts remained papered over. In some shop windows mannequins were still arrayed in winter clothes from last year.

We finished our coffees as we entered the Park and walked along the Seawall like proper tourists. There was already a group of people assembled by the Brockton Point Lighthouse.

"I've been waiting an hour," one bearded onlooker in a jean jacket told us.

The transient pod, eight whales in total, was spotted early in the morning from Deep Cove and had made it as far as the Second Narrows Bridge. They were hunting seals. They needed to double back to return to the open ocean.

The air became brisk as we stood by the water—neither Siddhu nor Tso had dressed properly. We spoke about Rieux's notebook, in part because everything that lay ahead for each of us was so provisional. Like many in the city, we also felt the events of the last few months haunting our consciousness. We needed to talk about it, to inscribe it, to externalize it. Otherwise these events lingered dormant in our bodies, like the bacterium, waiting for an opportunity to re-emerge.

"Did you really have that conversation in the car with Bernard?" Tso asked.

"Which one?" he said, pursing his mouth.

"*You know*. I can tell you know."

His eyes misted over. "It did happen," he said at last. "Were you surprised?"

"Does it matter?" she asked.

We were caught up in this particular speculation about missed opportunities when we heard gasps from the onlookers who had brought their telescopes and binoculars. We took our places along the stone lip of the wall. The whales came porpoising along the surface of the water as if performing for the whale-watching boats that followed them. A drone drifted up above them, looking silly as they always did. When it crashed into the water, we cheered.

Siddhu had lived all his life in the city and had never seen orcas this close. As a teenager, on a ferry to Vancouver Island, he chose to remain in his seat reading *The Stand* when the ferry captain announced that orcas had been spotted. Tso had only seen orcas bouncing beach balls on their snouts at Sea World.

"Aren't you glad we did this?" she asked Siddhu.

Tso chose to believe that the orcas were a sign. They arrived to celebrate her last day in Vancouver. She was reminded of one of the final entries in Rieux's notebooks. It was a definition of a cetacean-specific term used casually by Dr Orla Castello as a metaphor for the final throes of the outbreak.

A lobtail: when a whale slaps its flukes (the lobes of its tail) against the surface of the ocean, Rieux wrote in his diary. *The beginning of the end or the end of the beginning?*

Megan Tso waited for the whales to swim past them. She waited. She waited. The whales became specks in her vision, only their dorsal fins clearly visible.

Right before she lost hope, one of those orcas raised its tail in the air and splashed the surface of the water. It was far away, but she could hear the clap in her heart. *Goodbye, for now.*

Acknowledgments

My wife Holly.

My students at UBC and SFU, but especially my fiction cohorts
at The Writer's Studio.

John Li, Tom Hunter.

Arsenal Pulp Press: Brian Lam, Susan Safyan, Cynara Geissler,
Robert Ballantyne, Oliver McPartlin.

The BC Arts Council and the Canada Council.

Albert Camus.

Kevin Chong is the author of six books, including the memoir *My Year of the Racehorse* and the novel *Beauty Plus Pity*. His work has been shortlisted for the Hubert Evans Prize for Non-Fiction and a National Magazine Award. His writing has recently appeared in the *Walrus*, the *Rusty Toque*, and *Cosmonauts Avenue*. His books have been published in Canada, the US, France, Australia, and Macedonia. He teaches at the University of British Columbia's Creative Writing Program and The Writers' Studio at Simon Fraser University. Born in Hong Kong, he lives in Vancouver with his family.

kevinchong.ca